NORSE
CODE

Greg van Eekhout

BALLANTINE BOOKS • NEW YORK

A Spectra Mass Market Original

Copyright © 2009 by Greg van Eekhout

Published in the United States by Spectra, an imprint of The Random House Publishing Group, a division of Random House, Inc., New York.

SPECTRA and the portrayal of a boxed "s" are trademarks of Random House, Inc.

ISBN 978-0-553-59213-9

Printed in the United States of America

www.ballantinebooks.com

9 8 7 6 5 4 3 2 1

To Lisa

ACKNOWLEDGMENTS

It's often said that writing is a lonely profession, but I enjoyed so much assistance, support, friendship, and camaraderie during the making of this book that it didn't seem lonely at all.

My thanks go first to my best friend and best companion, Lisa Will.

For keen editorial and business guidance, I thank my agent, Caitlin Blasdell, and thanks also to my editor, Juliet Ulman, who turned a big shload of words into a book better than the one I initially sent her. Thanks as well to David Pomerico and the crew at Bantam for their care and professionalism.

I am deeply indebted to Sandra McDonald and Sarah Prineas, founders of the Harmed Fan Club, for constant encouragement, commiseration, ridiculousness, and friendship.

The members of the Blue Heaven novel workshop shared Brandy Alexanders with me on a snake-infested island and twice provided invaluable feedback on my manuscript, then titled "Greg's Damned Norse Novel." For that, my thanks to Paolo Bacigalupi, Tobias Buckell, Rae Carson, Brenda Cooper, C. C. Finlay, Sandra McDonald, Holly McDowell, Paul Melko, Chance Morrison, Tim Pratt, Sarah Prineas, Heather Shaw, William Shunn, Ian Tregillis, and Mary Turzillo.

Tim Pratt and Heather Shaw have been particularly kind to me through a Ragnarok or two, and their young nephew, Aleister Seiflein, provided me with the line "hole made of wolf" during a backyard cookout that involved watching a bee fly away with a chunk of meat, a sight that seemed plenty apocalyptic to me.

Thanks to Mike Jasper, David Moles, and Jenn Reese for providing helpful critiques of embryonic attempts at this story, some of which made it to the final draft. And thanks to Patrick Nielsen Hayden, who published my story "Wolves Till the World Goes Down," which got me started on wayward gods and nosy ravens.

I owe much gratitude to the ranks of additional friends and family who've boosted me in so many ways: Amy Creamer, Kirsten Hageleit, Karen Meisner, Robert Mitchell, Brian Tatosky, Aaron Vanek, Mom and Dad, Mike, Vicki, Sage, Mom Will, Dennis, Anita, Ashley, Amy, Renee, and the many awesome folks who have kept me company by leaving thousands of funny and lovely comments on my silly blog.

I'd go to war or dinner with this crew anytime.

PROLOGUE

ON THE LAST true day of spring the nine worlds will ever know, my brother and I fly recon through the land of the gods. From this high up, Asgard shimmers. The shields that roof the timber halls glimmer like golden fish scales. It's all green grass and fluffy white sheep and fresh red blood. A very pretty scene.

"One, two, sixteen, seven hundred and eighty-three," my brother intones as we fly over the wall where the heads of giants sit atop stakes, dripping blood. "Four thousand and eight."

"What are you doing?"

"Counting," he says, angling his wings to swoop down for a closer look.

"Counting what?" I ask, following.

"Everything. Five million and six."

My brother is good with questions of *what* and *when* and *how much,* and he remembers it all. His name is Munin, or Memory, and he annoys me.

As for myself, I'm better with questions of *why* and *how* and *what next* and what goes on in the minds of gods and men. I can see what happens in their skulls better than an electroencephalogram. I am Hugin, or Reason, or Thought, and we are the ravens of Odin. Every morning he sends us out to fly through the worlds, and every evening we return to perch on his shoulder and tell him what we've seen and heard. Sometimes I even tell him what I think.

We have been following one of Odin's sons today, the one called Hermod, who is coming home for the first time in several dozen years. Tall and thin, wincing as though the brilliance of Asgard gives him a headache, he approaches the gates of the city. He has walked far today. This morning he woke up on the shore of a white-sand beach in Midgard, the world of men, enjoying warmth and solitude. It's not that Hermod doesn't like people and gods; he just likes them better from a distance. For this reason, he spends a great deal of time in Midgard, for man at this time hasn't yet built his great cities and highways and shopping malls. He hasn't yet invented plastic and television. On the continent that will later be known as North America, humans are just starting to establish a toehold, chasing game across the Bering land bridge. Hermod is much more likely to encounter a woolly mammoth in Midgard than a human being.

Nothing makes Hermod happier than wandering with the broad sky above his head and stalks of wild wheat brushing his knees. Some consider his restlessness a fault. But before this day is done and a stake is driven through the heart of the Aesir's paradise, Hermod's gifts will be called upon.

So why has he come home? He's not sure himself. He felt something today, when he was lazing on that beach. Something changed. Something enormous, though Hermod can't quite put his finger on it. It's just a feeling, as though every particle in the universe suddenly changed state. And, strangely, he had a strong desire to see his brother Baldr. So he started walking. And he kept walking until he found a swirling arch of light, the rainbow bridge Bifrost. Now he approaches the city of his birth with dread.

"One hundred forty-six thousand, three hundred and two," says Munin.

"What's that now?"

"The number of hairs on Hermod's head."

Hours later, night has fallen, and Odin's hall of Valhalla is lit like a forge. Whirlwinds of embers spiral up to the rafters. Odin sits on his high seat, clutching his spear. His one eye glows like a fired coal. The hole where his other eye used to be is a dark chasm that knows no bottom. Beside him sits his wife, Frigg, soft and lovely and soothing as bread from the oven.

The hall is in a state of full-scale revelry. Gods and warriors drink tankard after tankard of the mead that squirts from the teats of a goat the size of a Midgard mastodon. They eat from an equally monstrous boar, who squeals piteously as meat is sliced from his flanks. Tables and chairs sail across the room. Cups smash together in toast. It is a good time. The party is not in honor of Hermod, who stands against the wall in shadow, trying and failing to stay sober. Instead, it is in honor of Hermod's brother Baldr.

Baldr, so handsome and fair he gives off a glow, sits at a table and indulgently drinks whatever his admirers put in his hands. Unlike Hermod, he can handle the strong drink of Asgard, and he will not disappoint those who have come to celebrate his life. If Thor is all the raging weather of earth compressed into bodily form, and if Njord holds the might of the seas in his eyes, then Baldr is all that is good and right and hopeful in the world.

Long ago a sibyl told Odin that Baldr's death would be the first link in a long chain of events culminating in the end of the gods and the destruction of the nine worlds. And then, earlier this week, Baldr had a dream in which he died. So there's been some nervousness in Asgard.

But as soon as she heard of the dream, Frigg, Odin's wife and Baldr's mother, had taken care of things. She exacted an oath from every creature living or inert, every animal, insect, fish, bird, every rock and chunk of metal—she took an oath from everything—that no harm would come to Baldr.

Well, she did leave out one thing. A small thing. Just a sprig of mistletoe growing on the outskirts of the city.

Too insignificant to be worth worrying about.

Which brings us back to Hermod.

# # #

REACHING OUT to grab an ale from a passing servant girl, Hermod slouched against the wall, watching the festivities from the shadows. He had entered the hall hours ago but hadn't yet paid his respects to his parents, and every moment that went by was making things worse. Maybe the best thing to do was slip out now, get back on the road, walk until his shoes wore out, and then walk some more and try to forget the murky anger brewing ever since he'd learned of Frigg's oath enchantment. Hermod hadn't needed a spell cast on him to get him to pledge no harm to Baldr. Why would he want to hurt Baldr? Nobody wanted to hurt Baldr.

He drained his cup and looked to the high seats where Odin and Frigg sat. Odin had many guises— mad poet-magician, gray wanderer—but tonight he was the great warlord, powerful, grim, and inscrutable. His wolf lay at his feet, and his two insufferable raven spies perched on his shoulders. Hermod couldn't even begin to guess what was going on in his father's mind as he watched over the proceedings.

Meanwhile, Frigg was in conference with some hunchbacked old crone, her face serious and intent as the old woman whispered in her ear. What was the crone doing in the hallowed hall of Valhalla? Who knew? In any case, his parents were clearly busy, and it would be rude to interrupt them. Good time to hit the road.

"You've returned!" Baldr was suddenly pulling him into a warm embrace, clapping him on the back and laughing in his good-natured way. "Please tell me you'll be staying in Asgard awhile, brother. We have missed you."

"Well, I . . . Yes, I'll be staying. Of course." And Hermod was surprised to find he actually meant it. It had been years since he'd entered his own hall, longer still since he'd sat in counsel with his Aesir kin, and perhaps it was time to settle down, at least for a little while, and reacquaint himself with Asgard.

And why had his thoughts on this matter changed so suddenly? he wondered.

"It *is* good to see you, Baldr. I trust there've been no more dreams?"

Baldr smiled, embarrassed. "Ah, yes, my dreams. I fear a lot of fuss has been made over nothing."

"Mother doesn't make fusses over nothing. That was a powerful piece of enchantment she worked on the worlds."

"And wholly unnecessary. But, then, she and Odin have been frightened by the idea of Ragnarok for some time."

Baldr almost, but not quite, rolled his eyes.

"Isn't the end of the worlds worth fearing?" Hermod said. For some reason, he found himself suddenly wanting to put a protective arm around his brother, but he resisted.

Baldr took two tankards from a serving girl and replaced Hermod's empty cup with one of them. "The final days are a very, very long way off, I think."

"Winter always seems a long way off in the beginning of spring," Hermod said.

They clacked cups.

A few hours later, when the host was even deeper in their cups, someone came up with the idea of hurling weapons at Baldr. The math was simple:

1. Baldr can't be hurt.
2. It's entertaining to throw weapons.
3. Weapons should be thrown at Baldr.

Tables and benches were dragged away to make room near the hearth, and Baldr stood alone in a circle of orange light, an indulgent smile on his face. He never sought to be the center of attention, but if it would satisfy others, he'd submit to it.

It began with Thor. He made his way down the

length of the floor, like a storm cloud gathering malice. Hermod took one look at the spear in his hands and knew this was a bad idea. Surely Frigg's spell of protection hadn't been cast for the Aesir's amusement.

Thor flung his missile with a clap of thunder. The spear struck Baldr's chest and exploded in a cloud of splinters. Baldr laughed and brushed debris from his tunic, and the hall erupted in cheers that made the flames in the hearth quaver.

Thor glowered. "Let me try my hammer."

After that, everyone wanted a turn. Arrows were shot. Swords were thrust. Cauldrons of boiling water and flaming torches and benches and tables collided with Baldr, much to the merriment of all.

Somebody tried to put a spear in Hermod's hands—that crone he'd seen conferring with his mother earlier—but he begged off, claiming he'd hurt his shoulder in a fall down a mountain. The woman released a high peal of laughter in response. In truth, dragged low by drink, Hermod was sure he'd miss and accidentally maim a serving girl.

That left only blind Höd among Hermod's brothers who were present and hadn't yet taken a turn.

Höd was the darkness to his twin Baldr's light. He stood tall and alone, his dark eyes like wells in a limestone face. Hermod didn't like to look too closely into Höd's eyes. They went a long way down.

Slumped over a table, Hermod watched the gray-cloaked old woman hobble toward Höd, leaning heavily on her walking stick. Seemingly aware of her approach, Höd shifted his posture uncomfortably.

"Why do you not join in the game?" she asked, her voice like a ragged talon.

"The last time I threw a spear," said Höd, "it went out a window."

Amid laughs, the woman persisted, wheedling; Höd continued to demur, but along with the weariness in his voice was a longing. How many times had he remained on the margins of things while his brothers and cousins played at contests and had adventures? Hermod sought those margins for himself, but Höd had been thrust into them, and it had been that way ever since they were boys, when Hermod and Baldr would race through the woods, bouncing off trees, chasing down wolves. Höd was ever left behind, a silhouette diminishing in the distance.

"I will lend you my stick to throw," the crone said, "and I will guide your aim. Come, what's the harm?" She placed her walking stick in Höd's hand. It was a twisted, leafy thing, clumped with dirt and grass and what looked to Hermod like mistletoe.

Höd could not have been more awkward holding the stick if it were a dead eel. He raised the rude spear, ready to throw it, but the woman put her hand on Höd's arm.

"Too low, dear. Let me help."

"I think this is a bad idea," Höd said, and Hermod tried to voice his agreement, but his drunken muttering was lost in the assembly's cheering. On her high seat, Frigg looked on, her peaceful smile matching Baldr's. Odin's face was blank stone.

Höd let the stick fly. It wobbled and corkscrewed, and when it punched through Baldr's flesh, he let out a squeak of pain and surprise. He laughed a little, as though he thought the dart protruding from his chest was a joke. Then he fell.

Later, people would say that color drained from the world at that moment. They would say that every living thing wilted just a little bit. But Hermod noticed none of that at the time. What he noticed instead was that Baldr looked like most other dead people he'd seen. His skin went gray. A froth of blood formed on his lips. There was a filmy red air bubble that Hermod couldn't take his eyes off until it finally popped.

His brother was just a corpse. No doubt the first of many to come.

CHAPTER ONE

ONLY TWO HOURS into Mist's first job, things were already going badly. For one, the duct tape had come loose over the recruit's mouth, and he was screaming so loudly that Mist was sure he'd be heard through the walls of the van, even above the roar of Route 21 traffic.

She turned to her companion in the passenger seat. "I thought he was supposed to stay out for at least another hour."

"Do I look like an anesthesiologist? Chloroform's not an exact science."

Mist shook her head at Grimnir. He did not look like any kind of *ologist*. Decked out in black jeans, quadruple-XL leather coat, and black homburg crammed over his head, he looked like what he was: a thug. *Her* thug, she reminded herself, still amazed at the idea of having her own devoted thug after having been with NorseCODE for only three months.

In back, the recruit pleaded for mercy. Mist steeled herself against his cries. Too much depended on the work to let a soft heart get in the way.

Grimnir slurped hard on the straw of his Big Gulp and popped open the glove box to retrieve a roll of tape. "I'll go back and redo him."

"Never mind," Mist said, aiming the van down the off-ramp. "We're almost there."

There was a vast, flat gray area of industrial parks and scrap yards, where a dummy corporation several steps removed from NorseCODE had prepared a warehouse expressly for this particular job.

Mist rolled down her window, letting in a blast of cold air and April snowflakes, and punched a security code in a box mounted on a short metal pole. A moment later, the automatic warehouse doors opened and she drove onto the concrete floor. The doors screeched shut and she killed the engine.

Grimnir got out and walked around to the side of the van. With reasonable care, he lowered the recruit's hog-tied form to the ground and used shears to cut the plastic ties that bound his hands and legs. The recruit had gone quiet, but Mist expected he'd start screaming again now that he was unbound. The warehouse was well insulated and equipped with fans and blowers configured to be as noisy as possible on the outside, in order to conceal interior sounds.

Tall and trim in workout pants and a New Jersey Nets sweatshirt, the man stood, shoulders hunched, like someone expecting a piano to fall on his head. "I don't know what this is about, but you've got the wrong guy." His voice quavered only a little.

"Your name is Adrian Hoover," Mist said. "You live at 3892 Sunset Court, Passaic, New Jersey. You're twenty-seven years old. You've been an actuary for Atlantic Insurance since graduating with a finance degree from Montclair State. I could also recite your Social Security number, driver's license number, cell phone, anything you'd like. You're definitely not the wrong guy."

Mist's boss, Radgrid, stressed the importance of establishing authority early in the recruitment process.

While Mist spoke, Grimnir removed two shotgun cases from a compartment beneath the van's floorboards.

Hoover's face looked green and clammy under the fluorescent lights. His eyes darted around the warehouse, at the ranks of port-a-johns and the glass-walled side office, its file cabinets full of authentic paperwork provided in the event that agents of some Midgard authority came knocking.

"You are about to undergo a trial," Mist said. "It's your right to understand—or at least be made aware of—the purpose behind it."

Grimnir opened one of the gun cases and withdrew a long sword. He rolled his neck and shoulders to loosen them and took a few practice lunges.

"Trial? But . . . I haven't *done* anything." There was at least as much outrage as fear in Hoover's voice. Mist took that as a positive sign.

"It's not what you've done, it's who you are. You and your fathers."

"My dad? He owns a dry cleaners'. Is that what this is about? Does he owe you money?"

"My name is Mist," she said, forging ahead. "I'm a Valkyrie, in the service of the All-Father Odin. My job is to help him prepare for Ragnarok, the final battle between the gods and their enemies. To that end, I'm in the business of recruiting fighters for the

Einherjar, the elite regiment of warriors who, when the time comes, will fight at the side of the Aesir, who are essentially gods. In short, if we have any hope of winning, we need the best army of all time. For reasons we can go into later, we have identified you as a promising candidate."

Grimnir's sword swooshed through the air as he continued to warm up.

"Are you guys in some kind of cult?" Hoover said, making an effort not to look at Grimnir. "Religion, I mean? I'll listen to anything you have to say. I'm open-minded."

Mist opened the other gun case and removed another sword. The blade glimmered dully in the flat warehouse lights.

"There are two qualifications for one to earn a place on Odin's mead bench. The fighter must be a blood descendant of Odin. Well, that's a preference more than a hard-and-fast qualification, but, anyway, we have determined that you're of Odin's blood. The second qualification—and this one is essential—is that the fighter die bravely on the field of combat." She presented the sword to him, bowing her head in observance of a formality she didn't really feel.

Hoover looked at her, appalled. "A blood descendant of . . . ? I don't even know what you're talking about, and you're going to kill me? You're going to *murder* me?"

"Murder?" Grimnir scoffed. "Hardly. It'll be a fair fight. And," he added with a wink at Mist, "there's always the possibility you could beat me. Now, take up your sword and prepare to be glorious."

Hoover covered his face with his hands. His shoulders shook. "Please, I don't understand any of this. I'm not . . . whatever you think I am. I'm an *actuary*."

Oh, crap, Mist thought. *I can salvage this. I'd* better *salvage it.* Maybe Hoover possessed the potential to become a great warrior, but nothing in his experience had prepared him to be captured during his morning jog, drugged, tossed in the back of a van, bound and gagged, and told he now had to fight a grinning ox with a sword to determine his postmortal fate.

She decided to go off script.

"I know how weird this is," she said, trying to avoid using a kindergarten-teacher voice. "Ragnarok, Odin, all that. I was raised Catholic, so this was all very strange to me too. But what you are one day doesn't have to be what you are the next. I wasn't always a Valkyrie. Just three months ago, I was an MBA student named Kathy Castillo. Then . . . something happened. My world flipped over, everything spilled out of its tidy order. But it's possible to go through that and thrive. Take the sword," she urged. "You don't have to beat Grimnir. You just have to fight him. You'll be rewarded. Trust me."

Hoover sank to his knees, convulsing with sobs. Mist continued to hold his sword out to him, awkward as an unreturned handshake.

She sighed. It cost NorseCODE a fortune in time and treasure to locate suitable Einherjar recruits, and nobody in the organization would be happy to hear they'd wasted their investment on Hoover. Least of all Radgrid.

"Grim, I don't think this one's going to work out."

Grimnir looked down at Hoover as if peering

beneath the hood at a hopelessly broken engine. "Yeah, I think you got that right. Well, stand him up, then. I don't like killing a man when he's on his knees."

Hoover looked up at them, his breaths catching in hiccuping gawps.

"We're letting him go," Mist said.

Grimnir pinched the bridge of his nose. "Kid, it doesn't work that way. We have to finish the job."

"We *have* finished the job. We're supposed to fill the ranks of Valhalla, not Helheim. He's obviously not fit for Valhalla, so I say we're done with him."

"Like it matters what *you* say? We work for Radgrid, and there's no way she'd be cool with cutting him loose."

"It matters what I say because I outrank you, and you've sworn an oath to me."

"I've also sworn an oath to Radgrid. And to Odin, for that matter."

"Great, and we can untangle that knot of obligations later, so for now how about we do what's right? Hoover's got no idea where he is now, no way he could find his way back. Let's drive him even farther out to the middle of bumfuck and dump him on the side of the road. We lose nothing that way."

"Yes," Hoover gasped, his eyes gleaming with hope. "Just leave me somewhere. I won't tell anyone about this, I swear. I wouldn't even know what to tell anyone if I wanted to."

Grimnir ignored him. "The test isn't facing death, the test is *dying*. You've been at this only three months, Mist, so maybe you still don't get how important the work is. But I'm Einherjar myself, and in the end it's gonna be guys like me with our asses on the line against wolves and giants. The system's worked in some form or another for thousands of years. You can't just start fucking with it now."

But Mist did understand how important the work was. Radgrid had impressed that upon her rather convincingly, and Mist lived in the world. It had been winter for three years now. She knew things were falling apart. And Ragnarok would be disaster beyond measure. Worse than the Big One, worse than an F5 tornado, worse than a city-drowning hurricane or a land-swallowing tsunami. Worse than a nuclear holocaust. The thin shield line provided by the gods and the Einherjar was the only thing standing between continued existence and Ragnarok. It was absolutely essential that the Einherjar have enough fighters for the war, and Mist was even willing to kill to see it done. As long as whomever she killed went on to serve in Valhalla. But sending them to Helheim was a different matter.

Grimnir took two steps forward, his boot heels echoing to the rafters of the warehouse. Rain clattered against the opaque skylights. Hoover was crying so hard now that Mist thought he'd vomit. Grimnir watched him with a pitying expression.

"Grimnir, don't—" Mist said.

Grimnir surged forward. Mist tried to block his thrust with the weapon meant for Hoover, her blade sliding off Grimnir's. She hacked downward, cutting through Grimnir's hat, and when her blade edge bit inches into the back of Grimnir's head, it sounded like pounding wet cardboard with a club. He squealed, his knees giving way, but not before his momentum carried him forward and his sword plunged into Hoover's belly. Grimnir fell on him, and Hoover released two loud, whistling breaths before falling silent.

Mist stared in disbelief at the corpses, their mingling blood gleaming like black oil in the queasy fluorescent glare.

The air grew cold and thick with a stretched cotton haze, and Mist knew what was coming. She'd experienced it three months earlier, when she and her sister, Lilly, had been shot on the way home from the grocery store. Mist never learned who'd shot them and why—thieves after their groceries, senseless drive-by, crazy drunk sniper-homeowner, it could have been anyone for any reason. Ragnarok was coming, and people were falling to all kinds of craziness.

An aching cold rushed through the warehouse, and then the road was revealed. The parade of the dead stretched as far as Mist could see, far beyond the walls of the warehouse. The dead shuffled forward, shoulders bent, eyes cast down, like slaves expecting the bite of the whip. Many of them were old and ill, dried out and hollow, their faces paper-white. Others had died more-violent deaths and shambled on with bullet holes in their bloody clothes. One teenage boy, dressed in the charred remnants of a T-shirt and jeans, trailed his intestines behind him like the train of a bridal gown. The dead were all around, dragging themselves in a queue without end, thousands, tens of thousands of murmuring dead, all walking the road to Helheim. Like Lilly three months ago. Like Mist, if Radgrid hadn't intervened.

If Adrian Hoover had died bravely, Mist's next job

would have been to escort him through the seam between worlds and bring him to the warrior paradise of Valhalla in the city of Asgard. There he would eat the finest roast meats, drink the richest ales, enjoy the flesh of willing and comely maidens. Instead, he would now walk the road north and down, to Queen Hel's realm of Helheim.

As one of the Einherjar, Grimnir would take a while to heal, but he'd be okay. Technically, he'd been dead for centuries.

"My stomach hurts," said Hoover. Rather, his spirit body said it, staring mournfully down at his own corpse.

"I'm sorry," Mist said. The words came out slowly, as though she had to carve each one out of stone. "I tried to stop him. He gave me some sword training, but I couldn't stop him."

Hoover's spirit body shuffled forward, toward the slow herd of the dead. "My stomach hurts," he said again. "When will it stop hurting?"

Mist thought of Lilly. The bullet had ripped through her sister's side, under her rib cage, and exited through her belly. She had not died instantly. Neither had Mist.

"Adrian, don't go with them." She grabbed his arm. He felt like thick slush, and she couldn't pull him away. He kept moving along with the other dead. "You don't have to go with them," she said, desperate.

"But I do," he said. "Don't you remember murdering me? I'm not sure why, but I have to go down the road."

She had to do something. She had to save him. Somehow. She'd failed Lilly, but she wouldn't fail

Hoover. What if she went with him, followed him to Helheim, claimed custody? Maybe she could bargain with Hel.

But the procession of spirit bodies was already fading to whispers of light, and when she reached out again for Hoover, her hand passed through his shoulder. She walked alongside him for a few more steps, and then he was gone, as were the other dead and the road itself. Mist found herself alone with the two corpses under the buzzing warehouse lights.

CHAPTER TWO

VENICE BEACH, CALIFORNIA: chalk-white sky, waves the color of lead, sand like wet cement. Hermod trudged south, his jeans soaked, his socks squirting water like a pair of sponges. Beside him, an Alaskan malamute trotted happily.

"Here I am, miserable," Hermod said, "and look at you, all smiles."

Winston barked in the affirmative and bolted off into white shrouds of fog. Maybe he'd sniffed out a body washed ashore and was closing in for a snack. Hermod grudgingly admired the dog's attitude. When the world was dying, it made sense to cultivate a taste for carrion. Hermod only wished he could do a better job of following Winston's example. His last meal was more than twenty-four hours behind him, and all he could think about were steaming piles of roast boar and warm ale, right from the goat's teat. But it had been several thousand years since he'd enjoyed that kind of home cooking.

Despite the grim weather, Hermod and his dog didn't have the beach to themselves. Figures moved in the fog like ghosts, picking through storm debris for wood to dry. Old men waved metal detectors over heaps of kelp, and whenever one drew close, Hermod would count the man's eyes.

"Hey, mister, you wanna buy a god?"

Hermod froze in the sand. A gray apparition stood several feet away in the swirling salt air. Hermod unslung his duffel bag and yanked hard on the zipper. He plunged his hand inside and wrapped his fingers around the hilt of his sword. Behind him, waves thudded against the shore.

"What did you say?"

"I said, do you want to buy a dog?" came a reedy voice. "Isn't he just the sweetest? Oh, silly, don't lick my face!"

The figure came forward. It was a girl, draped in blankets. Dirty blond dreadlocks framed a grime-streaked face. She cradled a small ball of white and gray fluff. It squirmed and tried to get at her chin with a pink and black speckled tongue.

"Thanks," Hermod said. "I've already got a dog."

"Not like this one, you don't. This one's gonna grow up big. *Real* big."

Hermod took a closer look. The dog's fur was a mixture of snow and smoke. Its ears tapered to points. Its paws were as large as the girl's fists.

"That's a wolf pup," Hermod said.

The girl squealed, "Oh, cold tongue! Not in my ear!"

"Where'd you get a wolf pup?"

"I know someone who knows a woman," the girl said, placing her hand gently around the pup's muzzle. "And she knows a woman who raises them. I'll trade for your jacket if you want him."

The waves broke like distant cannon fire, and an old song scratched at the back of Hermod's memory. Something about a woman who raised wolves. But was it a woman? Maybe it was a witch or a giant. He'd never had much of a head for music, and there were so many songs and chants and poems and incantations crowding his collected years that he could hardly hear an old bit of skaldic verse without it devolving into "Boogie Woogie Bugle Boy of Company B."

There lives a woman, there lives a woman who raises the wolves . . .

The wolf pup squirmed in the girl's arms, and she struggled to maintain her grip. "Hey, what's with you, fuzzy bean?" Losing her hold, she dropped it onto the sand, and it scampered off on its big clumsy paws. "Where are you going?" she cried, taking off after it. "I wasn't really going to trade you! Come back!"

Hermod stared after them for a few moments, until Winston trotted out of the murk to his side. Red sticky bits of gull feathers stuck to the malamute's jaw.

"Let's get off the beach," Hermod said to the dog. "You're giving me the creeps."

# # #

YOU EVER get an earworm?" Hermod started on his eighth beer, very much feeling the previous seven. His alcohol intolerance had always been a point of embarrassment back home, where his brothers and cousins could put down barrel after barrel of ale. They might vomit it all back up before sunrise, but the point was, they could down barrels of it first.

"An earworm? What's that, some kind of para-site?"

For the past hour he'd been enjoying relative comfort at the bar of the Venice Sidewalk Café, conveniently located mere yards from the beach. An open restaurant on the boardwalk was a rare find, most of the food stands and cafés having shuttered themselves against weather and vandalism. His companion was a woman in her early forties with hair the color of a highly polished trombone; he remembered she was named Roxie, or Trixie, or Linda. He liked her because she had a cute button nose and was willing to buy him more beers than he could handle (which appeared to be four), and he was hoping she'd take enough of a shine to him to invite him home, or at least buy him a second plate of chili fries.

"It's like a song you can't get out of your head," he said. "It just plays over and over and over 'til you want to jam a spoon in your ear and scoop your brains out."

Roxie or Trixie or Linda nodded. "Yeah, I get those. One time it was the first movement of Stravinsky's Symphony in C, for, like, two days. Thought I was gonna go bugfuck."

Hermod took a sip of his thin yellow beer. "So, you live near here?"

"I have to say, though, I still adore Stravinsky," she said, ignoring his question. "Those orchestral textures of his—nothing else like them. It's just that nobody likes a skipping record. When you know what's coming next, and then it does, again and again and again, it's painful."

Hermod drew his finger across the rim of the plate, picking up chili residue, and licked it. "Painful."

"What's your earworm?"

"There lives a woman," he sang tunelessly. *"There lives a woman who raises the wolves.* You recognize it?"

She sipped her own beer. It was only her second. "Not the way you're singing it." She gave his arm a playful punch, then rubbed his shoulder, as if to make the boo-boo go away. "You're not as skinny as you look," she said, giving him an appreciative reappraisal.

"I'm not as anything as I look."

"Ooh, Mr. Mysterious. Where did you say you were from?"

"Originally? Just on the other side of the bridge."

"Okay. And which bridge would that be?"

"The rainbow one."

The woman giggled. "You're so weird."

"It's just the beer. That, and this stupid song going through my head."

The woman flagged the bartender and held up two fingers. "My daddy always said the worst hell is inside a man's head."

"Oh, Hel's probably not what you'd expect," Hermod said. "At least not until you actually meet her."

"Of course," the woman sighed. "Hell is a woman, and you were married to her."

Hermod gratefully took the fresh mug of beer the bartender put in front of him, drained a fourth of it, and wiped away a foam mustache. "Hel's not married. You go north and down, for nine days and nine nights, into the sunless lands, through chasms with walls so high you can't see the top. You come to the freezing river. Beyond that is the corpse gate. It's a wall formed of corpses intertwined, arms and legs all tangled. They'll speak to you, and they'll want to touch you, because you're warm. Beyond the gate is the entrance to Helheim itself, and it's guarded by the hound Garm, huge and emaciated and terrible. And then Hel, queen of the deadlands: Half of her is pure flesh, soft and rosy as the most beautiful virgin's. And the other half is black like a rotten banana peel. I once asked her if I could take two of my brothers back home to the living worlds with me. She said I could take just Baldr, but I insisted on bringing Höd back with me too. I figured that was only fair. She wouldn't go for that, and then everything got really screwed up."

The woman looked at her watch and signaled the bartender again, and Hermod paid little attention to her as she settled the tab, because the song in his head wouldn't leave him alone.

"Thanks, Linda," he said, as she got up and put on her jacket. "Sorry if I creeped you out there."

There lives a woman. There lives a woman in Ironwood. There lives a woman in Ironwood who raises the wolves of Fenrir's kin, and one will grow to eat the sun and the moon.

Hermod raised his glass to finish his beer. Instead, he set it down and stared into the rising bubbles.

A raven hooked its claws over the seat Hermod's lunch companion had vacated. "Would you like to know how many women you've struck out with over the course of your life?"

"Tell your brother to fly off while he still has

wings," Hermod said to Hugin, who was perched atop a beer-tap handle.

"The girl on the beach had a wolf pup, and you let her go." Hugin's weight pulled down on the beer tap, dribbling Bud Lite.

"It doesn't have anything to do with me," Hermod said. "I'm just a pedestrian in this world."

"I'd say you're running out of sidewalk."

"Me and everyone else." Hermod finished his beer and rose, glancing at the raven's shiny black eyes to find his own reflection staring back at him.

"There's a seam to Ironwood nearby," Hugin said. "There are more wolves. Maybe you should follow the sidewalk there."

"I don't see why I should, really."

"Because you want to keep on walking. You like walking, don't you?"

"Hey!" The bartender rushed over, snapping his bar towel at the ravens. "Frickin' crows, Jesus! Shoo!"

The ravens flapped away out the open door, and once they were gone, the bartender gave Hermod a dirty look, as if he'd brought them in with him. He glared at Hermod's empty glass and empty plate and opened his mouth, but Hermod forestalled him.

"Don't worry, I'm on my way."

Outside, he retrieved Winston and strode off at a good pace. Hermod really did like walking. It helped take his mind off things. Such as the ravens, whom he hadn't seen in centuries. Of course, just because he hadn't seen them didn't mean that they hadn't seen him.

"Just keep walking," he muttered. "Doesn't matter.

None of it matters. It's got nothing to do with me. I'm a pedestrian." And for a while he managed to lose himself in the rhythm of his footfalls. This is what he was good at. He'd successfully let entire decades pass this way. Centuries, even.

Rounding a corner onto Venice Boulevard, he caught a faint whiff of hot pepper in the air. Winston growled irritably. At a strip mall, a pair of workers were replacing the front window of a laundromat. From the glass shards and the remnants of riot-control gas, Hermod figured there'd been some action here recently. Random acts of stupidity were becoming even more common as the months passed and winter refused to release its grip. And as bad as things were in Southern California, other parts of the planet were taking worse punishment. People blamed the freak weather on the cascade effects of global warming and retreating glaciers, and who was to say they were wrong? Hermod had experienced many long winters. Even ice ages. Just because things were cold in California and everywhere else didn't necessarily mean it was Fimbul-Winter.

Hermod spotted a plywood sign across the street, wired to an ivy-choked chain-link fence: IRONWOOD NURSERY.

He wondered how the people who lived around here experienced this place. Maybe to them it was just where they purchased their begonias. But some places looked different, depending on the angle from which you encountered them. Hermod spent a lot of time within these strange angles. It was the only way to approach the seams between worlds.

"You stay put," he said to Winston, reaching down

to scratch behind the dog's ears. "Find yourself a nice, plump squab to munch, if you want. But you don't cross the street after me, understand? And if I'm not back in an hour, you're on your own."

Winston whined and rubbed his muzzle against Hermod's pant leg. About a year ago, Hermod had picked him up in Churchill, Manitoba, the last survivor of his litter. They got along pretty well. Winston was a good traveling companion; he didn't ask questions.

Jaywalking across Venice Boulevard, Hermod checked the zipper of his duffel bag to make sure it wasn't stuck. It would be just his luck to die of a snagged zipper. Death was inevitable, but there was no sense in dying stupidly. Rusty hinges screeched as he pushed open the gate and entered the cover of the nursery. Marking the way toward a tangle of bushes, barren ornamental orange trees flanked a narrow path of cracked concrete paving stones. A hand-scrawled cardboard sign indicated the daily price increases on vegetable seeds. Withered potted plants raised on wooden pallets showed more evidence of the cruel weather. A few people went about their business here—a silver-haired Japanese man arranging bonsai trees and a boy setting rattraps by a palm tree—but otherwise the nursery felt abandoned. Hermod continued on through cottony fog.

Something called him off the path—instinct, or a spell, or a doom—and he stomped through ivy, whistling "Boogie Woogie Bugle Boy." When the sour tinge of urine touched his nose, he again checked the zipper of his duffel.

He came upon a peach-colored metal Quonset hut

edged with rust, like a flower past its bloom. Vines crawled up the sides and arched over the top, studded with yellow flowers and white fungal colonies and fly-specked spiderwebs. It was an entire ecosystem, an entire world.

From the duffel, he removed a bundle of stolen motel-room towels and unwrapped his sword. Its double-edged blade was scratched and stained, but he reckoned it would still do its job. He didn't require emerald-inlaid runes or curlicues, he just needed something that wouldn't shatter against swung steel and was sharp enough to bite through flesh and bone.

He wrenched open the door of the Quonset and took a step inside. The entrance behind him vanished in the gloom, as he'd expected. He coughed and batted at clouds of tiny flies with his sword, the reek of long-confined piss hanging in the steamy air. Sounds came out of the darkness. Snuffling. Mewling. Hermod lowered to a crouch as blotchy darkness gradually resolved into shapes, then into details.

In the center of the hut sat a giant, with a round spongy head like a mushroom and two dark little eyes, filmed over like those of an old fish. An irregular welt of a nose spread across her face, and, below that, thin, wet lips formed a ventlike mouth. Her flesh gleamed, clammy as wet clay.

Hermod counted five wolf pups clutched to her chest, suckling on floppy teats as long as his fingers. The pups pawed and nipped at one another to gain better access, and the giant stroked their coats of white and gray.

"Is it true what they say about a mother guarding her children?" Hermod said.

"Do you plan to earn fame that way, lesser son of Odin?" Her soft voice gurgled. "Oh, the songs they'll sing about you: Hermod the Nimble, mighty slayer of nursing mothers." She pressed the head of her smallest pup tight against a teat.

"I'm not here for that," Hermod said. Sweat trickled down the back of his neck. "I'd just like to talk."

"A visit to enjoy the warmth of my hospitality? I don't think so, when you barge into my mound, uninvited, sword in hand. So much for the vaunted manners of your tribe. No, the Aesir are cunning, and their city is built on a foundation of murder, and they offer the hand of fellowship only to their own. So why should I offer you mine?"

In truth, Hermod couldn't supply her with a reason. His kind had made war against giants and trolls since the earliest days. The Aesir had taken slaughter and made it a sport. Thor's hall was decorated with the mounted heads of this giantess's kin.

"If I had a hall in which to host you," Hermod said, "I'd offer you a seat by my fire."

"That is an empty offer."

"Yes. I'm afraid so."

Scratching sounds came from the matted roots at Hermod's back. His skin itched, but he wouldn't step away from the wall, wanting as much distance between him and the giant as possible.

The giant nuzzled her misshapen nose into the furry brows of her pups. "They say that when you returned from Helheim, having failed in the only significant task ever set before you, you left Asgard. You've never returned?"

"I've been traveling." He'd packed a sack with his pipe, a tankard, and a spare shirt, and though he'd lost all three many years ago, he'd never returned to his city. It wasn't home anymore.

"You must have seen much, given the length of your absence."

"Oh, you have no idea. And just when I think I've seen everything . . . This morning, for instance. There was a girl on the beach. She offered to sell me a wolf pup."

The giant's dark eyes narrowed to slits. "Are you saying I would allow my own babies to be sold, like pets?"

"Oh, I know they're not pets."

She sniffed, making a sound like a vacuum cleaner clogged with Jell-O. "If that's the most remarkable thing you've seen, you're touring the wrong places."

"Well, you know, the girl got me thinking," Hermod said. "She reminded me of an old song. I guess you wouldn't really call it a song. It was more like a prophecy. It was about a woman who raises wolves."

The giant shifted a little on her haunches. Muscles the size of basketballs bunched in her thighs. She hadn't seemed that big before. "Your kind are always making a villain of wolves. Another distasteful trait you share with men."

Hermod waved a fly from his mouth. "In the song, they're not actual wolves. They're other things, shaped like wolves, of a line belonging to Fenrir. You know of Fenrir, right? The great wolf son of Loki? There's a song about him, too, how at the end of days he devours Odin."

The giant did something that might have been a smile. Several hundred teeth lined her mouth, like pebbles. "I haven't heard that one, but I like it."

"Anyway, so this song I remembered this morning, it goes: *There lives a woman in Ironwood, who raises the wolves of Fenrir's kin, and one will grow to swallow the sun and moon.* So, the girl, the pup, the song, a path that leads to Ironwood, and here you are. You and your wolf-thing pups. I suppose it's all a coincidence."

"And if it's not, what is it to you? Some songs are sung not of a voice but of a truth that grows from the very soil of the World Tree. Some songs are older than us. Older than your All-Father, the gallows god himself. You were there when the Ragnarok doom was sung and your brother fell in blood. It was foreseen. It was prophesied. How you mighty Aesir must have quailed and wept to see the first hour of the end of the world struck. And yet you yourself journeyed to Helheim, and on your knees you begged before the queen for a reversal of fortune. Did it work? Did it set everything to rights? Hermod, little messenger, find the wisdom to see that the song will be sung, bray and flail as you might, and it will be sung to its very last note."

"Thank you," Hermod said, raising his sword. "That's all I needed to know." He charged and swung for a pup's head—any of the pups would do for the first blow—but the giant turned to protect them, and his blade bit instead into her shoulder. She threw back her head and roared. Twigs and clumps of dirt shook loose from the ceiling and clouded the air with filth. With the fury of an avalanche, she sprang forward, covering the distance between herself and Hermod in a single earthshaking step.

If there had been somewhere to run, he surely would have, but with no room at his back and the giant blocking any escape before him, he set himself into a stable stance and thrust his sword forward. The blade sliced neatly between two of her ribs, and she staggered backward, yanking the sword from his grip. Hissing in pain, she withdrew it like a splinter, inspected the blood-slicked steel, and then bent the blade across her leg until it shattered with a terrible glassy peal.

The giant hunched her shoulders and faced Hermod, panting a dank wind. "I take it you've really never slain a giant before?"

"You were going to be my first."

"You have to put more muscle behind a blow like that. That's why Thor was so good at giant-killing. He had the arms to swing that hammer of his. And he usually went right for the head, just dashed our brains out. Flesh wounds with us count for little."

"If only I had another sword." Not for the first time, it occurred to Hermod that many of his relatives knew how they were going to die. Odin in Fenrir's jaws, Thor poisoned by the Midgard serpent, Frey killed by the fire giant Surt. There was no verse about Hermod's own end. Usually he considered this a great blessing. But there were advantages to knowing how things would catch up with you in the end: For every other menace you encountered, you knew you'd get out with your skin intact.

Hermod sprang forward and dove to the ground, rolling and reaching for the largest of the shards of

NORSE CODE \ 35

his sword, about the size of a butcher-knife blade. The edge cut into his palm, a new addition to his lifetime collection of wounds. Using the giant's own knee for a foothold, he vaulted up and thrust the shard into her eye, smacking it home with the heel of his hand. The giant struck him on the side of his head, and Hermod crumpled to the ground.

The mound held still for a moment. Then the giant sat down slowly. "My babies," she said, only the last inch of the sword shard emerging from her eye socket. The pups returned to her, climbing up her body, sucking the very last milk she had to give them, even for a few moments after she'd died.

Climbing down, they approached Hermod, too much like puppies. But then they yawned, their maws growing wider and wider. Hermod pitched forward, and eventually all he could see was a gaping black chasm, and he was falling into it.

During his struggle with the giant, the roof of the mound had collapsed. It had been daylight when he'd entered, but now it was night. The moon shone yellow and fat, and the pups stretched their jaws yet wider and reached for it.

# # #

HERMOD GROANED and opened his eyes to see an elongated muzzle and sharp yellow teeth inches from his face. He scrambled away in a panic, his hand grasping for his sword but finding only mud.

Winston barked, and Hermod let out a gulping breath of relief. "Good boy," he croaked. Then the ground spun out from under him and he vomited.

He closed his eyes and made himself breathe. His

head was frightfully painful to the touch, and his fingers came away bloody, but his skull seemed to be holding his brains inside. He fished a bandanna from his jacket and bandaged his sliced-open palm.

A few yards away, the Quonset hut lay in ruins, all crumpled metal tangled in vines. He was sure if he dug through the wreckage, down deep, he would find the giant's corpse, but he was content to leave it there. Paw prints circled him in the mud.

Why hadn't the wolves killed him? They'd seen him murder their mother, and once they'd opened their mouths, he'd been entirely at their mercy. But, then, the moon still shone, a pale disk struggling to push its light through the clouds. Maybe the pups weren't quite up to sky-eating or god-slaying yet. The girl on the beach had said her wolf still had a lot of growing to do.

And Hermod had a lot of questions for that girl. Finding her should be a priority. Instead, he lay back in the mud. A giant had broken his sword and given him a concussion, and he deserved to lie in the mud and sleep.

Cursing, he forced himself to his feet. He thought he was going to vomit again but managed to hold it in, swaying on his legs. The wolf tracks led back to the paving stones, marking a muddy trail for a dozen or so yards. The trail blurred as the path led farther from the Quonset, away from the overhanging trees. It had probably rained while Hermod was unconscious. Beyond the gate, outside the nursery on Venice Boulevard, there was no trace of the pups at all.

"Well, boy," he said to Winston, "once again it looks like I've taken a mess and made it a disaster."

The malamute wagged his tail, which Hermod took as polite agreement.

CHAPTER THREE

NORSECODE GENOMICS WAS housed in a three-story cinder-block cube in the back of a Needham, Massachusetts, office park. Its only distinctive architectural feature was the logo etched into the glass doors of the front entrance: a DNA double helix entwined around a tree with nine roots. Mist pushed through the doors into the reception area, where some dozen men sat on stylish but uncomfortable chairs. Most of them had clipboards and were busy filling out forms. Since NorseCODE was paying fifty dollars to males willing to complete a questionnaire and provide a mouth-swab DNA sample, the waiting room was usually packed with people willing to brave the snow and ice. Fifty dollars could buy gas or oranges or batteries.

Mist gave the men a quick visual assessment as she crossed the floor. They represented a broad range of age, race, dress, and body type, but none looked particularly impressive.

The ice-queen receptionist behind the granite-slab desk gave Mist a respectful nod and buzzed her through another door. Mist paused in the doorway. "Is Radgrid in today?"

"She's at the home office," the receptionist replied, and Mist concealed a breath of relief. Radgrid was the last person in the worlds she wanted to encounter right now, and having her as far away as Asgard was better than she'd hoped for.

She continued down a long corridor lined with glass partitions, behind which bleary-eyed technicians in lab coats manned computers and centrifuges and gene sequencers. Everything gleamed white and clean, so far removed from the actual sweat and blood and urine that their work culminated in. NorseCODE maintained branches in São Paulo, Singapore, London, Johannesburg, Dubai, and Basel, each staffed by Valkyries, Einherjar muscle, and techs. As far as the techs knew, NorseCODE's work focused on genomics for pharmaceutical application, not on recruiting soldiers for Odin's army. That dirty business stayed hidden in places like the New Jersey warehouse where Mist had left the bodies of Grimnir and Adrian Hoover.

An elevator delivered Mist to her third-floor office, overlooking a landscape of office parks and, just beyond them, a freeway overpass half lost in the fog, like a ghost road. A dim line of brake lights barely moved down the snow-choked blacktop.

Mist eyed her coffeemaker longingly, but this office visit had to be a surgical strike. Considering the severity of the wound she'd dealt Grimnir, she figured on three days until he'd recover enough to report in to the office—less if he had been injured on the fields

outside Valhalla, where the Einherjar trained for battle by disemboweling and dismembering one another.

Mist settled behind her desk and keyed her computer to life. Logged in, she searched NorseCODE's intelligence dossiers for references to Helheim. She'd
read some of the material before, but Radgrid had kept
her too busy over the last three months to spend much
time in the office, and these records weren't accessible
off-site.

Helheim was one of the nine worlds that made up
Yggdrasil, the World Tree, which Mist tended to
think of as some kind of metaphor for the cosmos.
But every Asgardian at NorseCODE, from Grimnir
to Radgrid to all her Valkyrie sisters, insisted that it
was an actual tree, that its roots ran through all the
worlds, and that the worlds themselves were part of
the tree's living tissue. Mist figured that this concep-
tion was a product of some ancient worldview rather
than literal truth, but she allowed that she might be
indulging in comforting, self-serving thought.

The reports didn't offer much more than some de-
scriptions of Helheim and a few cryptic mentions that
Mist couldn't make sense of. No map, no hints about
the route or anything about how to walk the road if
you weren't among the dead claimed by Hel. Nothing
about how Helheim was guarded, how it was orga-
nized, nothing that would help her find her way in
and then back out.

And maybe that was just as well. The fight over
men's souls was an eons-old feud waged between
Odin and Hel, and sometimes just knowing that these
gods existed was enough to make Mist doubt her own
sanity. Radgrid and Grimnir called her a Valkyrie,

she'd seen and done things that challenged her ideas of what the world really was, but she was still Kathy Castillo, UCLA student, granddaughter, sister. Maybe she wasn't quite mortal anymore, but she felt mortal, and she had no business challenging gods and death.

She almost shut off the computer but instead resorted the file listings in reverse chronological order and opened one named *Hermod*.

"Back so soon?"

Mist barely managed to conceal a startled gasp at the sight of Radgrid in the doorway. Red curls spilled over the shoulders of her ivory pantsuit, a contrast so sharp that Mist expected to see clouds of steam rising in the air. She met Radgrid's eyes, bright as burnished steel, and knew the same jolt of fear and mute wonder she'd felt the first time she encountered the Valkyrie, three months earlier.

To this day, Mist still didn't understand why she'd been selected as a Valkyrie while Lilly, a kind of warrior in her own right, who'd braved bullets while trying to help farmers plant trees in the Congo, who'd been Tasered and beaten by police batons in dozens of protests across the globe, was left to meekly walk the road to Helheim. Kathy had tried to stop her sister from leaving, but, as with Adrian Hoover, the road had faded from her sight, and Lilly with it. And then Radgrid had appeared, towering over Mist in white furs and chain mail, glimmering in the colorless morning like a polished knife.

Radgrid entered Mist's office and took the seat across the desk. Casually, Mist closed the window on her computer. "I thought you were in Asgard," she said, congratulating herself on managing to sound only mildly interested in Radgrid's unexpected presence.

"I was, and longer than I'd have liked. The Einherjar are deserving of their honors, but, truthfully, I have more pressing matters than serving them drinks in Valhalla."

Mist felt fortunate to have mostly avoided that duty, and on the one occasion when she hadn't been able to duck out of it, Grimnir had assigned himself as her menacing bodyguard to make sure nobody harassed the new girl. Grimnir had been a loyal friend. And she'd rewarded him by slicing his head open.

"How did things work out with Adrian Hoover?"

"He didn't work out," Mist said flatly.

She watched Radgrid's face warily, waiting for an explosion. But Radgrid's expression barely changed. "That's too bad. I had high hopes for him. His Y-chromosome match was as close as they come."

A Valkyrie's job had always been to find soldiers for the Einherjar, and the corpse-choosers' traditional method had been to pick their way through combat zones, sorting through burned bodies and piles of guts and limbs, selecting the best of the fallen to be brought to Valhalla.

Radgrid had devised a new way to find recruits. She realized that many of the best warriors among the Einherjar—like Volsung, and Sigurd the Worm-Slayer—were descendants of Odin, from a line established on earth in the early dawning of man. Over the ages, the records of lineage had been lost, but Radgrid believed the bloodline was still unbroken. If geneticists could learn the deep language of blood and find the descendants of Genghis Khan, then couldn't they also find the many-generations-removed sons of Odin? So she'd built and staffed the NorseCODE labs.

"How's Grimnir?" Radgrid asked, setting her valise on the floor. It was a black kidskin number, thin as a blade.

I should just confess now, thought Mist. Admit to trying to save Hoover's life, to splitting open Grimnir's head, throw herself on Radgrid's mercy.

"He's okay, I guess. I think he was heading for Atlantic City or somewhere." That was a vague-enough lie, consistent with Grimnir's proclivities. He liked to spend his time where the drinks were cheap, where he could relax by intimidating gangsters and security goons. She knew Grimnir's habits well, having spent most of the last few months in his company, either being trained by him in everything from horse riding to hot-wiring cars or surveilling Hoover from inside the van, the air filled with his jovial grumble and the smell of take-out pizza grease.

She could still fix this, somehow. She could make things right with Grimnir and get back on track with NorseCODE's work and do her bit to counter the end of the world. And kill and leave the innocent to waste away in Helheim.

Radgrid idly removed a letter opener from the cup on Mist's desk and ran a long white finger along its edge. "It really is a shame about Hoover. Grimnir hates it when recruits don't work out."

"What if we gave them a little training before the test? No army just shoves a gun in a new recruit's hands and sends them into battle without some training first."

A tiny shift in the angle of Radgrid's head was the

closest thing she had to a shrug. "I prefer to concentrate our efforts on the ones who have already proved themselves worthy of Valhalla. Our resources are finite, and time is the least plentiful among them."

"But if we could determine if they were Einherjar without killing them first . . . it would be more humane. Killing men needlessly, men who might have families, loved ones . . . does that make sense?"

Radgrid's eyes glinted like icicles in sunlight. "The sense of it was determined when our ancestors were still living in caves. The sense of it was formed by beings who count among their elders only the ground you walk upon and the stars above your head."

Radgrid returned the letter opener to the cup. Then, from her valise, she withdrew a file folder and slid it across the desk toward Mist. It lay there, dark against the warm oak.

Mist opened the file. The assignment specifications took only a few pages. She flipped through them, glancing at a printout of fuzzy pink caterpillars—chromosomes—and phenotype data with references to the O-Prime sample. There was an 83 percent likelihood that this recruit was descended from Odin, which made him a high priority. The recruit's name was Lucas Wright, of Las Vegas, Nevada. He was smiling in the surveillance photo, riding a skateboard, his braces gleaming. He was fourteen years old.

"I'll get right on this," Mist said, her voice steady and confident.

Apparently satisfied, Radgrid stood and took her leave with only a brisk nod. The office seemed to warm by a degree or two a few moments after her departure.

Mist sat motionless in the dark room for several more minutes. The turnpike traffic outside her window had become a blurry trail of brake lights slowly engulfed in the fog. Eventually Ragnarok would manifest itself in spectacular ways, with disasters and monsters, but now it was more like a lingering whimper. A lot like what Grimnir had once told her Helheim was like.

She reopened the dossier on this Hermod character, and when she finished reading the report, her heart was pounding. According to the file, Hermod had ridden to Helheim to retrieve another of the Aesir, his brother Baldr, and though he had failed, he had come back alive. He'd severed his ties with Asgard long ago, but last week an agent of NorseCODE had spotted him in Los Angeles.

Across the country lived a god with the proven ability to travel in and out of Helheim.

Mist knew that, if their positions were reversed, Lilly would be on her way to Los Angeles right now.

# # #

GRIMNIR WOKE up in the warehouse to the sound of his own groans. He gingerly felt the back of his head. It had been a long time since he'd been so badly injured, and for a while all he could do was sit with his head between his knees and force himself to breathe. If this had happened to him in Valhalla, Odin's hall in the city of the gods, he would have been healed in time for supper. In the men's world of Midgard, recovery took longer.

Grimnir badly missed Valhalla.

Mist had done this to him. He couldn't believe it. She'd seemed like such a nice kid.

Well, actually, that was the problem. She *was* a nice kid. He'd known that three months earlier, when Radgrid had assigned him to be Mist's assistant, her trainer, her mentor. In the time they'd spent together, he felt they'd become friends. And now here he was with a split skull, plus a ruined hat. He picked up his homburg and stared glumly at the fissured brim. He loved that hat. He'd looked very smart in it.

He reached into his pocket for his cell phone, only to find it missing, and laughed a little. Despite his disappointment in Mist, he was proud of her for having thought to nick his phone. Any delay in his ability to notify Radgrid about what she'd done would buy Mist a bit of time.

Slowly, he got up and stood over the corpse of Adrian Hoover. Judging by his color and smell, he'd been dead for a few days. Mist had given herself a good head start.

"Buddy," Grimnir said to the dead man, "Mist really put her ass into trying to save your life. I hope you appreciate it."

Leaving the warehouse, Grimnir started looking for a car to steal. He had a renegade Valkyrie to track down.

CHAPTER FOUR

HERMOD WALKED DOWN Centinela Avenue into drilling rain. He disliked the lightness of his duffel bag and missed his sword, not that it would do him much good at the moment, when his most formidable opponents were the buses that huffed by, kicking up rooster tails of dirty water.

Ahead, Winston darted from puddle to puddle, his tail wagging off globs of water. A late lunch of two grackles had put the dog in a particularly chipper mood, but Hermod's head was pounding too much from the beating the Ironwood giantess had given him to feel chipper. And there were wolves on the loose, very dangerous ones, and he'd helped set them free. Ragnarok was inevitable, Hermod understood and accepted that, but that didn't mean he wanted to be the one who finally set it off.

He needed to find those wolves.

And once he did, then what? What could he do? Nothing, probably. But should he find himself facing down a sky-eating wolf, doing so unarmed was definitely worst-case. So, there. One relatively simple errand to focus on: find himself a blade. And for that, he needed a dwarf.

Several hours of walking brought him to a neighborhood of payday loan services, nail salons, liquor stores, and a great many boarded-up storefronts. Nothing about the area distinguished itself from the rest of LA, but Hermod came to a pensive stop. There was something weird here.

Winston barked and cocked his head inquisitively.

"I don't know," Hermod said. "But I've got a feeling. I think there's a seam close by."

Winston barked again.

"Why do I even bother talking to you? It's not like you understand what I'm saying. I could have just said, 'I think there's a dancing banana close by.'"

The dog squatted and shat.

After another several blocks, Hermod halted before a boxy stucco building beside a fenced yard. HOLLYWOOD SCRAP AND SALVAGE, read the sign in front. Hermod's legs shivered, registering danger, and he checked the zipper of his duffel before remembering that he was unarmed. These late days were not a time to squeeze between seams without protection, but a powerful impulse drew him along. It was in his nature to explore.

Inside, he stood on a cracked tile floor, water dripping from his sleeves and pants legs. A roly-poly Hispanic man with a Dodgers ball cap leaned against a cluttered counter, sipping Pepsi from a bottle. He gave Hermod a skeptical glare.

"I need one of those things," Hermod said, gesturing vaguely with a hooked index finger. "One of those plumbing fixtures, you know? I don't know what it's called."

"Looks like what you need is one of those, whatchamacallits, umbrellas." The man chuckled at his own joke.

"Yeah. Well, first the plumbing thing. Mind if I take a look out back?"

With a slight jerk of his head, the man indicated the door leading out to the yard. Then, "Hey, is that your dog out there? In the *rain*?"

"Yeah, he's fine. He likes it."

"That's cruel, man. Let him inside. I got some chicken."

Hermod's stomach clenched with jealousy.

"That's very kind of you, but he just ate. He'll be fine."

"A person who can't take care of himself shouldn't have a dog. If you want your plumbing 'thing,' then you let me feed him."

Hermod relented, lingering inside while Dodgers Cap ruffled Winston's coat. When the man stripped the breading off a fried chicken breast and started feeding Winston strips of white meat, Hermod could stand no more of this display of human decency and went back into the rain, into the metal and rust world of the scrap yard.

Gutted washing machines, water heaters, and refrigerators bounded muddy lanes. Rain plinked against hills of copper tubes snaking like exposed roots. Hermod wandered a random path, trusting instinct to guide him to his unknown destination, and wished again for the comforting weight of his sword.

He came to one heaping mound of scrap composed

of radiators, oven doors, cracked car mufflers, dented and gouged stainless-steel sinks. It looked no different from the other mounds in the yard, but Hermod knew his seam was here.

Cautiously, he removed a stained white monolith—the lid to a big freezer—and set it down in standing water. He remained motionless for a moment, fearful that the towering hill would collapse on him, but when no avalanche followed, he continued disassembling the mound, pulling free a wire birdcage, a patio-table top, a battered coffee percolator. Eventually he revealed a fissure in the jumbled mass. He leaned forward, poking his head into the black space, and felt a wave of dry warmth drift over his face. His vision couldn't penetrate the darkness.

If there was another giant down there, or a litter of wolf pups, he would end up with much worse than a bump on the head. He sighed and squeezed through the fissure.

Feeling his way along the wall of metal junk, he shuffled forward carefully. After several paces he thought his eyes were adjusting to the darkness, but, no, there was light ahead, a faint orange glow that grew stronger the farther he went. His feet found a stairway, and he followed it down. The tangle of junk on either side of him gave way to plates of metal, joined together by rivets and bolts and welds like scar tissue. The steps under his feet were at first diamond-plate, then unfinished slabs of black iron, and then uneven lumps of thick, pitted metal. The light here was much stronger, like the inside of a wood-fired pizza oven. A metallic tang that reminded Hermod of blood hung in the air. His footfalls sounded echoing clanks.

He landed on the final step, and before him was a door, heavy and mighty as a bank vault but of a darker color. There was no knob or handle, so he pushed on it, and it swung open with buttery smoothness.

He walked through. Pots and pans and kettles and cauldrons hung by hooks from the ceiling. Hermod had to bend to avoid striking his head on them. A low workbench the size of a Ping-Pong table bore a messy array of tools—hammers, wrenches, tongs, clamps. Finer tools were arranged on a smaller table. Hermod didn't recognize most of them, but they had the look of a jeweler's precise instruments. He found a bicycle clamped upside down to a rig. He found a pile of golf clubs. And on a table of its own, beneath a silvery cloth, he saw a long, slender object that he knew would be a sword. He peeled back the cloth.

The blade was difficult to look at. Something about the way it reflected light was fundamentally wrong, as if the photons were taking strange detours on their way to Hermod's eyes.

"Burglar!"

"Thief!"

Hermod dropped the cloth back over the sword. A pair of dwarves glared at him, their eyes coal-dark and rimmed with red. Standing chest-high to him, they wore leather aprons over breeches of thick cloth, revealing bunched muscles in their powerful arms. Their faces were dark and furry, like big coconuts.

"I'm not a thief. I'm a customer. My name is Hermod."

The two dwarves—brothers, Hermod suspected—exchanged a look.

"That name means nothing to us," one of them said. His chin was fringed with a copper-colored beard. The other had a beard of silver.

"At the very least it means I've told you my name and you haven't told me yours," Hermod said in the dwarves' own language.

If the pair was impressed by Hermod's ability to speak in their tongue, they gave no indication of it.

"How did you get in here?" demanded the copper-bearded one.

"I walked. And then I went through your door. Which was unlocked."

"You idiot, Gustr!" spat the copper-bearded one, striking his brother with a hairy fist. "What's the point of having a door if you don't bother locking it?"

The other was uncowed. "I'm *working* on the lock, Úri. I'm *improving* it."

Úri raised his fist again, but then apparently thought the better of it. "Really? What did you have in mind?"

Gustr rubbed his palms together and revealed a smile of silver Chiclets. "What's the tightest, most closed-up thing you can think of?"

Úri scratched his chin. "My jewel chest?"

"That flimsy thing?" Gustr said with a guffaw. "I could break into it with my fingernails."

"Oh, could you? Then I have to wonder why you've never bothered."

"How do you know I haven't? Maybe I did and just didn't find anything worth taking."

Úri cracked his knuckles, a sound like smashing walnuts. "If you did, you'd be cackling with ceaseless glee, because you're a braggart with no self-control."

Gustr seemed on the verge of a scathing comeback, but Hermod interrupted him with a cough. "Gentlemen? Perhaps you could settle this later. I was hoping we could do business."

Both dwarves gave Hermod long, probing glances.

"Business usually implies an exchange of some sort," said Gustr. "You look like you'd be hard-pressed to exchange a pleasantry."

"You've really never heard of me?" Hermod asked.

The dwarves checked with each other silently, then shook their heads no.

"I'm Hermod," he said again, trying not to sound as exasperated as he felt. "Hermod, of Asgard. Of the Aesir. Hermod, son of Odin. I trust you've heard of Odin?"

"Of course," said Úri, "but that hardly recommends you."

Hermod realized that if he'd spent more time building a reputation for recreational violence, people might be more impressed with him. It was hard to deny at least a grudging respect to someone who left mountains of bloody corpses wherever he walked.

"I would like to negotiate the purchase of a sword," he said, tight-jawed.

"We don't have any swords," said Gustr.

"We're not in the weapons trade," agreed Úri.

"What about that one?" Hermod shot back, his voice ringing off the pots suspended from the ceiling. "The one under the cloth?"

"It's a commission," said Gustr.

"Already spoken for," said his brother. "Anyway, it's not finished."

In truth, Hermod didn't want that sword. That one was embedded with something he didn't understand, a deep enchantment of some kind. Enchanted blades were as likely to draw blood from those who carried them as from their enemies.

"And it's a very interesting blade," said Hermod. "The sort of thing crafted by wise, experienced hands. I can't believe it's the only sword you've got in the entire shop."

The brothers leaned their furry heads close together and exchanged low muttering. Then, "We may be able to dig something up," said Úri. "What have you got to pay with?"

Hermod knew he didn't have much to interest them. They'd be unimpressed by his meager bag of coins, and, besides, he needed to save his money; a sword wasn't the only thing on his shopping list. But maybe this was an opportunity, a chance to test just how badly he was bound in a chain of events. Somebody or something had wanted him to find the giant in Ironwood, had put him in a place and at a time in which he couldn't help but find the wolf den. It had also been awfully easy for him to find this seam to the dwarves' workshop. Yes, it was time to test his bonds.

And, of course, maybe that's how they—or it, or whatever—got you, by convincing you that you were acting of your own free will when you were really just dancing on the strings.

He rummaged through his duffel bag. It was pretty slim pickings in there: the hotel towels that had formerly swaddled his sword, a slim bar of soap, his canteen, a spare shirt, a hardened old piece of Hel cake. For this to be a proper test, he reasoned, he should select the most worthless possession he had. He withdrew a tattered postcard.

"There is a place in Midgard where many worlds collide," he said. "Egyptian pyramids, New York skyscrapers, the Eiffel Tower, the canals of Venice— all within sight of one another. Anything you could want, they can provide." He held up the postcard. The words *Viva Las Vegas* ran across the photo in pink script. "This image was captured with a device that grabs light and holds it, frozen for all time. If you have a sword worthy of my hand, I will trade you this for it."

Gustr looked at his brother. "What about that one I saw you toss on the scrap heap yesterday?"

"I was going to melt it down for nails."

"Let the Aesir have it instead."

Úri considered this for a moment. "I don't think we're getting the better part of this deal."

"Of course we're not," said Gustr. "It's just a postcard. But at least then we'll be rid of him."

The brothers scowled at each other in silent consultation, and then Úri stalked off, disappearing behind a row of scrap bins. He emerged a moment later with a mutt of a broadsword. The hilt was wrapped in scarred hide. A number of nicks ran down the length of the blade, a few so deep one could tuck a poker chip inside. Úri held it in one hand. He held his other hand out toward Hermod, twitching impatiently for Hermod to hand over the postcard. The exchange was made.

It was a poor blade, but it was simple metal, and Hermod liked that. "I don't suppose you'd throw in a scabbard?"

The brothers made only rude noises, so Hermod wrapped the blade in his towels and stashed it in his duffel bag. He turned to take his leave, again feeling vaguely ill as he passed the strange sword.

"Who's this one for, anyway?"

Gustr opened his mouth to say something, but the other dwarf drove an elbow into his side.

"I wasn't going to tell him," Gustr protested.

"I know," Úri said, "because I wasn't going to let you."

And Hermod left the brothers to bicker, their voices echoing in the metal passage as he climbed the iron stairs.

The weight of the sword in his duffel bag felt good. He didn't suppose there was much chance he could leave it in there for long.

CHAPTER FIVE

GODS SHOULD BE easier to find. After two days in Los Angeles, Mist had seen no sign nor turned up any leads concerning Hermod's whereabouts in the places where the NorseCODE files said he'd been spotted. She'd thought a god walking around in Midgard would leave more of an impression.

As early darkness approached, she dashed down the sidewalk through hailstones that clattered against the pavement like molars. She dove out of the cold into a warm, dry place called Café Lascaux. As she peeled off her raincoat and hung it on a rack by the door, the smells of dark, loamy coffee and cinnamon enveloped her. She sighed with pleasure. It had been almost a day since her last coffee, and if she was going to continue her search, she needed a little time for nourishment and regrouping.

She'd covered her tracks as well as she could, drawing funds from her own savings to buy a used Toyota Corolla in Boston and then paying cash for gas and food in a sprint across the country. The expenses had almost broken her, but she couldn't risk using her NorseCODE credit cards.

Nobody noticed as she walked to the counter; the other customers were absorbed in their laptop screens, their copies of *Daily Variety* and *Advertising Age*. Then Mist noticed a bearded man in a leather jacket across the café, looming over his little round table like a bear over a pancake.

She ordered a quadruple-shot Americano and waited for it to appear on the counter before joining Grimnir.

"So. You found me," she said, blowing ripples across the top of her drink.

"Found you? Come on now, give me credit, kid. I did better than just find you. I planted myself somewhere you've never been, before you even got here." He'd bought a new homburg, which he wore over a black bandanna covering the back of his head and neck.

"Neat trick," Mist said. "I didn't know you could predict the future."

"Anyone can predict the future. Some people don't even stink at it." He leaned forward, going into his tutor mode. "I snuck a GPS tracker into the lining of your jacket months ago. I've been following you since Ohio."

"And you figured I'd be coming in for a cup of coffee before too long." Mist sipped her Americano. It was thin and still too hot.

"Well, I know I sure as shit needed one. That was mean, by the way, betraying me and cutting my head near off. But nicely done. Looks like I managed to teach you something after all." He took a sip from his mug. Whipped cream and chocolate sprinkles clung to his mustache.

"What happens next, Grim? Do you kill me now, or do you take me to Radgrid first?"

"Radgrid. And there doesn't have to be any killing. I'll tell her . . . I dunno, that you were drunk, or whatever. She'll be pissed beyond pissed, but we'll talk to her, and you'll face whatever punishment she hands you, and maybe there'll be enough time for you to get out of her doghouse before the world ends." Grimnir looked out the window thoughtfully. "Actually, I've been thinking. Maybe we don't have to tell her anything about your extreme betrayal of our friendship after all. I told her the Hoover kid fought like a ninny and I slew him, which is technically true. And she believed me when I told her I cut my head in a dispute over a restaurant check, because it's not like that's never happened before."

"You mean . . . she doesn't know I did it? You didn't tell?"

"Didn't see a reason to. I mean, you committed an extreme betrayal of our friendship, but I didn't want to see Radgrid strap you to a rock and have a serpent drip toxic venom on your face for whatever's left of eternity. Maybe you can still go back to NorseCODE and redeem yourself with productivity. Of course, I don't want to work with you anymore, on account of your extreme betrayal of our friendship. Not sure how I'll sell that part of it. Maybe I can convince Radgrid that I just miss working with Thrúdi, who's a very good lay, by the way. I'm really going out on a limb to help you, kid, because . . . I don't know. You're a mess, but I like you. I gotta tell you, Mist, I'll be worried about you, not having me to cover your ass. Radgrid'll probably assign you to work with Targad the Steel-Nosed, and there's something wrong in the head with that guy. He scares me."

Mist's throat grew tight. She'd buried a sword blade in the man's head, and he was still worried about her. She was reminded of the way Lilly had always tried to protect her when they were kids.

And that, she thought, was what she should have been doing for the last three months, since she'd died. She should have been trying to do for other people what she couldn't do for Lilly. Instead, she'd kidnapped and terrorized. No more.

"I've been looking for Hermod of the Aesir," she said. "He knows how to get in and out of Helheim, and once I find him, I'm going to convince him to help me bring my sister and Adrian Hoover back to Midgard."

Grimnir made a noise halfway between a groan and a laugh. Flecks of whipped cream flew off the top of his drink. "Why stop there? What about your parents? And their parents? And all their brothers and sisters and aunts and uncles? And all the Make-A-Wish Foundation kids and . . . and Robert Kennedy and Martin Luther King? What about Bruce Lee? What about Sinatra? People die, kid."

"We died, but we're still breathing the air, drinking coffee. We're proof that there're other options."

The mirth left Grimnir's face, leaving his expression as serious as Mist had ever seen it. "You're being stupid. Odin claims his share, Hel claims hers. That's the handshake deal. You and me, we may not be exactly mortal anymore, but we ain't much more than

NORSE CODE \ 61

little specks in the universe's eye. It's not up to the likes of us to screw with things. I've lost people, too, you know. Enough of this shit. Finish your coffee."

He reached for another sip of his drink, but Mist grabbed the cup from his hand and set it firmly back on the table.

"I'm not going to go quietly, Grim. I swear, try to take me back to Radgrid and I will fight you every step of the way." She dug her phone out of her purse, holding her thumb over the keypad. "I've got 911 programmed into speed dial. Try to take me by force and you'll have to deal with me *and* the hassle of LAPD. If you manage that, I'll consider it my job to survive, escape, and sabotage. I will be the biggest pain in the ass you've ever dreamed of."

He rubbed the back of his head and winced. "You already are."

Mist said nothing, and Grimnir stared at her for a long moment. He closed his eyes. "You're serious about this."

"Help me find Hermod. That's all I ask. Once I've done that, you can go back and tell Radgrid whatever you want. She doesn't have to know about you helping me. You can just say you looked and couldn't find me, that you taught me too well."

Thunder shook the windows and set off car alarms. Outside on the sidewalk, a couple of men started beating on each other for no reason Mist could discern. Nobody else took much notice. "Come on, Grim," she said. "The world's coming apart at the seams. What've you got to lose?"

"My honor, my job, my limbs, my afterlife . . ."

"Do it anyway."

"Because?"

"Do it because it's a grimly hopeful thing to do instead of grimly hopeless. You haven't been knocked around too much to believe in hope. I know you haven't."

"Kid, I've had a really shitty couple of days." He rubbed his eyes with hands the size of boxing gloves. "And thanks to you, I have a feeling I'm in for a whole lot more."

"You're a good man, Grim. I mean that."

"Save it for my funeral."

They spent the rest of the day crawling across the greater metropolitan area in Grimnir's Jeep. They visited a bowling alley in Sylmar, a Chinese seafood restaurant in Monterey Park, a prostitute in West Hollywood, another in Culver City, a gorgeously androgynous sculptor living in a downtown loft who was surely from Alfheim, and more prophets and seers living out of shopping carts and donut shops than Mist could keep track of. She'd had no idea there were so many people existing where the edges of Midgard blurred into the other eight worlds, but when she mentioned it, Grimnir only shrugged.

"It's always been this way," he said, "but, yeah, it *is* getting more common. The structure of the World Tree is getting chewed up as Ragnarok approaches."

Grimnir inquired about Hermod's current whereabouts at every stop, sometimes relying on charm, other times going into his more comfortable mode of looming intimidation. Neither approach gained them more than a passing of the buck to yet another informant.

The task reminded Mist of one of those road rallies

she'd sometimes undertaken with her friends in high school, where you'd have to race across town and do things like snap pictures of yourselves in a Hot Dog on a Stick girl's hat or nab a matchbook from Spago. At least those old car rallies usually came to an end around midnight, at Bob's Big Boy, with sundaes and fries. That was back when the roads of Los Angeles had been more passable, without untended earthquake fissures and sinkholes.

In Beverly Hills, Grimnir parallel parked the Jeep between a Mercedes and an Audi, bumping both. The stretch of Wilshire Boulevard hosted an unusually active string of businesses, including a nail salon done up in postmodern severity. Behind a counter of unfinished concrete and artfully rusted metal, the receptionist greeted Mist with a look of cool disinterest that morphed into full-scale alarm when Grimnir came in behind her.

"Do you have an appointment?" she asked, managing to wrestle her mouth into something like a smile.

Grimnir leaned with his elbows on the counter. The receptionist took a nervous step backward. "An appointment? Here, at such an exclusive salon? Oh, if only!"

"I'm afraid we're not accepting walk-ins just now."

Mist glanced around. The receptionist didn't appear to be lying. All the stations were filled with luxuriating clients being attended to by masked manicurists. While Rome burned, a whole orchestra got their nails done.

"My claws are fine, honey. I'm just here to talk to that guy." Grimnir aimed a frankfurter-size finger at a man receiving a pedicure. He was in his fifties, eyes hidden by aviator glasses, and was dressed in a blue polo shirt and black shorts that revealed a long bypass scar running down his thigh and calf. A younger man, twenty-something and blond with an objectively perfect face, stood with his arms crossed behind the pedicurist's chair. While the older man stared at the ceiling, nodding his head as though listening to music, the blond stared openly at Grimnir.

The receptionist tried to send Mist and Grimnir away with apologetic noises, but when the blond man approached, she gratefully let him deal with the unwanted visitors.

"Can I help you?" he asked. His turtleneck clung to a body contoured with lean muscle.

"Cutting to the chase," Grimnir said, "your boss has information I want, and if you don't move out of my way, I'll be picking my teeth with your ribs."

"You know, it takes only eleven pounds of pressure to break a knee."

Subtle shifts in stance signaled that Grimnir and the blond were getting ready to have it out, right in the middle of a Beverly Hills nail salon. Sometimes it was hard for Mist to remember to be grateful for Grimnir's presence. "Grim—"

Still staring up at the ceiling, Mr. Bypass Scar held up a hand. "André, this is the last goddamned decent salon on this side of town, and I will not see it wrecked. Bring the man over."

Disappointment registered on the faces of both Grimnir and André. Neither moved for a moment— André refusing to step aside, and Grimnir unwilling to walk around him—until Bypass Scar barked at his assistant/bodyguard again. André shuffled aside a couple of inches.

The pedicurist continued to nip the man's cuticles as Grimnir towered over them both.

"You're another one of those Asgardians, aren't you? Your girlfriend too?"

"She's my boss."

"Harvey Silver." The man held out his hand to Mist, looking on expectantly, as though the name should mean something to her. His nails gleamed. "Aren't you a fan of the movies, dear?"

"Some of them. Are you an actor?"

"No, I'm a professional godparent."

"Like, Mafia?"

He laughed. "No, dear. Name your favorite actor, favorite hip-hop artist, favorite studio exec, if you have one, and odds are that I'm godparent to at least one of their children. People feel secure knowing that a man like me has their kids' best interests tucked in his back pocket."

"And do you?"

Very seriously, he said, "I'm an exceptional godparent. I go to great lengths to take care of my children."

Grimnir picked up a pair of nail clippers and held them to the light. "Harvey hasn't always been such a nice man. Six years ago, when he was a veep at Sony, he was known as Harvey the Scythe. But then all the caviar and cream puffs caught up with him, and his heart exploded. To put it in less polite terms, Harvey croaked."

"I was dead for only a minute or two," Harvey

protested. "But long enough to walk a few steps down the road and to see what's on the other end."

"And Harvey was sharp-minded enough to remember his glimpse of Helheim. So, once he came to in the hospital, before he was even up and around, he decided to devote his very considerable resources to finding his way back to the road."

Mist suddenly felt a kinship with this man. "I lost someone down that road," she said. "If you know anything about how to get to Helheim and back . . ."

To Mist's surprise, Harvey's chin quivered, just briefly, before he regained control. "Who did you lose?" he asked, his voice gruff.

"My sister. We were both shot."

Behind his sunglasses, Harvey seemed to be looking at something off in the distance. "When she was nine, my daughter, Brooke, died of acute lymphoblastic leukemia. Her mom did a lot of praying and crystals, a lot of talking about seeing her again in our next lives. I just kept nodding until the divorce. But then the heart attack happened, and I saw the road, and I realized that if there was another place, an afterlife, I'd have to be a real son of a bitch not to get my daughter the fuck out of there. It took a lot of time and a lot of my money, but eventually I learned about Hermod, and after even more time and more money, I actually found the bastard."

Again, Mist wondered about Radgrid's selection methods. Any mortal commanding the wherewithal to track down a god was someone to be reckoned with. But it was highly doubtful that Harvey Silver was all that decent with a sword, and his reconfigured heart probably didn't pump Odin's blood, so a man like him would be of no interest to Radgrid. If only the Einherjar were a meritocracy.

"Will you tell me where Hermod is?"

Harvey Silver shook his head. "Won't do you any good, dear. Hermod may be a god, but he's not any useful kind of god. I followed him around the globe for two straight years, and let me tell you, the guy gets around. But even after I offered him everything I could think of—cash, stocks, gold, girls, a house in Malibu, executive-producer credits on anything he wanted—he wouldn't work for me."

"Are you still having him tracked?"

"I get reports, sure."

"Tell me where he is."

"You're wasting your time, dear."

"It's my time to waste. And if it turns out I can convince Hermod to help me get my people back, I'll work on him to bring your daughter back too. I'm bringing back as many as I can."

Grimnir sighed.

Harvey Silver's eyes remained hidden behind his dark lenses. "André," he said after a time, "give me a pen."

# # #

MIST HAD hoped for an address, but, instead, Harvey Silver had given her a list of instructions. She and Grimnir were to look for a tall, thin, shabbily dressed man. These days he reportedly had an Alaskan malamute with him. He would likely be found near the beach, because he was drawn to shorelines. He had a tendency to walk along the borders of places. Look for him where the homeless were common and not likely to be evicted. Look for him in places where underground economies thrived, where nobody took credit cards.

Grimnir said he knew a few places like that, and they spent the next two days fruitlessly checking them out.

On the third day they came to Palisades Park, a crumbling ridge of grass and dirt perched above the Pacific Coast Highway. A concrete barrier had been erected to keep people away from the precipice, but much of that had itself tumbled down the cliff side, and the city ultimately relied on nothing more than signs warning people to stay at least six feet from the edge. Many of the signs had gone over the edge themselves. Was this Ragnarok, Mist wondered, or just California? All it ever took was a decent rainstorm to dissolve half the city.

Makeshift shelters constructed of wood scraps and shopping carts and plastic garbage bags sagged in the saturated air. Men in filthy donated clothes lay in the shadows of lean-tos, or on benches, or on bare ground.

Mist and Grimnir walked north, wading through mud and wet grass, past the merchants. Their setups ranged from stalls of plastic tarp and PVC pipe to mere blankets spread on the ground. Racks were hung with used clothing—winter coats, flannel shirts, bootleg UCLA sweats—draped in clear plastic sheeting to guard them from the wet. There were vendors hawking hothouse tomatoes and amateur apothecaries selling everything from vitamin C pills and Chinese herbs to home-brewed antibiotics. Other merchants sold batteries or gas-powered generators, always in demand since most cities' power grids hadn't been reliable for three years. With street performers playing guitars and drumming on plastic buckets for change and vendors roasting satay on hibachis, the atmosphere was almost festive.

Mist scanned the crowd. "I've got a few other places on my list we can try," Grimnir said, leaning over a merchant's display of switchblades with a connoisseur's eye.

"Not yet. Let's split up to cover more ground. You mill around the south end of the park and I'll take the north. Call if you find anything."

She checked her cell phone to make sure it was getting a signal.

North, the market seemed less flea than black. Mist suspected that the girls and boys hanging around the restrooms weren't selling anything other than themselves. What some of the merchants were dealing in, however, was a little harder to figure out.

The stalls here were sparser and less friendly to the casual browser, so to give herself something to do while visually scanning the place, she dug out a few coins to hand to a man huddled up against a tree.

"Have you seen the ocean lately?" he said, palming her coins.

Mist glanced beyond the cliff. The waters were calm today, a flat, steel-colored slab. "It's quiet."

"That's because the worm's sleeping. But he'll wake up before too long. I'm here, day in, day out, and I've seen him reveal himself. He shows the thinnest bit of his spine. Just a long, dark line on the horizon. It happens before a storm, usually a crazy one, like the one that took out the marina. He's testing the air, seeing if it's time."

"Time for what?" Mist had to ask, even though she generally tried to avoid conversations with schizophrenics.

The man winked, as if revealing a juicy slice of gossip. "When he gets restless, the world cracks apart. And he's starting to get restless."

"Yeah, I have heard this one, actually."

She spotted a tall man conducting business a few stalls down and moved closer. He was dressed in stained jeans and a black longshoreman's coat. Flecks of gold glittered in the gray stubble on his cheeks and chin. Over his shoulder he carried a long duffel bag patched with duct tape. An Alaskan malamute stood alertly beside him.

He seemed to be in the middle of a negotiation with a man at a card table. The merchant held a ball about the size of an apple, wrapped tightly in brown paper.

Now she wished she hadn't split off from Grimnir. The man fit Hermod's description, but he didn't give off . . . whatever it was she thought a god of the Aesir ought to give off. She reached for her phone, but at that moment the man turned his head and stared right at her with eyes the color of wet slate.

She left her phone in her pocket and strode up to him. "I'm Mist," she said. "A Valkyrie under Radgrid's charge."

"*No hablo inglés,*" he said.

The merchant snorted. "He was *hablo*-ing *inglés* just fine a minute ago."

Hermod gave him a dirty scowl and then directed

the very same look at Mist. "I'm trying to do something here, and you're interfering. Please go away. And don't come back. And don't send anybody else. Thank you very much."

This could not possibly be Hermod, Mist thought. Gods were supposed to be wrathful or capricious, not cranky.

"I've given you my name," she said, drawing on the lessons in Asgard protocol Radgrid had given her. "Won't you have the courtesy to tell yours to a servant of your father's?"

"I don't owe my father anything, much less his servants. If you won't go away, then at least be quiet, okay? Thank you."

He turned back to the other man and gestured to the paper-wrapped ball in his hands. "So how does it work? I don't see a fuse."

"No fuse," the man said, showing him a plastic tab curling from the ball. "You just yank this."

"Okay. Nice. I'll take four."

"That's eight hundred dollars."

"I'll give you six hundred."

"Eight hundred dollars."

"Seven—"

"Eight. Hundred. Dollars."

Hermod muttered and dug into his duffel bag. Out came a jingling, knotted tube sock, which he untied to retrieve a handful of something. He opened his palm under the merchant's nose. Gold coins glittered, even under the gloomy sky.

"Hold on a sec," the merchant said. He produced a balance and set of weights, and with the attention of a neurosurgeon working on a patient's brain, he weighed the coins. "You're a few short," he announced.

Hermod grumbled some more but placed another coin on the balance tray and leveled the scale.

"Four grapefruit at two hundred each," the merchant said. "You want a bag for these?"

Hermod did, and the merchant placed them with considerable care in a brown grocery sack, the paper worn soft as leather. Meanwhile, Mist quietly took her cell phone out to call Grimnir, but the LCD displayed no bars.

Hermod placed the grocery bag in his duffel and took off with long strides. "Are you really a Valkyrie?" he said over his shoulder as Mist struggled to keep pace.

"Honestly? Not in good standing, and I've been one for only three months, but I *am* a Valkyrie."

"Hmm" was Hermod's only reaction.

He stopped at the edge of the cliff, where a pedestrian bridge crossed high over the Pacific Coast Highway to the beach on the other side.

"Who sent you to bother me?"

"Nobody. It was my own idea."

"Why?"

"You can find people in Helheim."

His face didn't change, still set in a frank frown of displeasure.

"My sister died with me and took the road, and I want her back. And a man I was supposed to recruit for the Einherjar . . . I want him back too."

"Why just them? Something like one hundred billion people have lived and died in Midgard since the beginning of the human race, and nearly every single one of them has ended up in Helheim. So why are you concerned only about your sister and this man, your recruit? Why are some lives worth more than others?"

Mist decided not to tell him of her ultimate intention, to free as many dead as she could. Not yet.

"I seem to have touched a sensitive spot with you."

Hermod's expression shifted enough to let her know she'd landed a blow. He turned and began crossing the bridge.

This stretch of Highway One was the main artery between Santa Monica and the rich enclaves of Malibu, but uncleared mud slides left the road impassable more often than not. Only rare islands of asphalt in the mud indicated that there was a road down there at all. Again, Mist wasn't sure if this was the result of the world ending or just business as usual in Los Angeles. Earthquakes, wildfires, and landslides were the trinity of natural disasters in this part of the country.

Mist decided to play on what she suspected might be Hermod's vein of fairness. "I want my sister, Lilly, back because I love her and it's not right that I got to live and she didn't. She's more of a fighter than I ever was, and if anyone should get to be a Valkyrie—"

"Yeah, life's arbitrary and capricious."

"And the man, Adrian Hoover: I helped kill him, and I need to set things straight—"

"Making up for past mistakes, I get that. But, no, sorry, I don't do retrievals. I tried that once, and it was a disaster." They reached the other side of the suspended walkway. Hermod jogged down the steps.

"Would you stop long enough to look me in the eye when you turn me down?"

"No, sorry, really, but I'm in kind of a rush. There are these wolves I accidentally freed. Not wolves, really, so much as monsters. And at least one of them is fated to devour the moon and the sun, as sure a sign of Ragnarok as I can think of. So I've got to clean up my mess, and I don't have time to chat."

"Are these wolves nearby?" Mist asked.

"That's what I've been led to understand."

"What if I help you?"

Hermod came to a halt. "How can you help?"

"Well, like I said, I'm a Valkyrie. I can swing a sword."

Now she had him thinking. Mist suppressed a satisfied grin.

"Even if you help me, I'm not agreeing to get your sister and your recruit out of jail. But we can talk about it, I guess."

Better than nothing. And, truly, if the wolves of Ragnarok were free, didn't she have an obligation to help Hermod do something about it? Trying to prevent the end of the world, after all, was why she'd agreed to serve Radgrid as a Valkyrie in the first place.

"Deal," she said, surprised to see relief wash over Hermod's face.

\# \# \#

WHAT LUCK! Hermod thought, stomping across the sand with Winston and the Valkyrie in tow. Whether the luck was good or bad, he wasn't sure, but allying himself with a Valkyrie—and a cute, modern one at that—had to be auspicious in one way or another.

The lifeguard stations were little blue huts on stilts that reminded Hermod of lunar landers. He still remembered where he was when astronauts first walked on the moon—rumbling through Western Siberia in a boxcar, between Kormilovka and Ekaterinburg, sharing a bottle of vodka with half a dozen fellow hobos. One of them had a transistor radio, and he declared the mission of Apollo 11 a great folly. "All the suffering on earth, and here's man, trying to become a god of the skies. The old gods won't look kindly on that."

"It's too late for the old gods," Hermod had said, taking a long pull off the vodka bottle. "You little guys outstripped us a long time ago. Tyr's something else with a sword, but let's see him take an AK-47 round in the face. Even Thor—I doubt there'd have been much left of him at Hiroshima. The only real difference between mankind and my lot is that you won't destroy the world unless you decide that's what you really want to do. But us gods? We think we have no choice but to blow everything up, like it's our job. So go ahead and walk on the moon. Get your footprints all over it. Get your hands grubby with moon dirt. Enjoy it while it's still there."

After that, his fellow passengers wouldn't let him have any more drink.

Nearing Lifeguard Station 9 with Mist, Hermod saw bundles lying among the wooden supports: people sleeping, wrapped in blankets and coats. He'd spent the morning asking around the beach until a cluster of homeless men singing doo-wop had interrupted their rendition of "Duke of Earl" long enough to tell him where they'd seen a girl with dreadlocks who kept a big puppy with her.

"You hang back and out of the way," he said to Mist. "I'll have my hands full with the wolves, so if you see a girl with blond dreadlocks stealing away, you tackle her and don't let her go. Clear?"

"Well, it's a very intricately detailed plan, but I think I can keep it all straight in my head."

"Good enough." He continued toward the life-guard station. The wind carried a strong, stinging odor, something like an amalgamation of piss, wet fur, human body odor, and other smells more diffi-cult to identify. The stink reminded Hermod that the wolves weren't exactly wolves. Their grandfather, Loki, was neither man nor god but a giant and a shape-changer, and other things.

Winston slowed to a hesitant walk and started to whine.

"That's fine, boy," Hermod said, reaching down to scratch the dog's ear. "You stay back." But when Hermod resumed his pace, Winston followed, and Hermod felt an embarrassing wave of affection for the dog.

They continued on across the cold sand, and when they came within a few yards of the station, Hermod unzipped his duffel bag.

"Wolf girl," he called. "It turns out I *do* want to buy a god. Let's talk."

There was movement among the bundled forms. "Fug off," someone muttered. A figure crawled out from under a pile of blankets. Dreadlocks hanging in her face, she hugged the wolf to her with both arms. It was bigger now, nearly half Winston's size. Hermod slipped his hand inside his duffel bag and gripped his sword. He glanced quickly over his shoulder and saw

Mist standing alert. She'd unbuttoned her coat, revealing a nylon scabbard and the grip of a short Chinese saber.

The girl shuffled closer, peering up at him with bleary eyes. Her face seemed thinner than it had been just a few days before.

"Hey," she said.

"Hey. Do you remember me?"

"Nuh-uh."

"You offered to sell me your wolf."

The girl's eyes flicked away, as if she was looking for an escape route. She spotted Mist and looked back at Hermod. "I didn't mean it," she said. "I wouldn't sell him for a million bucks. He's my darling." The wolf sagged heavily in her arms.

"I see you two have developed an attachment. Where'd you get him?"

"Found him."

"Hear me," Hermod said. "I've got a sword in this bag, and if you're not more forthcoming, I'm going to take Little Darling's head right off. Do you believe me?"

The girl looked at him with fear and smoldering hatred. "Yes," she whispered.

"Good. You found him where, exactly?"

"Here," she said with contempt. "On the beach. He was just a tiny ball of fluff with sand fleas in his fur, crying for his mama. I know I can't take care of a wolf. I can barely take care of myself. But what could I do? It's so cold. And people . . . We've all gone crazy. There's people who'll eat him." To Hermod's alarm, tears stood in her eyes.

She set the wolf down and threw an arm around

his neck. "Beautiful boy, look at those eyes. How could anyone want to hurt you, hmm? But don't worry, I won't let them."

Maybe there was no problem here, Hermod thought. The wolf might just be someone's lost exotic pet. This was Los Angeles, after all, where people kept ocelots in their backyards. True, the pup looked like the ones in Ironwood. And, yes, it had tripled its size in only a few days.

Hermod sighed as the grim thought came to him: He'd have to kill it in front of the girl.

The wolf shot a jet of piss, barely missing the girl, who jumped back with a squeal. Steam rose from the sand where the urine landed. There was a great deal of movement now beneath the lifeguard station. The blankets fell away, revealing not people but five more lean-muscled pups. They stretched their jaws wide in horrible yawns, their teeth like little white knives set in black gums. A gust of wind disturbed the sand at Hermod's feet, or maybe it was gravity drawing the grains toward the wolves.

Winston vibrated in a low growl, remaining at Hermod's side. Mist came forward, closer to Hermod, widening her stance to keep her footing. "Jesus," she whispered.

"More little balls of fluff you found?" Hermod called out. His own voice sounded distant to his ears.

"No, they just showed up. I think they're my sweetie's littermates."

The girl must have caught the look of murder in Hermod's eyes, because she moved around in the sand to put her body between Hermod and the pup. "Don't you hurt them!" she said with a snarl. "Don't you dare!" She tilted her head back, and Hermod thought she was going to start howling, but instead she screamed, "Help! Rape! Murder!"

The other wolves moved around the girl and their sibling, like slow-moving water around a rock.

"I don't want to hurt you, miss," Hermod said, "so you'd better get out of my way."

"I hate you," the girl spat. "You're a terrible man. We haven't done anything to you. This isn't *fair*."

With the world-ending wolves approaching, Hermod could only agree with her. Nothing was fair. It wasn't fair that Baldr had died. It wasn't fair that Höd had been killed in punishment when the crime had been Loki's. It wasn't fair that Hermod couldn't spend the last days of the world on a warm beach with nubile island girls, drinking fruity drinks and being fed ham sandwiches.

At least the wolves were nowhere near fully grown yet, and Hermod allowed for the remote possibility that he could kill them, maybe even all of them, and not suffer a fatal wound. Stranger things had happened.

They continued their slow approach, almost cat-like in their deliberation, and Hermod felt his balance slipping, their attraction increasing as they grew closer. He almost pitched forward and just managed to plant a leg in front of himself to prevent a fall. Winston flattened himself, digging into the sand. With a small cry, Mist flew past him. Hermod reached out and grabbed her by the arm just in time. She fell to her knees, holding her shoulder. He hoped he hadn't dislocated it.

The five pups formed a circle around them.

"Heel," Hermod said. "Play dead."

One of the pups let loose an ear-gouging yip, and the others took it up, stabbing the air with rising notes that became fully voiced howls.

Hermod waited it out, sweating.

Then, the wolves spoke in words, all joined in a breathy, high-pitched voice that wavered in tone, a wolf howl repurposed. "Is the moon out?" they asked. "We're so hungry."

"It's daylight still," Hermod said, though there was little light and even less warmth on the beach. "Guess you'll have to come back later."

"But we're hungry *now*," they whined. "You killed our mother, and, oh, we want the moon so badly. The sun too. We'll chase them both until they're tired, and then they'll be ours."

Hermod tried not to look into their open mouths. It was so dark in there.

"What about the girl? She feeds you."

"She can't keep even one of our bellies full. She's such a tiny morsel." And the pup the girl was protecting opened its jaws and leaned forward, and the girl's head was in its mouth. Screaming, she went down slowly, like a rat being devoured by a snake, disappearing up to her shoulders, then her elbows.

"Hey, leave her alone!" Mist struggled to her feet, and Hermod reached out to restrain her but missed.

The other wolves stretched their jaws wider, and Mist shot forward, helpless. She stumbled and fell, somersaulting like a leaf in a windstorm. Hermod dove for her legs, managed to catch them, and held her down in the blast of flying sand grains.

The girl kicked and thrashed to no avail as the wolf

continued to draw her down its gullet, until she was gone from the thighs up. Her sobs came in a faint echo, now only her feet sticking out from the pup's mouth, and then it snapped its muzzle shut, and the girl was vanished from the earth.

The pup turned two drowsy circles in the sand and lay down, resting its head on folded paws.

"Will it be night soon?" the other cubs asked.

Hermod's lips moved silently. It took him a moment to find his voice. "Soon enough," he said.

"We'll eat you now. We're so hungry."

"If you want to snack on me," Hermod said, "better digest me quick, because any mutt that eats me is getting cut open from the inside."

"There are six of us," the wolves said.

"Suits me fine. Take turns. I'll slice you one by one."

The wolves pulled their lips back in snarls, displaying their incisors. Their growls made Hermod's eyes hurt. He wondered what it would be like in a wolf belly. Tight, he figured. Hot. Acidic. Would there be enough room to swing his sword? He had reasonable hopes that there might be. The wolves were probably bigger on the inside than they were on the outside.

"The mutts will eat just about anything," Hermod whispered to Mist. "Those balls I bought at the black market are hand grenades. When I give the signal, grab a couple from my duffel, yank on the pull tab, and toss."

"Excellent," the Valkyrie said. She seemed a little bit impressed with him, and Hermod caught himself grinning. "What's the signal?" she asked.

No sooner had she posed the question than the wolves sprang forward.

"Signal!" Hermod screamed, and they both plunged their hands into the duffel and came out with a grenade each. Simultaneously, as though they'd drilled the maneuver together, they pulled the tabs, tossed their grenades underhand, and dove down in the sand. Hermod covered Winston with his body, peering up to see two of the pups leap to swallow the grenades.

And then nothing happened.

Hermod pounded a crater in the sand with his fist. "Damned unreliable black-market munitions—"

The rest of his words were interrupted by a pair of concussive blasts, followed by the plopping of sticky red chunks hitting the ground.

"Two more," he shouted, again reaching into his duffel.

But the four remaining pups turned tail and sprinted away, yipping and barking with lunatic laughter. Hermod pulled the tab of his grenade and lobbed the ball into the middle of the pack, but this one turned out to be a dud, and by the time Mist handed him another, the wolves were just tiny black dots in the distance. Hermod knew he'd never catch them; they were going too fast.

"Can't you toss it that far?" Mist asked with obvious impatience.

"Not with any accuracy. I'd be as likely to hit a hot-dog stand as the wolves."

Mist responded with an ambiguous *hmm*, scraping blown-up wolf bits from her boots and pants. "They're not quite animals, are they?"

"They are, in a sense, but they're also packed with other things, like chaos and entropy and emptiness."

Mist shuddered. "Wish we'd killed them all."

"Yeah. There's not much worse than a half-defused bomb, and now that I've made it clear I'm out to get them, the wolves won't be as easy to find the next time. I hate to say it, but I think we need to see the sibyl."

Mist held up her hand. "Wait a minute, who's this 'we' you're talking about? You said if I helped you out here we'd discuss you guiding me to Helheim."

"Well, sure, I said we could talk about it."

"So," Mist said, "let's talk."

Hermod sighed and rubbed the back of his neck. It had felt rather fine to have the Valkyrie at his side while fighting the pups; it'd been so long since he'd had an ally. And merely talking had never hurt anyone, right? He laughed bitterly in answer to his own question.

"We can talk," he said. "But let's do it somewhere else, okay? This beach hasn't been very good to me."

Mist nodded and they set out for the pedestrian overpass.

A thought occurred to Hermod: "Hey, you can also buy me breakfast."

CHAPTER SIX

THE WORLD TREE grows from the roots of worlds, and down at the bottom of a deep depression between two of the roots is a sea, and in the sea is a single island, which has no name. The island's sole inhabitant is a wolf, and the wolf is called Fenrir. His fur is ice-white. His eyes, cold midnight.

Munin and I fly circles over the island, half-frozen rain striking our feathers. Munin recites from memory every word he knows for this kind of rain, asking me repeatedly which word I think most accurately describes it.

"For the last time," I squawk, "it's slush, all right? Cold, nasty slush."

"In Alfheim they call it slow-stinging darts. Don't you think that's a better term for it, Hugin? More descriptive?"

"Fine, that's fine, that'll be fine."

"But the giants in Jotunheim call it the frost kiss. I think I like that. Hmm."

Hidden behind a wall of gloom, waves collide ceaselessly with the ghostly outline of towering crags.

When a longship fetches up on the beach in a crunch of timber on gravel, the wolf whines with apprehension.

The wolf is helpless, but this hasn't always been the case. Fenrir, closer in size to a bear than to another wolf, and much larger than that if viewed with a squint from certain angles, long ago bit off the arm of the Aesir's mighty warlord Tyr. The gods feared Fenrir, so they imprisoned him here on this rock, and gagged him, and fettered him. A sword keeps his jaws from closing, the pommel jammed against his tongue, the sharp tip of the blade poking the soft roof of his mouth. His legs are bound with a silken ribbon. The ribbon's name is Gleipnir, and it was crafted with great cunning by a pair of dwarf brothers.

Two figures emerge from the fog. One is Vidar, eldest of Odin's sons. Many consider him most like his father, in strength second only to Thor, but stingy with words and always deep in the wells of his own thoughts. So deep that even I have a hard time seeing them. His eyes are the dark gray of far northern skies, his face lean, almost gaunt. Strapped to his hip is a long scabbard. His hand rests lightly on the pommel of his sword.

The other is a child, chubby-kneed and hyper. This is Vidar's brother, Vali. After Höd was duped into killing Baldr, Odin sired Vali for the sole purpose of vengeance, and when Vali was scarcely a day old, he strangled Höd to death.

"You look uncomfortable, smelly old dog," Vali says. "I bet if we free you, you'll try to eat us. But you better not, because if you eat us I'll kick you from the inside and make your tummy hurt, and then I'll bite my way out of your belly and pull all your tubes out, and then I'll whip you with your own guts, do you wanna see my bug collection? It's right here in my pocket, only some of them aren't bugs, some of them are spiders, plus some ears and tongues from people I don't like—"

Vidar puts a restraining hand on Vali's shoulder, and while Vali doesn't exactly fall silent, he does lower his volume.

Vidar draws his sword, and Fenrir squirms and whines, longing for freedom. He does not want to die this way, helpless as a blind newborn. It's not merely fear that fills him with a sense of dread. It's that his death is supposed to occur in a way otherwise, after he has accomplished certain tasks, among them the killing of Odin the gallows god.

Vidar raises the sword above his head and closes his eyes, gathering himself. His blade hurts to look at, as if it's made of things that should not be, and Fenrir knows what it reminds him of.

Gleipnir, the ribbon binding him, is made of six impossible things, from the roots of a mountain, to the breath of a fish, to the sound of a cat's footfalls.

Vidar's sword is made of seven.

Vidar swings the blade down. The island shivers as the sharp edge cuts through the sound barrier, and then through the ribbon, and Fenrir is free.

The wolf doesn't move. He's craved freedom for so long that, once his uncanny restraint is gone, he doesn't quite know what to do. His breath rises in plumes, and he remains still when Vidar reaches into his maw and carefully removes the sword gag.

Cautiously, Fenrir tests his strength, drawing a

paw across the stony ground and digging runnels as deep as graves. He extends his forelegs before him and bows his back in a mighty stretch that feels so good he nearly howls with joy. Then he yawns, and Vidar and Vali stagger forward, while Munin and I flap our wings harder to remain airborne.

"What time is it?" Fenrir asks.

Vidar takes a moment to recover himself. He holds his sword before him, and it suddenly looks ridiculously small, like a swizzle stick.

"It's really late," Vali answers.

Fenrir imagines he could swallow the sword without trouble, and its owner too. He turns a circle, sniffing the ground. "It would have to be late, yes, as I've been here a very long time. But not too late for games. You Aesir were always up for games. Is that why you freed me, little sons of Odin? To play? Tyr played with me once."

Fenrir begins to salivate. He raises a leg and gushes a spray of urine. "I've been confined for a long time, and I'd rather my first conversation in ages not be entwined in riddles. Why did you unbind me, Vidar Odinsson, when I am bound to kill your father?"

The wolf craves the taste of the All-Father's intestines. He knows the flavor will be rich.

"Once you kill Odin," Vali says, "Vidar will kill you right back."

"Of course," says Fenrir. The wolf pulls his lips back in something resembling a smile, running his tongue over teeth like scimitars. "I think you enjoy games, Vidar. But you no longer wish to be a piece. Instead, you've found a way to be a mover of pieces. That makes you very mighty indeed."

Vidar bows his head slightly. With that, the two gods take their leave, pushing their ship back into the surf. Vidar vaults over the gunwales to take the tiller, and Fenrir watches the boat fade into the swirling mists. Then he compresses his body into a tight ball and releases, leaping high up into the near sky.

"These late days are very curious," the wolf says.

CHAPTER SEVEN

WHAT RADGRID REALLY wanted to do was shoot them both in the heart and get on with her busy day. She didn't have time for guests, let alone gods. She was running into difficulties obtaining permits for another NorseCODE office in Shenzhen. There was a promising candidate in Vancouver whose testing awaited an available Valkyrie/Einherjar team. And Mist had gone missing. It was this last bullet point on her list of action items that troubled her most. She'd had such high hopes for the girl.

"Can I offer you anything else to drink?" she asked, using her facial muscles in a way that she hoped would form a convincing smile.

Magni raised his glass. The small movement caused alarming squeaks and creaks in his chair. "More of this green stuff. What'd you call it?"

"It's Mountain Dew," Radgrid said, a model of patience. "It's very popular with my younger programmers."

"Yeah, I'll have some more too," put in the other god, Modi.

The need to show the brothers courtesy went beyond protocol. The two sons of Thor were stupid but incredibly mighty, and Radgrid couldn't afford to anger them. They had the trust of Vidar and Frigg, gods for whom Radgrid's respect was unquestioned. So she made sure not to laugh at Magni's and Modi's broad faces and the little pale raccoon masks around their eyes; apparently the gods had been visiting a tanning salon.

Radgrid buzzed her secretary to have the gods' drinks refilled. They finished them in one gulp each and belched.

Radgrid closed her eyes, counted to three, and opened them again. Something in her look made the gods sit up a little straighter, and that pleased Radgrid. She might not be an Aesir goddess, but she was a Valkyrie, a chosen servant of Odin, and she deserved their respect.

"So, here's the thing," Magni said, jiggling the ice in his glass. "We're concerned about your progress with this whole NorseCODE project. You've been doing this for, what, almost four years now, and what have you got to show for it? Eighteen recruits?"

"Nineteen," Radgrid said tightly. "Which is almost double the number of recruits found using the traditional methods in the same period of time."

"Maybe so," Magni said, "but you're using more than double the resources of your more traditionalist sisters. You've got eight Valkyries devoted one hundred percent to NorseCODE endeavors, an equal number of Einherjar, and two dozen Asgardian slaves and servants who are too busy with NorseCODE to keep up with their normal duties. Not to mention all the gold it takes to keep you in test tubes and Mountain Dew."

Radgrid frowned. She did have a gun in her desk drawer. She really could just belly-shoot the both of them. Though she doubted it'd be enough to kill them.

"Is Asgard tight for cash?" she asked, no longer caring if her displeasure registered.

"It's not about having the money," Magni said. "It's about the trouble of moving it to Midgard. It's not like you can electronically transfer a ton of dwarf gold from Asgard to Geneva. Magni and I are breaking our backs to handle the logistics that fund your little project, so if we're not getting sufficient results, well, that's a problem."

"I see," Radgrid said. "Thank you for voicing your concern. Is there anything else? I do have matters requiring my attention."

"Not anymore," said Magni. "We're taking over NorseCODE, my bro and I. You'll stay on as our executive assistant, helping us get settled and stuff. We'll be working out of LA, mostly, so you can keep your office here, but we're taking some of your staff; we want the best people working directly with us."

He paused, waiting for Radgrid to say something in response. Instead, she reached into her desk drawer, took out a .45 Luger, and shot both brothers in the forehead. Her ears rang, so she barely heard what Magni said as he held his ham-size palm to his bleeding brow. She didn't suppose he was saying anything complimentary. She shot him again, and then Modi again, and she continued to squeeze the trigger until the magazine was empty, although she could already see that the bullets weren't penetrating their skulls. A misshapen slug from her last shot bounced on the carpet near her feet. The gods stood.

She wished she'd poisoned their Mountain Dew.

"Bitch, we're gonna shred you," Magni said, as Radgrid took a sword from the umbrella stand next to her desk. She didn't wait for the brothers to advance but drove a thrust toward Magni's right knee.

A tremor shuddered the walls. The floors vibrated, and the windows jiggled in their frames, and through the sounds of all the shaking rose a hum, ringing like a bell struck deep in the earth. The tones shifted, and though they didn't form words, they expressed an undeniable intelligence. Its will was clear enough, and Radgrid listened, as did the Aesir brothers.

Radgrid hadn't been born yet when Frigg exacted her pledge from everything in the universe, but there was no mistaking this voice, or its power, or its simple message: Magni and Modi would do whatever Radgrid told them to do, because Frigg had just said they must.

The voice faded, and the tremor subsided.

The brothers glowered furiously at Radgrid, massive fists clenched. Muscles writhed in their wrists and forearms like boa constrictors, but they didn't dare touch her.

She put her sword back in the umbrella stand and went to the phone to raise her secretary.

"Ingrid, I need a car from the motor pool for Thor's sons."

"Where are we going?" asked Modi, blood dripping down the bridge of his nose.

"One of my Valkyries is missing, and the Einherjar

I sent after her is causing me concern. You're going to find them for me. And don't abuse your expense account. As you reminded me, NorseCODE needs to observe financial prudence."

Once the brothers, sulking, left the office, Radgrid returned to her desk with the sunny realization that Frigg had just promoted her over Aesir. That must mean Frigg considered Radgrid worthy of being a god herself, which would be a nice position to be in after Ragnarok, when there'd be a new, green world to rule.

Now Radgrid could concentrate on devising a way to rule it all by herself.

CHAPTER EIGHT

MIST AND HERMOD returned to the black market, where they found Grimnir chatting up a couple of prostitutes. "My lady friends say they've seen a guy with a dog matching your Aesir's description," he said to Mist, and then he looked over her shoulder and saw Hermod for the first time. "Oh," he said, favoring Hermod with one of his more unfriendly glares. "Huh."

Mist made quick introductions, and as they walked back to the Jeep, she filled Grimnir in about the wolves on the beach.

"Kid, you shouldn't be getting involved in that level of thing," he grumbled, settling in behind the steering wheel. "You've gone so far off the reservation that I'm not sure how you're ever going to patch things up with Radgrid."

"Later," Mist said. She didn't want to have this argument in front of Hermod, who was fumbling with the seat belt in the backseat and trying to keep his face away from the malamute's wagging tail.

Grimnir keyed the engine. "Fine, but you're not

the one calling headquarters to give Radgrid updates. She's starting to find it suspicious that I haven't tracked you down yet."

"Why should she be suspicious of you?"

"Because I'm too good not to have tracked you down yet. So, where to?"

Hermod directed them to Venice Pier, or the remains of it, saying he wanted to go there to contact an old consultant of Odin's. He had questions for her about Ragnarok.

Minutes later they were picking their way across the debris-strewn beach, stepping around snapped pylons and concrete slabs. City services, already overwhelmed, hadn't gotten around to hauling away the remnants of Venice Pier, and at low tide the wreckage provided small, private coves. Hermod led them to one, about twenty feet across. "This'll do," he said. "Seawater, privacy, and an easy surface to write on."

Mist picked up a few marooned starfish and frisbeed them back into the ocean, not sure if she was saving them or if they were already dead.

"You're a regular lifeguard," Grimnir said.

Hermod patted his pockets. "Anybody have a knife I could borrow?"

Like a magician conjuring a bouquet of flowers, Grimnir provided a frightfully large Bowie knife. Hermod regarded it skeptically. "Thanks, but I've already got a sword."

Mist offered her Swiss Army knife, which he accepted. "I'll want it back," she said. A gift from her sister, it was one of her few possessions that predated her existence as a Valkyrie.

Hermod hinged open the larger of the two blades

and lowered himself to his knees. He drew a vertical line in the damp sand and then spread the line out into nine roots. Next, he drew an eye.

"It's some kind of rune spell," Grimnir explained for Mist's benefit. "The World Tree, and Odin's eye, which he sacrificed at Mimir's Well in exchange for knowledge."

"I wonder who got the better end of that deal?" Mist said.

"I dunno. Odin's eye has seen a lot, I bet."

Hermod cleared his throat. "Do you mind? I need to concentrate here."

He drew a half-decayed rune, which, from the little bit of rune lore Radgrid had given her, Mist recognized as a reference to death and to Hel. Hermod worked quickly as the tide gradually came in. When he finally stood and handed the knife back to Mist, he'd drawn a circle of runes that surrounded them.

"What happens now?" Mist asked.

Hermod shrugged. "Magic is a little like pulling the pin on a grenade and then stuffing it down your pants to see what happens."

"How reassuring."

Fog thickened in the cove, simplifying the world to the fundamental elements of sea and land. Shrieking wind raised whitecaps over the water like floating ice. Minutes passed, clouds roiling above. The sky took on a cold, metallic sheen, and Mist lost track of how long they'd been standing there.

A wave came over the debris wall, and suddenly Mist found herself chest-deep in a churn of water that took her legs out and pressed her to the sand. With no time to draw a breath, she clenched her jaw tight and struggled to regain her footing. *Magic demands knowledge,* she remembered Radgrid telling her once, *and knowledge demands sacrifice.* Odin gave his eye for knowledge, had hung on the World Tree for knowledge, and some said he'd died there.

Hands lifted her by her armpits, and she opened her eyes to find Hermod holding her up. He was as soaked as she was, as were Grimnir and Winston. She coughed and sputtered.

They weren't alone. An old woman stood in the center of the rune ring, naked and red-eyed, with gray ropes of wet hair plastered to her fat breasts, like some primeval Venus statue. Mist felt that she knew this woman somehow, as though she were a figure from a recurring dream.

"Sibyl," Mist croaked.

"Oh, damn," Hermod said. "You weren't supposed to speak first."

Mist coughed. Salt water dribbled out her nose. "Why not?"

"Now she'll talk only to you."

"You could have warned me."

Hermod had no answer to that beyond a sheepish expression.

Despite the waves, the runes still stood out clearly in the sand, as though carved in cement. The sibyl began rubbing them out with her heel. "You're one of Odin's little lovelies, aren't you? Daughter, lover, or both?"

"Employee would be more accurate," Mist said. "I'm a Valkyrie."

"We're all in his employ. Even me. Who else but Odin could have dared call me from death and kept me in thrall 'til he knew all I knew? Well, you dared, I suppose."

Mist pointed to Hermod. "*He* dared, actually."

Hermod dug a brown paper bag from his duffel and handed it to Mist. "She won't talk to me. The rune spell's not designed that way. Give her this gift, and maybe she'll tell us what we want to know."

Mist unrolled the soggy paper and peered inside. "This is supposed to be a gift?"

The sibyl frowned at her with a scrunched apple-doll face. "Gifts?"

Mist removed a ziplock freezer bag from the recesses of the sack and withdrew an object the size of a walnut.

The sibyl sniffed. "What's that?"

Hermod told Mist, and Mist repeated it to the sibyl: "This is a prince who died in the body of a mouse."

"Not bad," the sibyl said, reaching out to grab it from Mist's hand. She clutched the mouse to her bare chest. Seawater dripped from her hair and ran in rivulets down her belly and thighs. "You are not entirely without manners, little corpse-chooser. What is it you wish to know from me? If true love lies in your path? If life grows in your womb? If the cows will give milk this year?"

Mist's nose was running. She sniffed and looked expectantly at Hermod.

"Let's see," he said. "Okay, try asking her this—"

The sibyl seemed to take notice of him for the first time. "I don't like him," she said to Mist. "He has the stink of bad news."

Grimnir laughed. "You got that right."

"Ask her about the wolves," Hermod said. "Where can we find them, how do we kill them all? And what about the other Ragnarok portents? What can we do about the Midgard serpent? And ask her about the ship of dead men's nails, and can we find Loki and kill him before he busts loose and pilots the ship of Hel's soldiers? And what about the sons of Muspellheim? And also find out if someone's controlling all this, manipulating events, and so forth."

"Anything else?"

"That's it, for starters."

Mist took a deep breath and repeated Hermod's laundry list of questions.

Crabs scuttled over the sibyl's feet. "I won't answer a thing," she said. "Your runes aren't powerful enough, and your gift isn't pretty enough. You're a rude picker of corpses. You have nothing I need, so nothing will I give you." With that, she turned her back and took several steps into the surf.

"She *has* to answer the questions," Hermod insisted. "Otherwise we're just thrashing around here instead of knowing what and where to attack. You have to make her answer."

"Do I?" Mist shot back. "You said you'd help me get my people out of Helheim, and as far as I can tell, none of your questions has anything to do with my objectives."

"When the worlds are destroyed, Helheim will be one of them. If you want to rescue your sister and your recruit, then the best thing you can do is to make sure there's still a Helheim to rescue them from, not to mention a living world for them to return to."

"Dammit," Mist growled. She called to the sibyl,

but the old woman just pushed deeper into the waves. Mist jogged into the cold foam and called out again. "Forget the spell, forget the stupid mouse. Please, tell me what you want that I can give you."

The sibyl stopped, waves breaking over her shoulders as though she were a rock. She turned and put her hands on her ample hips. "You *could* offer an old, dead lady a cup of tea."

# # #

GRIMNIR WAS typically resourceful in finding something for the sibyl to wear, though Mist was afraid to ask him exactly how and where he'd obtained the purple sweatshirt, yellow pants from a rain slicker, orange sparkly boots, and Minnesota Vikings ball cap with one sagging gold lamé horn.

Sibyl, Valkyrie, warrior-thug, god, and Alaskan malamute made for an odd party when they arrived at the Novel Café, which occupied part of the bottom floor of the old Masonic lodge on Pier Avenue in Santa Monica. Hermod gave Winston instructions to remain outside on the sidewalk, and the group installed themselves around a corner table, flanked by chipped-wood bookcases stuffed with paperback best sellers from the 1970s. Mist left to get tea for the sibyl and black coffee for the rest of them, as well as a poppy-seed muffin for Hermod, who'd reminded her that she'd promised him breakfast. The total cost of the drinks and muffin shouldn't have astonished her as much as it did, considering how the prices of fuel and food had been climbing in inverse proportion to the average temperatures. When she returned to the table, drawing on past waitressing experience to balance everything, the sibyl was immersed in a copy of the *Weekly World News*.

She looked up at Mist and snorted. "Just who is this Nostradamus character?"

The front page displayed a scowling, bearded visage in grainy black and white. Two-inch type had him predicting a Miami buried in snow and mammoths charging through the streets of Santa Fe.

"He was a prognosticator, like you." Outside, hail clattered on the sidewalk.

"A prognosticator?" the sibyl barked. "He was a spouter of non sequiturs. Listen to this: *The young lion will overcome the old one on the field of battle in single combat and put out his eyes in a cage of gold*." The sibyl threw the paper down on the table. "What in Niflheim is that supposed to mean? What a phony."

"Not like you, though. Your pronouncements always come true."

The sibyl's smile was tight and smug. She squeezed honey into her tea from a plastic bear. "I'm more than reliable. I prophesied that a son of Odin would kill another, and wasn't Baldr slain by Höd? I predicted all of this: three winters, each longer than the last, with no summer between."

Mist took a sip of watery coffee. At least it was hot. "There've been ice ages before."

"Three winters," the sibyl boomed, "each longer than the last. Man forgets the bonds of kinship. Battle-ax and sword rule, and an age of wolves 'til the world goes down. The rust-red cock will raise the dead in Helheim, and the golden cock Gullinkambi will crow to the gods. The wolves of Fenrir's kin swallow the sun and the moon. Earth breaks and mountains crumble, and the Midgard serpent, venom-spitting, rises from the sea. *Naglfar,* the ship of dead men's nails, breaks its moorings and sets sail. The Aesir's enemies meet them on the battlefield of Vigrid, and the nine worlds fall to fire and ice."

The sibyl caught her breath. "Forgive an old woman for admiring her work. It's so nice to chat like this." She slurped her tea.

Mist gazed out the window and tried to imagine the sky on fire. She tried to imagine monsters striding over the horizon, leaving gravel and dust in their wake. But she couldn't, really. It was all too big, too abstract. Easy enough, however, to picture the Irish pub across the street engulfed in flame. She'd spent a first date there during her sophomore year at UCLA with a classics major named Jared. After dinner, he'd taken her back to his car, parked on this very street, and they'd made out for three hours. She remembered his hazel eyes and the way he seemed genuinely interested in learning everything about her, about how her grandmother Catalina had raised Lilly and her, how she'd been a band geek with a tenor saxophone at Venice High, about how Lilly dropped out of high school to travel the world and protest the World Trade Organization and whaling and half a dozen other things, and how alone she'd felt when her grandmother died. Now she imagined Jared's hazel eyes shriveling in the heat of conflagration and Catalina's little house burning to cinders—all just collateral damage in the fight between gods and monsters who wouldn't even notice.

"I don't believe it," Mist said. "I will not believe

that the world can go on for four and a half billion years, and we can go from living in caves to building the Taj Mahal and sending probes out to Jupiter and making music and law and antibiotics . . . and it's all for nothing."

The sibyl tore open a sugar packet. "Take heart, carrion-lover. There will be a new world, all fresh and green, run by the Aesir who survive: Vidar and Vali, and Thor's sons, and Baldr and Höd. It just won't be *this* world, and you and those you love won't be around to enjoy it."

"Ask her what happens to me," Hermod said around a bite of muffin. "No, wait, changed my mind, I still don't want to know. Ask her about all those things I told you on the beach."

The sibyl dumped sugar in her tea. "You don't have to speak through the girl, Aesir black sheep. Your spell may have called me from the fringes of life, but it's not enough to bind me. I remain here out of choice, and I'll speak to whomever I wish."

Hermod gaped at her. "Well. Fine, then. First question: Can we stop the wolves from eating the sun and moon?"

The sibyl swatted Hermod's coffee cup to the floor, where it burst apart in ceramic fragments. Coffee splattered his legs.

"Can you make it so that your cup never shattered?"

"No, but I could cut your arms off." Hermod made the threat so matter-of-factly that it gave Mist chills.

"But that wouldn't unbreak your cup," the sibyl said with a calm that equaled Hermod's.

"I could have cut them off back on the beach when I first summoned you, before you spilled my coffee."

"Perhaps, but you would still be without your coffee now. The chain of events through time is made of stronger links than your sword can cut through. Baldr fell, and therefore the wolf must eat the sun and moon, and since the wolf eats the sun and moon, the nine worlds must die. Each event falls irrevocably from the previous and triggers the next."

"It's like a domino effect, then?" Mist asked.

"We had something like dominoes in the early days," the sibyl said. "We carved them from the bones of our enemies and burned the markings in. We called them something else, though. I had a nice set when I was a girl."

"The domino effect," Mist pressed on, trying to keep the sibyl on topic. "If you tip one over, the others all fall. Unless you remove some down the line before they topple."

"That's not how we played the game."

"I'm not talking about a game. I'm asking you how things work. I'm asking if we can change it."

The sibyl ripped open five more sugar packets and let the contents fall into her teacup. She drank without stirring. "You need a better metaphor. Think of it as a ball of string. It can be a big, knotty ball, all convoluted, but it's still one single strand. Tug here, tug there, just one string."

"But . . . what if you cut the string and break the connection?"

"Oh, girl. You don't have shears sharp enough." Her gaze crossed everyone at the table. "None of you does. Accept it, as I do. Where you hear a pink newborn crying out its first breath, I hear the death rattle of the brittle-boned man it will become." She drained the sludge from her cup and rose to her feet. "Thank you for the tea."

"We're not done here yet," Hermod said. "I still have questions."

"You keep asking the wrong ones."

"What should I ask you, then?"

"First of all, how about, 'Can I offer you the rest of my muffin?'"

Hermod sighed and pushed his plate toward her. "Dig in. What else?"

The sibyl returned to her seat. Hermod watched mournfully as she plucked away at his muffin. She seemed very satisfied. "Because I was given honey and pastry," she said, smacking her lips, "I will say one last thing to you: Go to Hel. In her realm, where even Odin won't tread, you will find the links in the chain at their weakest. There, if you will, you might still grasp a few dominoes."

Mist carefully watched Hermod's reaction. He looked resigned, and Mist realized she'd won. With Hermod, she could make it to Helheim. Only now, having achieved her small but important victory, the ramifications of what they were going to do hit home. Making an incursion into death's realm was no small thing.

"Thank you for breakfast and for these lovely clothes," the sibyl said, pushing her chair back from the table. "But I'll be leaving now. I'm missing my shows." Straightening the horn sagging off her hat, she walked out of the café, into a curtain of rain.

After a time, hail struck the windows as hard as machine-gun fire.

CHAPTER NINE

LILLY CASTILLO REMEM-
bered dying. She'd been walking
home from grocery shopping, argu-
ing with her sister, Kathy, as usual. Lilly had been
back in California for only a month, but she was already thinking about leaving again. She knew some
people in Oregon who were smuggling vegetable
crops from government-funded hydroponic farms
and distributing them to those without money or connections, the sort of thing that was right up her alley.

Naturally, Kathy hadn't been shy about telling
Lilly what she thought about contraband networks,
and they'd been on the edge of a major fight when
Lilly felt a pinching pain in her ribs, accompanied by
a heavy blow that knocked the air out of her.

She'd found herself on the ground, her cheek
against the pavement beside her sister. Kathy said
she'd been shot, and that's when Lilly understood
what was happening.

She and Kathy were being killed.

She'd tried to shield her sister with her body
against further shots, while Kathy had tried to do the

same for her. Then a second shot slammed into Lilly's belly. A moment of blood-red pain drained to a milky haze, and the road of walking corpses appeared.

Lilly hadn't wanted to join the other dead, but she'd known she had to. Death was just fucked up like that.

Kathy had called to her, reached for her, tried to join her, but there'd been someone holding Kathy back, a tall redheaded woman outfitted in white furs and silver chain mail. She'd said things to Kathy, things that Lilly had caught only part of before the murmuring of the dead drowned out all other noise. Something about being a Valkyrie, about claiming Kathy for Odin's service. She'd called Kathy "Mist." It sounded to Lilly like a porn-star name.

Carried along in the current of the dead, Lilly waved back to Kathy, blew her kisses, tried to tell her she was sorry for every slight, every wound, for every time she'd run away. But it was too late for that. Being dead meant never getting to say sorry.

Since arriving in Helheim, Lilly hadn't stopped moving. She walked across endless plains of gray dust until her body dragged with hunger. But there was no food. Her head ached and thirst made her tongue feel like an old sock, but there was no water. Her side and belly hurt from the bullet wounds, but she was getting used to the pain.

She missed green. She missed the sun's warmth on her cheeks and eyelids. She missed orange juice.

She thought she was doing a little better than many of the other dead. Most everyone else stood around like herds of sheep, quietly moaning or weeping or

staring into the featureless distance in a state of cata-
tonia.

It wouldn't do. Prisoners had obligations: survive,
escape, sabotage. She understood that survival was
out of her hands; she was dead, after all. And if there
was some kind of deeper, more permanent death after
this one, she didn't know how it worked or how to
avoid it. Despite her ache for it, food and water didn't
appear to be necessary, and if it was, she'd seen no evidence of sustenance in Helheim. So she focused her
attention on escape. That meant she needed to get a
sense of her prison's landscape. From what she'd been
able to gather from the more experienced dead
around her, she now dwelled in the world of Helheim,
ruled by Queen Hel. Here, there was the queen's
palace, the corpse gate, some perpetually frozen
rivers, cold plains, and some rock formations, like the
eroded bones of mountains. The corpse gate apparently went all the way around Helheim's border, posing a formidable obstacle. And there were also fearful
mutterings about Hel's dog, a terrible hound named
Garm who served to keep the dead inside bounds.

Actually, the existence of Garm comforted Lilly. If
there was a need for a guard dog, then escape must be
possible.

What Lilly needed, then, was a plan.

Cresting a ridge, she came to a wary halt. There
was some commotion down below, angry shouting
coming from the center of a knot in the crowd. What
could possibly ignite people's passions in Helheim?
She jogged down the path from her ridge to investi-
gate.

Pushing through the mob, she found a towering,

gaunt figure surrounded by people wielding sticks and stones. The man at the center of the crowd wore loose trousers tucked into boots of an archaic style, and his hip-length shirt opened at the collar to reveal a ring of deep purple bruises around his throat. Narrow cheekbones curved down to a pale-lipped mouth set in a sardonic smile. His shriveled eyes were nearly lost in dark hollows.

He was leaning on a tall, skinny tree branch, and Lilly realized he was blind.

"I tell you it's him," said a man. "He's the reason we're all here."

"That's Judas?" said someone else, wearing modern jeans and a T-shirt.

"Not Judas," said the first man. "It's Höd, the one who killed Baldr, on account of being a jealous dog—thanks to him, we're all cursed to rot in Helheim."

The blind man shook his head and released a bored-sounding sigh.

Lilly had heard murmurings about Baldr—some kind of god or something—and that his murder many thousands of years ago had been some kind of watershed moment of cosmological something-or-other. All of it was so far removed from her that she didn't much care whether this Höd person was guilty or not of doing what the mob accused him of. But Lilly thought she knew scapegoating when she saw it, and when a baseball-size stone flew from the crowd and struck Höd in the temple, she couldn't stand by and do nothing.

As a man beside her moved to throw a rock of his own, Lilly grabbed his wrist and elbow and made him drop it. She swung him around to use as a shield as she moved closer to Höd.

"Rather gotten yourself in the thick of things, eh?" Höd said.

"I have a habit of doing that." Lilly picked up a rock that had narrowly missed her and speedballed it back into the crowd. She heard the satisfying impact of rock on bone.

"Well, at least they can't kill you," Höd said as a rock whizzed past his ear. "But they can render your body such that it will be little more than a bag of pulp or a scattering of debris, yet even then you will remain conscious."

"God, you're cheery."

"I am of the Aesir tribe, true, but there's no need to call me God."

"I think you misunderstood what I meant."

"Very likely. Now, please, crouch down."

Höd lifted his stick, and Lilly saw what he had in mind. She ducked and heard a great whoosh of air as his stick circled overhead like a helicopter rotor blade. He hit those closest and batted away a few hurled stones. The mob scattered.

"They'll be back," Höd said. "And now that you've identified yourself as my friend, they'll come after you as well."

"Who said I was your friend?"

"You didn't need to. It doesn't take much in Helheim to find yourself the target of blame. Blame for Baldr, blame for death, blame for lack of good footwear. Now they'll blame you too."

"Terrific. So we should get out of here."

"Yes," Höd said.

"Where to?"

Höd pointed off in the distance with his stick, but

Lilly didn't think he was pointing at anything in particular.

She set off with him, not knowing what he was all about, or where they were going, or what they'd do when they got there. Höd didn't know either. "We're going that way," he said. "We can do there everything we can do here, but hopefully with fewer rocks being flung at us."

"Yeah. Okay. That actually makes sense."

Besides, staying on the move made her feel a little less dead.

# # #

T HEY MADE slow progress down a packed-dirt path wide enough to be a two-lane street. Höd swept his crooked stick before him to determine his way. She'd gotten out of him that he'd spent a long time in the custody of Hel, though what a long time meant in a land of gods and dead mortals was something she was still having trouble calibrating. He claimed he'd recently escaped Hel's palace, with the assistance of Baldr's wife, but he refused to say much more about that matter.

In return, Lilly gave him the online-dating version of her biography, with brief sketches of some of her felonies thrown in to make herself sound more interesting. She'd left home at sixteen, finding Los Angeles too tainted by Hollywood and Beverly Hills. After trying out life as a barista, a bass player, but mostly a sofa-surfer, she'd fallen in with a group of anarchists in Washington State who were saving up to fly to Geneva to protest a G8 summit. She'd come back from that trip with a broken wrist, Taser scars, a criminal record, and a life's calling.

"How did your family feel about all this?" Höd asked.

Lilly's feet shuffled through the dust. "My grandmother died when I was in Switzerland. Kathy never really forgave me for that. I wish we'd managed to settle that stuff before I died."

"And your grandmother? Have you sought her out here?"

"No. It would be . . . I don't want to see anyone I knew when I was alive. I guess that's cowardly."

Höd was quiet for a while. Then, "No," he said. "I understand completely."

They walked on together. Vapors swirled around them, occasionally thinning enough to reveal low, one-story structures built of piled stones and limbs from dead gray trees. Gaps in the piles suggested windows and doorways, and some of the buildings had awnings woven from thin boughs. Not so much buildings, Lilly judged as they passed a pile of rocks arranged to resemble a fire hydrant, but abstract simulacrums of them.

"Who built this place?" she asked.

"They were mostly dead from your lands, perhaps two generations removed from you. Iowans, they called themselves. Many of them had died together in a tornado. In Midgard they had built a town, and they sought to build it here again, as best they could. It took them longer to gather the materials than you might believe."

Lilly shook her head in bemusement. She could imagine hardened, determined, Depression-era townsfolk trying to reconstruct Main Street, dreaming of one day building a library and a city hall and a little park with a statue, schools and houses, all of it. They dreamed of building an America with sticks and stones.

"What happened to them?"

Höd's stick scraped the dirt. "I'm not certain. I heard that Hel put them in the corpse gate."

They went on for a while, only the sound of their footfalls disturbing the silence.

"Is that what she'll do with us if we're caught trying to break out?" Lilly said.

"She'd probably make you part of the gate," Höd said matter-of-factly, "but I'm of the Aesir, one of her prized possessions. I imagine she'd want to keep me around, probably in chains, possibly tortured."

Better that than be tangled up in the writhing mass of bodies in the gate. The idea of getting cuddly with other corpses made her empty stomach quiver.

Of course, she herself was a corpse. Or was she? If she managed to breach the wall and get out, what would she be? A ghost? A zombie? Nothing at all?

A ragged growl cut off her thoughts, and she felt a jolt shoot through her legs. Whatever the state of her existence, that sure as hell had felt like an adrenaline spike.

"Do you see anything?" Höd demanded in a hoarse whisper, his staff raised. Lilly realized he was afraid.

"No. What was that? It sounded like an animal."

"Garm. Hel has sent her best servant after us."

Lilly tried to analyze their situation tactically. Except for Höd's stick, they had no weapons. And

Höd's blindness ruled out a fast retreat. Their best bet was to take cover in one of the nearby buildings.

She hooked Höd by the arm and pulled him through a doorway. Inside were more stones, arranged into shelves against the walls. When she spotted a waist-high stack of rocks, atop which sat another stack in the unmistakable shape of a cash register, she came to the heartbreaking conclusion that the place was supposed to be a shop of some kind. The shelves were bare; apparently the townspeople had not gotten around to sculpting stone merchandise.

"We can duck down here," she said, hunkering behind the counter.

"Garm will smell us out," Höd said. "He probably already has. He'll squeeze through the doorway and bring the walls down with him. The last thing you will see before he tears your head off is blood and slaver dripping from his jaws. Hel will probably have your head placed such that you will be able to view your own decapitated body. Thankfully, being blind, I will be spared the sight of my own corpse."

"Thanks, Sunshine," Lilly hissed. "But as long as my head's still attached to me, I'm staying attached to it. What's Garm's weakness?"

Höd considered this for a moment. "It is said he can be subdued with Hel cakes, which never fail those who gave bread freely in life."

"I used to collect cans for food drives. Does that count?"

"I would have no way of knowing," Höd said. "I don't write law."

Another growl ripped the air. It was a nasty, terrible sound, a force of nature driven by hunger and malevolence. Lilly wiped her palms on her thighs, though she wasn't sweating. She hadn't perspired or wept or pissed or shat since dying.

"What are Hel cakes, anyway?"

"I'm not sure," said Höd. "But it seems unlikely that Garm could be dissuaded from his pursuit by mere morsels. Some lore is only invention."

"So our best option is throwing rocks?" said Lilly, incredulous.

"Now, now, it's not that bad. We also have sticks," Höd chided, shaking his staff at her.

And then the front wall caved in, and an enormous beast stood among the wreckage and billowing dust. Emaciated, with cobweb-gray fur stretched over ribs as thick as bamboo poles, the hound vibrated with anger. When it stalked forward, its blade-sharp shoulders six feet off the ground, Lilly could see the movement of every muscle and tendon. She tried to draw her eyes away from its scab-red eyes and yellow, blood-smeared teeth, but she couldn't look away. The dog's low growl seemed to come from all directions.

"I have a plan," Höd said in a conversational tone. "I'll need your help. Throw a stone at the dog to make him bark. That will help me locate him. Then, when I attack, you run."

The hound's ears snapped flat against its skull.

"That's suicide," Lilly whispered. "For both of us."

Höd's brow drew down over his abysmal eyes. "Stop thinking like a living person and throw a damned rock, will you?"

She lifted a card-deck-size stone from the counter and, with a grunt, chucked it at the hound's head.

The dog let out a shrieking, stomach-gouging bark

and sprang forward. Höd leaped high in the air to meet it. Swinging his staff overhead in a circle, he brought it down with a snap across the hound's muzzle. The ground shook as both god and monster returned to earth. Höd's stick wheeled as he backpedaled, striking the hound with each end of it. Another bark collapsed into a choked screech as Höd thrust his staff into the hound's throat. Again and again, with snapping jaws, bloody foam spraying from its mouth, the hound tried to get around the blurring motion of Höd's stick, but again and again Höd drove it back with quick strikes.

Lilly hurled rocks at the dog, but even when one connected with the hound's eye, there was no discernible effect. That was not the case with Höd's blows, which drove the hound back and had it yelping with pain. Lilly watched the Aesir fight, fascinated. So this was what it meant to be a god.

The hound ceased its attack and backed against the rubble of the fallen wall. Bloody stripes from Höd's blows marked its fur. The violent canine madness had left its eyes. Now it lowered itself to the ground and merely looked sad.

Höd was still unbloodied, but he looked worse off than the dog. His breath came in ragged sobs, his alabaster flesh looking like wax. "I thought I told you to run," he said between gulps of air.

"That's chickenshit," Lilly said, not willing to admit to him that it had been fear and awe that had held her in place.

"Then I just spent myself for nothing. I suppose that's fitting, this being Hel's realm, but mortals should follow the counsel of gods."

"I don't think the dead should be counted as mortal. But, anyway, what do we do now? Fido looks like he's catching his breath."

"Indeed, I believe he is. And when he does, I shall again go on the attack, and this time you will flee like a startled rabbit. Garm will catch you soon enough, but if delaying the inevitable is good enough for Odin, it's good enough for you."

As if on cue, the hound rose from its haunches, towering atop its polelike legs. It pulled its lips back and showed its teeth. Ropes of blood and saliva stretched to the ground.

Terror shivered down Lilly's thighs, but she would not run, would not abandon Höd to this. She'd faced death before, she reminded herself. She'd even died. Why should she fear anything now?

A sound drew her attention down toward her feet. A flat stone the size of a pizza box slid aside and revealed a man's face looking up at her from a dark hole. "I'd drop down here, if I was you," the man said, before vanishing back down the hole.

Lilly wasted no time. "Back over the counter," she shouted to Höd, rushing to yank him by the arms. Still clutching him, she stepped into the void. Together, they fell.

It turned out not to be very far to fall. Following the weak greenish halo of the man's torch, Lilly and Höd trailed him down a narrow rock passage—the ceiling so low they all had to crouch to avoid scraping their heads. After what seemed like several minutes of turning sideways to squeeze through the corridor, rock walls abrading their skin, they followed the path sharply downward. The sounds of Garm's anger faded only a little.

Finally, the man came to a stop and turned to face Lilly and Höd. In bib overalls and a plaid shirt, he was as stocky as a bale of hay. He wore a wide-brimmed straw hat, the entire left side of which was the autumnal rust of old blood.

"You'll have to tell me who you are if you want me to take you another inch," he said, furrowing his push-broom eyebrows.

"Höd, son of Odin," said Höd wearily. "And Lilly Castillo, late of Midgard."

"Venice, California," Lilly supplied. "Get us away from here and we'll owe you."

"Owe me? That sorta implies you have something to pay me with."

More grating sounds. Garm was digging through the rock.

"Didn't you hear my friend?" Lilly said, grasping at straws. "He's a son of Odin. Wouldn't you like to curry the favor of gods?"

The man laughed and spat at the same time. "Aw, hell, we know all about Höd in these parts. Skewered his own brother, fouled things up for all of us. I'd say he already owes us more than three times my last mortgage."

Höd smiled bitterly and offered a shallow bow.

"We're going to follow you wherever you're headed, no matter what," Lilly said. "So you can either proceed or wait here for Garm to mine through the rock and tear us to shreds."

"Garm? Oh, no, that ain't Garm. That's just one of Garm's pups." The man shook his head, incredulous. "Haven't you ever *seen* Garm?"

"I don't see much," Höd answered.

The low ceiling seemed to shiver as the noise of the hound's labors grew louder.

"Well, I suppose you did answer my question. Follow me." He turned on his worn boot heels and led the way with his light.

The route became more complex and disorienting. After a time, the dog's digging was no longer audible, and the passage opened onto a chamber the size of a three-car garage. It was lit by about forty men and women carrying sticks smeared in some sort of bioluminescent slime. They seemed more costumed than clothed, the men wearing jeans and shirts of cuts and fabrics that Lilly associated with the Dust Bowl and Woody Guthrie. Most of the women wore aprons. Their faces, whether lean or fleshy, carried the weight of hard times. And, like the other dead, they wore their old wounds—lacerations and bent limbs and caved-in heads. Lilly noticed that many of them had made repairs to their clothing, the rips patched up and stitched tight. Lilly fingered the hole in her own shirt, near her ribs.

"Who are you people?" she asked.

The man who'd rescued Höd and Lilly turned to the others. "The blind fella's a god," he said, ignoring her question. "The gal says she's from California."

"California, huh?" said a handsome woman with gray streaks in her black hair and a small cleft at the tip of her long nose. Little blue flowers decorated her apron. "My brother went to California. Men with shotguns turned him away at the Kern County border. They fired shots over his truck even while he was driving away, didn't care that his kids were in back with everything they owned."

Another woman stepped forward, squinting at Lilly. "Are you a Mexican?"

"I was born in Los Angeles," Lilly said carefully. "My family's from Mexico."

The woman turned to face the group. "Mexicans in California ain't got it no better than folks like us," she said. "But I don't know about the blind one. Maybe we should have a vote."

"He handled Garm's pup pretty well," said their rescuer.

A bark echoed down the length of the chamber.

"You sure that's just one of the pups, Henry?" asked the woman with the cleft nose. "That sounded awful big."

Henry's bushy eyebrows went up and down in a little shrug. "I dunno, Alice. Sometimes monsters get bigger."

Alice accepted this fact unhappily. Returning to the business at hand, she said, "I'm not sure about the girl, but we've learned everything we need to know about gods. The bitch-queen Hel's a god, ain't she? Everything that's ever gone wrong since we died is because of a god. Jesus excepted, of course." She crossed herself, as did several of the others. "And this blind one, we've all heard stories about him, how he killed his own brother out of jealousy and brought on blizzards and dust storms and twisters. He might be the very one who killed us all."

Lilly looked at Höd, waiting for him to speak up in his own defense. But he just stood there with a small, patient smile on his face, a silent observer to his own character assassination.

Lilly had no reputation with these people, so there

was no way she'd be able to talk them into accepting Höd out of a sense of pathos. She'd have to opt for practical arguments.

"Höd's been in Helheim longer than any of us," she said. "He knows things about this place that could be crucial. And he's a fighter. Whatever dangers you people are facing out here, he can be useful."

"I think she has a point," said Henry.

"And if she's wrong? Or lying?" said Alice.

A man in a striped shirt raised his hand. A strip of bloody cloth covered his left eye and most of his nose. "I move we let the both of 'em in. And if it turns sour, then we put 'em out and Garm and his kin can chew on their carcasses."

"Seconded," said Alice.

"All in favor?" said Henry.

He counted raised hands. The motion passed by two votes.

"Okay, then," Henry said. "Let's move on."

The group began filing through a fissure in the rock that opened into another passage.

"Hey, who are you people?" Lilly asked again, tugging on Henry's shirtsleeve.

Smiling apologetically, he said, "We're citizens of the town of Ellhead, Appanoose County, Iowa." He wiped his hand on his pants and offered it to her. "We're the resistance."

Lilly shook her head and laughed. Then she grinned broadly and clasped his hand in both of hers.

CHAPTER TEN

HERMOD DROVE ACROSS the endless city, down surface streets, past train yards and warehouses and mile after mile of liquor stores and nail salons and storefront loan services. The buildings were in ruins, burned and boarded up, dead-eyed streetlamps curving over the broken road. There were no road signs to mark the way.

"I'm lost," Mist said from the backseat. "I've lived in LA all my life, but I have no idea where we are."

Grimnir started rummaging in the glove compartment for a map, but Hermod told him not to bother. "We're not in LA anymore," he said. "We're not even in Midgard. We crossed into a crack in the World Tree about an hour ago."

"What does that mean, exactly?" Mist asked.

"It means we're between worlds, where everything gets mixed up."

The terrain had changed since the last time Hermod journeyed to Helheim, when he'd come to ransom Baldr. Instead of stone canyons, now there were blighted apartment blocks, soot-stained hospitals, prisons, and stucco house after stucco house on dead-end curving streets. The lines between Helheim and Midgard had rubbed away.

"I'm starving," Grimnir said after a time. They didn't have much food—some broken Fritos, a pack of jerky, a box of graham crackers.

"I wouldn't eat any of that if I were you," Hermod told him.

Grimnir ignored him, tearing open the jerky wrapper and filling the Jeep with the sweet, chewy perfume of rotting meat. Grimnir gagged and tossed it out the window while Hermod patiently explained to Mist that all the food from Midgard became inedible the closer one came to Helheim. Nothing from the living world was quite right here.

The first dead they encountered was an old man with slicked shoe-polish-black hair and a tuxedo. Hermod rolled down the window and said, "Hey."

The man turned his head. He had a steak knife jutting from his neck. "Are you lost?"

"I don't think so," Hermod said.

"I only ask because you don't seem dead. I thought this road was only for the dead."

"Where are you headed?"

"The corpse gate. I have to go through the corpse gate and then I'll be in Hel's embrace. Say, could I get a ride?"

"Sorry," Hermod said, rolling up his window.

More dead walkers soon appeared on the road, and the farther Hermod drove, the more certain he felt that he was on the right course. Behind the wheel, guiding his companions into a place from where no living being other than himself had ever returned, he felt a strength and a certainty he hadn't known since the first time he'd come to Helheim. If Thor was for protecting earth from giants, and if Odin was for storming across the sky and goading men into battle, then this was what Hermod was for: going into forbidden places.

Then he looked at his companions. Grimnir and Mist both looked gray, their eyes haunted. Even Winston, in the backseat with Mist, was quiet, his head resting on folded paws.

"I really shouldn't have brought you here," Hermod said.

Mist breathed a weary laugh. "You're the god of self-recrimination, aren't you?"

"I'm old," Hermod said. "Being old means making the same mistakes over and over. Sometimes I just get tired of it."

"What's the biggest mistake you've ever made?"

"We're supposed to have these conversations late at night. And we should be drunk."

Mist rubbed her face with her hands. "It seems plenty late, and we're not lucky enough to be drunk. Come on, entertain me." When she pulled her hands away, Hermod caught sight of her face in the rearview mirror. Those sad, dark eyes of hers were distractingly lovely.

He wondered if Mist and Grimnir were lovers, and with alarm he saw the trajectory these thoughts were taking him on. *Stop it,* he told himself. Falling for the Valkyrie was the very last thing he needed.

"Everyone knows my big mistake," Hermod said, expecting to hear some kind of disparaging noise from Grimnir, but he'd nodded off, slumped in his

NORSE CODE \ 125

seat and snoring. "I promised the Aesir I'd get on bended knee before Hel and bargain for Baldr's life. I made a really convincing case too. She was ready to give in. But then I went and demanded Höd as part of the deal."

In the mirror, Mist's expression revealed nothing. "Actually, I didn't know the part about Höd."

"That's the part nobody likes to talk about. My family made him the scapegoat for Baldr's death. Then Odin had him killed. And then we promptly forgot about him."

"*You* haven't forgotten him."

"Höd got screwed. There was no way I was going to beg for Baldr's life and abandon Höd to this place."

Mist gently petted Winston's head. "So that's your big screwup? Acting out of fairness and mercy?"

"Well," Hermod said after a long silence, "I didn't say it was my *only* screwup."

A body crashed through the windshield. Hermod found himself staring in shock at a leering face draped over the steering wheel. Then he began pounding it with his fist. He could figure out what was going on later. Now was a time for punching, and he did not stop punching until the face opened its mouth wide, caught Hermod's fist in it, and bit down. Hermod hit the brakes and shoved the thumb of his other hand in the draugr's eye—it *was* a draugr, of course, one of Hel's mindless dead, what else could it be?—but the dead monster bit down yet harder.

Mist kicked the back of his seat as she struggled to get her sword free, while Winston tried to squeeze in front, his jaws snapping at the draugr. Between Mist's kidney punches and the malamute's bites, Hermod feared his friends would do him as much harm as the draugr.

"Everybody calm down," Grimnir said over the screaming and barking and the draugr's dead-moaning. "I'll handle this."

He lifted his sword from the floorboard, struggling in the tight quarters to turn the blade toward the draugr, and accidentally nicked Hermod's earlobe.

"Could you be careful with that thing?" Hermod yelled.

"Maybe hold still a little?" Grimnir shot back.

With his shoulder jammed against the door and one leg braced against the cup holders, Grimnir sliced into the draugr's neck. The draugr thrashed but didn't release its biting grip on Hermod's hand. Hermod was now certain that the draugr intended to eat his fingers. He repeatedly slammed his free fist into the draugr's face. There was a satisfying collapse of skull bones, but the draugr's bite didn't loosen until Grimnir methodically sawed through the creature's neck and separated it from its body, which hung through the shattered glass of the windshield. Even then, the decapitated head clamped down on Hermod's fist, but, with Grimnir's help, Hermod was able to pry it loose.

He kicked the accelerator to the floor.

"Holy shit," said Mist from the backseat. "What the fuck was that?"

"Draugr," said Grimnir. "Shambling dead."

"You mean a fucking zombie?"

"Yes," Grimnir said, "I mean a fucking zombie."

Hermod shoved Winston out of the way before the

dog could start eating the draugr's remains. Groans roiled in the fog.

"Let me guess—they travel in mobs," Mist said.

Grimnir nodded. "Sometimes. Back in the day we thought they were people who hadn't been given proper burial rites and had come back to haunt their loved ones. But once you've seen them come over a hill like a rotting tide, you start to think maybe something else is going on. Some think they're under Hel's control, maybe even her creations, but nobody's really sure."

"What I'm sure of is I don't want to fight any more of them," Hermod said. "That bastard near chewed my hand off." The Jeep sped forward, tires bouncing on the rough terrain as Hermod tried to steer around the parade of dead clogging the road.

A leathery pop sounded, and the steering wheel jumped in Hermod's hands. They'd lost a tire. He pulled on the wheel to compensate, and the front bumper collided with a cluster of dead. The rest of the windshield fell in, and Hermod found himself fighting at least two draugr, who reached in through the gap for control of the wheel. Then the Jeep was logrolling, and he screamed, "Hold on to the dog, Mist!" With an explosion of glass and the crunch and shriek of collapsing steel, the Jeep came to rest on its roof.

Arms reached inside and violently dragged Hermod free of the wreck. He knew better than to consider this a positive development and looked up to find himself staring into the gruesome, hungry faces of at least a dozen draugr. They clawed and clubbed and bit one another like a pack of wild dogs fighting over a kill. He struggled in vain to gain his footing, but it seemed every time he managed to kick one draugr away, three more came to replace it. Dimly, he heard shouts that sounded like Mist's, and then Winston's vicious barks, but he could only think they'd soon fall silent.

"Enough."

The voice wasn't particularly loud or distinct in pitch, but it cut sharply through the sounds of the struggle. To Hermod's surprise, the draugr moved off him and backed away.

Hermod shot to his feet in a defensive crouch, glancing around in search of his sword. He was bleeding from his hand and head. Everything hurt. Mist stood just a small distance away, bleeding circles of tooth marks on her cheek and neck. Winston, with a torn ear, snarled by her side. Grimnir was grunting with the effort of trying to free his sword, which was embedded in the ground through an impaled, wriggling draugr.

Just a few feet away from Hermod, his brother Baldr stood, arms crossed like a stern principal who'd just broken up a schoolyard brawl.

Baldr was still beautiful but not the same as on the day he'd died. He hadn't aged, exactly, or even weathered, but his time in Helheim had changed him. His face now was flawless white stone, his eyes a pale, glacial blue. He stood, cold and magisterial, in a shirt of white wool marred only by a spot of red in the center of his chest.

Hermod had so many questions, so many things he wanted to say. His words came out thick, and he managed to dislodge them only with great effort.

"I'm sorry, Baldr. I couldn't let her keep Höd any more than I could let her keep you."

Baldr blinked in surprise. "Oh, that? But it was so long ago."

"I let too much time pass. I should have come back sooner and tried again."

Baldr dismissed that with a wave. "Hel wouldn't have let you back into her kingdom. If you'd tried again she would have rent you limb from limb and used your corpse as building material."

"But she let me in this time," Hermod said, disliking the tone of helpless confusion he heard in his own voice. More firmly, he said, "I'm here now, and I've come to stop Ragnarok." He indicated Mist and Grimnir. "These are my associates."

"Yes, of course. The Valkyrie Mist and her Einherjar servant, Grimnir. Not to mention brave Winston."

Hermod caught Grimnir's glance, and then Mist spoke for all of them: "You knew we were coming."

Baldr smiled slightly, a shadow of his old, gentle humor showing through. Then, "Bind them," he said.

The draugr swarmed in, gripping Hermod's and the others' wrists and arms and legs. A knee in the back brought Hermod down, and though he managed to throw a few draugr off, ultimately he couldn't stop them from pinning him in the dirt. They forced his arms behind his back and clapped rusted shackles around his wrists. An iron collar went around his neck.

Mist and Grimnir got the same treatment. A few draugr held them fast while another connected their collars with a chain. Even Winston was collared and leashed and had a strap tied around his muzzle.

Hermod spat dust. "Baldr, what is this?"

Baldr said nothing. He wouldn't meet Hermod's eyes.

He turned to the draugr. "Let's go."

\# \# \#

HEL'S HALL was not constructed of bones, as some poets insisted, and the roof was not made of woven serpents. Her hall wasn't terribly large, it wasn't a hive of congealed blood and shit, nor did its angles defy the fundamental norms of Euclidean geometry. It was just a hall made of gray timbers, perched on a mesa of gray stone, and what made it dreadful was the simple fact that Hel resided within.

"So, how long have you been Hel's bitch?" Hermod asked for perhaps the tenth time as the party made their way up steep, narrow switchbacks, the draugr walking them on their leashes. Despite the exhausting march of the past three days, Hermod had managed to badger Baldr almost nonstop, increasingly more determined to goad his brother out of the silence he'd maintained since their capture. Baldr rode a few yards ahead on a cigarette-ash gelding. He dropped back to pull up even with Hermod.

"Some advice for you, brother. You're entering the hall of Helheim's ruler. You'd do well to observe the courtesies here." His voice was mild, his tone sincere. This was not a dressing-down. This was helpful guidance. Baldr was always so helpful. Hermod couldn't believe he used to fall for it.

With the draugr constantly keeping tension on Hermod's chain, the collar bit into his skin, and it was painful to look up. But he wanted to see Baldr's face as they spoke. "There's something funny about you lecturing me on courtesy when your zombies are dragging me and my friends around in chains."

Baldr didn't respond.

"Brother, what's *wrong* with you?" Hermod said plaintively. Watching Baldr fall with a spear embedded in his heart had been bad enough. Seeing the cold thing he'd become was almost unbearable.

Baldr brought his horse to a stop, and the procession halted with him. He turned in his saddle and faced Hermod, his face like a funereal statue. "I *died*," he said.

Grimnir snorted. "I've died plenty of times. Doesn't mean you have to be an asshole about it."

Upon reaching the top of the mesa, Baldr dismounted and commanded his draugr to remove the prisoners' chains. Then, with a draugr escort, he led the party into Hel's hall, a high-roofed space filled with dead soldiers standing shoulder to shoulder in ranks. They were as motley a crew as the Einherjar, a living museum of military uniforms and arms, from spears to blunderbusses to automatic rifles. Most warriors entered Helheim without their weapons, but Hel's handpicked army carried quite an arsenal.

The ranks parted to leave an aisle that led to the front of the hall, where a pair of wooden thrones loomed before a cold hearth. Baldr made his way up the aisle and assumed his place on one of the chairs. Beside him, on the other chair, sat Hel, regal and somber in voluminous black robes. Her hands rested lightly on the chair's arms, the left hand delicate with long, tapered fingers, the flesh a pale, healthy pink.

The right was grotesquely swollen and rotted black. With great effort, Hermod forced himself to look up at her face, the left half of which was pleasingly shaped, the cheek blushed with a rosy glow. The right half was dark, mummified skin. But it was her eyes that seized Hermod's heart, for they contained every sorrow suffered by every denizen of Hel's kingdom, and it was impossible to look upon them and not weep. Staring into them, Hermod felt his mother's suffering at his own birth, and the first time he'd ever felt hungry, and the first time he'd been scared, and the first time he'd been lonely. He felt Baldr's death anew and his shame at coming home alone when he'd been sent to bring his brother back to Asgard, and he felt every hopeless night of his long life. These were not memories but pains felt just as strongly as though the events were happening now.

But, no, they weren't happening now. This was Hel's doing. He made himself look hard into her eyes. *I see you. I know what you're doing. I've already faced these things down, and I'm still walking, you half-rotted bitch.*

"Where's Höd?" he said.

Baldr glanced over at Hel before answering: "We have had a parting of ways."

"That speaks well of Höd," said Hermod, drawing a sleeve across his nose. "What happened?"

For the first time ever, Hermod saw an expression so alien on Baldr's face that it took him a moment to recognize it for what it was: peevishness. And then his placid expression resumed.

"I begged Höd to accept the queen's hospitality,"

Baldr went on, unperturbed. "He could have been a prince here."

"And what is he instead?"

"He is a fugitive. But we will have him back before the last day is done. And, in the meantime, we have you."

"Collecting the whole set, are you?" Hermod addressed this to Hel. Things squirmed beneath her rotten skin. "We are still alive. You have no right to hold us."

There was a graceful movement to Hel's robes, like a billowing of smoke, as she rose to her feet and spread her arms wide. "You think me covetous," Hel said in two voices, a sensuous alto and a thick, viscous rasp that coated Hermod in clammy sweat. "But I have never asked for more than my due. I was cast into this land, and to me was given stewardship of the dead. I have never complained. For the second time you make an incursion into my kingdom. You rush to my embrace. Every step a man or a god commits brings him closer to death, so do not complain, seam-walker, when you arrive at the destination you set out upon."

Hermod sought a derisive reply, but standing before Hel, in her own hall, in the center of her own kingdom, all he could do was gesture at his surroundings and murmur, "I never wanted this."

"There are many who do not know what they want until it is lost," Hel said. "But in my kingdom, late reunions are often possible. I am generous. Those who dwell in my realm will find me a good gift-giver. Here, Valkyrie, I have something for you."

From the folds of her robe, Hel produced a gray cloth bundle. Hermod could make out the writing and logo on the cloth. It was a New Jersey Nets sweatshirt.

Hel lovingly unfolded the cloth. A man's severed head blinked.

"Adrian Hoover?" Hermod asked Mist. She nodded in mute response.

"Is this not the man you came for?" Hel said.

Mist's lips moved silently before she found her voice. "You decapitated him."

"His body became separated in transit," Hel said. "I don't know how, exactly. It happens."

"Put him out of his misery."

The soft, living half of Hel's mouth smiled. "But how, Valkyrie? Shall I remove his brain? He would still live and feel. Living death 'til the end of the worlds. That is the gift I bestow upon all who come here."

Hel folded the cloth back over Hoover's head. "Let our guests retire now," she said to Baldr.

"Please," said Mist. "I'm begging you. End his suffering. He's done nothing to deserve this." She lowered herself to her knees. "I'm *begging* you."

Hermod saw no cruelty in Hel's eyes, or pleasure in suffering. What he saw was resignation.

Baldr made a gesture, and a detail of draugr and Hel's soldiers escorted Mist, Hermod, Grimnir, and Winston from the throne room. Hands prodded them along, and just before exiting the chamber, Hermod glanced back at Hel and Baldr, elegant and somber on their high seats. Hel idly petted the bundle containing Adrian Hoover's living head as though it were a lapdog.

# # #

A LONG TIME ago on an Asgard seashore, Munin and I are perched high in a tree overlooking Baldr's funeral. It is a grand affair, worthy of the Aesir's most beloved son. Frey comes in a chariot drawn by a boar, and Freya is there with her cats. Her dress is very pretty. Everyone is there: all the gods, and dwarves and elves and trolls, and even mountain giants and frost giants. The Aesir weep. Thor keeps blowing his nose, making a great *schnoork* sound that shakes the leaves from our tree.

Baldr's corpse, dressed in his finest white, is laid atop a pyre built on the deck of his ship. He manages to look beautiful and magisterial in death but also very cold. A slave stands by with a burning torch, ready to ignite the pyre, and logs are already in place to serve as rollers. Once the ship is lit, the Aesir will launch Baldr's body to sea.

Odin climbs the pyre. He has always hoped that the sibyl was wrong, that he wouldn't have to see blood on Baldr's breast. Sometimes witch babble is just witch babble, after all, but now here's the shocking white corpse of Baldr, whom Odin loves not in the way a war god loves a warrior but in the way a father loves his son.

Odin whispers something in Baldr's ear, but what he says, not even Munin and I can hear.

A woman wanders through the crowd of mourners, her hair in disarray, dark rings around her eyes. This is Nana, Baldr's wife.

"Do you think he'll be all right?" she asks Thor, grabbing his massive forearm.

"All right? Nana, he's dead."

"Yes, but Hel will be kind to him, won't she? And Hermod will bring him back."

"I don't know, Nana." Thor gently withdraws his arm.

"Hermod will bring him back," she says, with utter conviction.

The pyre is lit, and soon Baldr's ship roars in full conflagration. It is a grand, beautiful pyre. According to Munin, in terms of thermal output, it is the best pyre ever.

I watch as Frigg says something to Vidar, and moments later he is at Nana's side. He is speaking to her, which is rare, for Vidar guards his words like a dragon guards its hoard.

Nana swoons and falls into Vidar's waiting arms. Carefully carrying Nana over his shoulder, he climbs the burning ship and lays her in the fire, where she dies in the flames, crying weakly.

"She died of a broken heart," Frigg says.

The Aesir all nod in agreement.

# # #

HERMOD, MIST, and Grimnir were taken to some dimly lit apartments and left there without chains, though a company of armed guards remained posted outside the door. A table of meats and cheeses and bread and wine and cakes was laid out near the dead fire, untouched. Not even Winston would go near it.

Mist sat in a chair and stared at the dirt floor.

"That . . . really sucked," said Hermod. He came over and took her hand. He knew what it was like to fail in Helheim.

"Yeah," she said.

After a time, Grimnir lumbered over. "So, we gonna get out of here or what?"

Hermod rubbed his face, trying to see if he could force his skin to feel blood circulating beneath. "There's a whole platoon of Baldr's goons outside. What do you suggest?"

"I could act really sick, and then when someone comes in to check me out, we lower the boom."

"Why would anyone in the land of the dead care if you got sick?" Mist asked.

"Good answer, kid," Grimnir said. "I was just testing you."

"Thanks. What's wrong with breaking the door down and fighting them with overwhelming force?"

"Baldr took our weapons," Grimnir pointed out. "Without them, our overwhelming force is going to be somewhat lacking in the *over* department."

They each floated a number of ideas for escape. Grimnir offered an impressive variety of them, but by the time he got to setting off fire-suppression systems, it became clear that he was no longer trying to form a plan as much as he was reminiscing about fonder days.

I could let you out.

The papery rasp came from the hearth. Pale flames wavered there.

I know all the ways here, Hermod, and I know the ways out.

Mist raised her eyebrows at Hermod. "The fireplace seems to know you."

"Funny. I don't think I know any fireplaces." Hermod took a step closer to the hearth. "Who are you?"

The flames danced an inch or two higher. *Have you already forgotten the daughter of Nep, Hermod, my kin?*

Hermod hissed air through his teeth. "Nana?"

Ah, good. I was afraid everyone had forgotten that I ever lived.

Hermod came closer to the fire and crouched before it. "Where *are* you?"

I am in the fire, of course.

He shivered a little.

Mist came up beside Hermod. "Who is it?" she whispered.

"Baldr's wife," he said, peering into the flames. "So, uh, Nana, how've you been?"

A little lonely. Baldr doesn't spend much time with me anymore. There aren't any fires near Hel's high seat.

In Asgard, Baldr had been a loving and devoted husband to Nana—but Hermod supposed thousands of years in the deadlands would strain even the best marriage.

"How long have you been a fire elemental?" he asked.

The flames popped and crackled. *I've always had an affinity for hearths. I like hearths. They're the center of good homes, where men and women mate and have healthy children. I like homes. I like children. But I couldn't speak through flames until I burned up and died on Baldr's pyre. It was very hot. It hurt.*

"I'm sure it must have," Hermod said. "I'm sorry you had to go through that. It was very unfair."

Yes. It was kind of you to ask Hel to release Höd. Höd

and I used to keep each other company here, after Baldr decided he liked Hel better than me.

"Do you know where Höd is now?"

Not exactly. Looking for a way out. Wherever he is, there's no fire. There's hardly fire anywhere in all of Helheim.

Grimnir circled his index finger in a hurry-up gesture, which Hermod was inclined to ignore both on general principle and out of sympathy for Nana. But the thug did have a point.

Hermod cleared his throat. "Nana, you said you could help us escape?"

Yes. I know the way. Just take my hand.

Mist and Hermod exchanged a glance, and Hermod could only shrug. "Nana, you don't seem to have hands."

Oh, of course. I'm sorry. It's been so long since I've had to think properly. I usually talk to the dead, and they don't think properly either, so I don't often bother. I will manifest my body for you.

The little fire drew in on itself, shrinking but glowing slightly brighter. Then, with a sizzle that sounded like a hiss of pain, the flames shot five feet in the air and took on a flickering, not quite opaque, but distinctly human form.

Hermod had feared she would appear as she looked at the time of her death, her clean flesh charred and bloody, but she looked as he remembered her.

She held out a slender, wavering hand. *Come with me, and I'll take you outside through the fire.*

"Right, hold the phone," Grimnir said. "How does this work, and where are we going?"

You take my hand, Nana said very patiently. *And we go through the fire. Outside.*

"And then we'll be a pile of ashes or something?"

I am the closest thing Helheim has to a goddess of the hearth, Nana said. There was now only the slightest hint of imperiousness in her tone. *I will not harm you.*

"That's reassuring," Grimnir said. "And I mean no disrespect, but why are you helping us?"

I don't like Hel. Baldr doesn't like me. I like Hermod. I'm not sure I like you, but Hermod seems to like you. I neither like nor dislike the Valkyrie. Oh, and I like your dog, she added as an afterthought.

"Convinced?" Hermod said to Grimnir.

"No. You go first."

Hermod grasped Nana's hand. It was quite hot, but it didn't burn. Mist took her other hand, and then, with a mix of hesitation and bluster, Grimnir latched on to Nana's wrist.

"Wait," Hermod said, letting go. "What about my dog?"

Nana told Hermod to take Winston by the collar. A moment later his vision went orange, then white, and it *did* burn, everything burned, searing pain, and he was sure he'd been suckered again, but he held on anyway. They emerged in a small ring of stones, where a campfire lapped against the chill air outside the hall. Only after hopping out of the flames did Hermod notice they were surrounded by a half dozen guards.

Startled, the guards scrambled to their feet. They wore an assortment of ragged military uniforms, and all were armed with wicked-looking serrated spears.

Grimnir took the initiative, grabbing one of the guards' spears with both hands and twisting it away. He impaled the man through the chest, pinning him to the ground. The guard wiggled, angrily screaming, "Oi! What's this? Oi!"

I'm sorry I couldn't get you farther away, Nana said. *As I told you, there aren't many fires burning in Helheim. But I did find the men guarding your things. They were trying to warm their hands.*

While Mist and Winston struggled with another of the guards, Hermod risked a glance down into the fire. Their bags were piled there. He dove away from a spear thrust, rolled through the flames, almost smothering them, and grabbed the bags. Another guard attacked, but Hermod managed to duck under his spear and swing his bag, with his sword inside, into the guard's face. He heard bones crack.

He removed his sword from his duffel and thrust up through the armpit of the next attacking guard. It felt obscenely good.

With the guards temporarily out of commission, no more assaults came. Hermod looked around.

"Did we get them all?" he asked the others.

"Yeah," Mist said, coming over to get her own bag. "They kinda sucked."

Those weren't guards, said Nana in a tiny voice. The campfire was barely alive now. *They were keepers.*

"Keepers of what?" Grimnir said, testing the weight of his sword in one hand and a captured spear in the other.

A gust of wind moaned across the mesa, and the flames wavered and died, and there was no answer from the fire. A howl rose in the air, a hornlike lament. Winston whined and turned over to submissively show his belly.

Down a crooked narrow path, nestled into the rock, sat a pen built around the mouth of a cave.

Hermod pried his dry lips open with his tongue. "Run."

He led his group down the switchback, the jagged rock wall beside them sharp enough to cut flesh and the edge of the path sheering off into a steep drop. Looking over his shoulder, Hermod caught sight of an enormous hound loping after them. Easily fifteen feet at the shoulders, with a corrugated rib cage and small, expressionless black eyes, Hel's hound gave chase.

There was no way to outrun Garm. With every lunging stride down the narrow slope, the hound closed in by yards. They would have to stop and fight it, and after his trials with the wolves in Midgard, and the long journey to Helheim, and even the scuffle with Garm's keepers, Hermod wasn't sure how much fight he had left in him.

Still sprinting forward, he reached into his duffel and dug out a small leather pouch. He'd probably transferred that parcel from one carrying bag to another a hundred times without ever opening it up. He unfastened the leather thong.

The Hel cake, as hard as wood, still smelled of honey and spice. It was a souvenir from his first visit to Helheim, taken as a trophy to show his Aesir kin that he'd completed his journey; by the time he'd gotten back to Asgard, though, he'd lost all interest in proving anything. Still, he'd kept it all these years.

Hermod skidded to a halt and waved the others to run past him. Holding his ground, he looked up the path to face Garm. Puffs of dust flew up every time the dog's paws slammed the ground. Saliva cascaded down his jaws.

Hermod shook the cake as though it were a tennis ball and Garm an excited retriever. With the hound thundering toward him, he told himself to wait. He'd once gotten in the path of a charging woolly rhinoceros. The horn had gone through his chest, puncturing a lung and missing his heart by a quarter of an inch. It'd taken him years to heal. Garm was bigger than a woolly rhino.

When Hermod could smell the dog's breath and feel the saliva spray in his face, he hurled the cake off the path into empty air. Garm switched direction and lunged at the cake, his momentum propelling him to the edge of the path. His nails tore deep scars in the ground as he tried to scrabble to a stop, but with a piteous yowl he fell, twisting head over tail.

Hermod peered over the ledge, watching mists swirl in the wake of the hound's descent.

# # #

IT FELT as though they'd walked through a season. The road stretched ahead in a long, brutally straight line along a dusty plain, the monotonous scenery broken only by the occasional cluster of piled rocks, some of them as large as houses. Hermod imagined unpleasant things using them for cover.

He led the group east, heading for a distant ridge of sharp rocks on the horizon that never seemed to grow closer. He remembered that a river ran parallel to the other side of the rocks, and he reasoned that if they followed the river, they might eventually find a portal out of Helheim. Rivers in all the worlds flowed from the same place.

Several dozen yards ahead, in the middle of the road, stood a boy with eyes too big for his face. He leaned on a tree branch roughly the shape of a rake, beside a field of rows drawn in the powdery dirt with rulerlike precision. Nothing living could grow in the fields of Helheim, but the dead weren't spared hunger, and in their desperation some of them tended hopeless plots of land. Others made attempts at building towns and villages like the ones they'd come from. Helheim was unfathomably vast, but Hermod could imagine it one day crowded with dead—men and women never stopped dying. The habitations would grow into cities, and the cities would sprawl to the deadlands' borders. And what then? If the World Tree stood long enough, there would be so many dead that they'd start spilling over into the other worlds, in greater numbers than the occasional stray draugr.

It occurred to him that Ragnarok had a purpose: to end the world when it reached carrying capacity. Death and rebirth formed a natural cycle—isn't that what the sibyl had tried to tell him? Why couldn't he just accept that? Let the wolves eat the sun and moon. Let the worlds burn.

As they approached the boy, both Hermod and Grimnir reached for their swords. Mist moved in front of them. "Let me handle this," she said. Hermod had to admit she made a more agreeable presentation than either himself or Grimnir, especially when they were brandishing weapons at a little boy.

He nodded at her. "Be careful."

She took a few more steps toward the boy. "Hi, there. My name is Mist. What's yours?"

The left side of the boy's skull curved inward. "Steven," he said. "I'm a farmer."

Mist nodded appreciatively. "Did you rake this field yourself? Those are really straight rows."

"I rake 'em every day. The hounds always leave paw prints, and I gotta rake 'em over."

Hermod and Grimnir exchanged unhappy glances.

"That's a big job for one farmer," Mist said. "Don't you have anyone who helps you?"

The boy smiled shyly, dust mottling his blond crew cut. Then he dropped his rake and took off running as fast as his spindly legs would carry him.

"Wait!" Mist shouted. "I'm not going to hurt you!"

Grimnir grinned. "Leave this to me."

Mist shot a warning look to both him and Hermod. "You will stay here and let me handle this," she said, before taking off after the boy.

"Sure, kid, you're the boss," Grimnir said.

He let Mist get a bit of a head start. Then he launched himself in a heavy-footed jog after her.

Hermod watched the boy lead the chase toward a stack of sharp-edged, Cadillac-size boulders in the distance.

"Stay," he commanded Winston. The malamute barked once and joined Hermod as he set off across the field after the others.

The boy scrambled over the crest of the rocks. A moment later, Mist and Grimnir climbed up after him. When Hermod got there, he moved around the pile instead of going over it, and when he came to the other side, he found Mist and Grimnir surrounded by a dozen men and women with sharp sticks. The boy peered around the legs of a woman with a face smashed in so badly that, when viewed straight on, her nose was in profile.

"I got 'em, Ma, I got 'em!" the boy said, dancing on the balls of his feet.

She ruffled his hair. "You did real good, Steven. But hush up now and keep still."

"That goes for you three as well," said a plump man. In overalls, a plaid shirt, and a bloodstained straw hat, his robin's-egg-blue eyes were the most colorful things Hermod had ever seen in Helheim.

"I've got a sword," said Grimnir. "So does my pal Hermod. The woman's got one too. And as for you, you've got . . . sticks. The friggin' dog could take you lot all by himself."

The man in the straw hat nodded thoughtfully. "There's more of us than you see here, and we know this terrain better than you. Think about it: One boy led you into our trap. So maybe your swords aren't giving you the upper hand you think."

The others in the group gave approving nods.

Grimnir turned around in a slow 360, arms spread to indicate the miles of fields and rocks around them. "Not that it matters much, but you're bluffing."

Putting two fingers to his mouth, Mr. Straw Hat whistled sharply. Hermod admired that whistle. He'd never managed to develop a good whistle himself. Out from a gap between two potato-shaped boulders, half a dozen others emerged. Hermod wanted to call these newcomers *townsfolk,* the men dressed in cotton shirts and denim, the women in plain, practical dresses the colors of pale spring flowers. They all bore injuries—broken limbs and cruel lacerations—but they held their crude spears with confidence.

"Let's not have any unnecessary fisticuffs," Hermod said. "So, what is this, highway robbery? Piracy on the plains?"

"We'll ask the questions," said Mr. Straw Hat. "For starters, where'd you come from?"

Hermod hooked a thumb over his shoulder. "Down the road."

"We know that. Steven saw you coming for miles. I meant before that."

"We're from California," Hermod said. "Died of drug overdoses."

"My condolences to your families," Mr. Straw Hat said with possible sincerity, though others in the group frowned at Hermod and his companions with disapproval.

Hermod wondered if he should just cut off all their legs at the knees right now. The longer he conferred with these fine townsfolk, the more likely they would dispatch a messenger to Hel to let her know the whereabouts of her wayward Aesir prize.

"Tell them the truth, Hermod."

Hermod's brother Höd squeezed between a gap in the rock pile. He brushed dirt from the knees of his charcoal wool pants. Directing the dark pits of his sightless eyes at Hermod, he leaned on his stick and said, "Trust these people, brother. You'll be bringing more trouble to them than they to you."

A woman followed through the gap, but other than to register that she seemed familiar, Hermod was too taken aback to pay her notice.

"Höd," he said.

"Yes. How flattering you still recognize me."

Definitely Höd, thought Hermod. "Why aren't you at Hel's hall, with Baldr?"

"Because he is a pretty-mannered traitor. Why aren't you with him?"

"I'm neither a traitor nor pretty-mannered," Hermod sputtered back, offended.

"No," said Höd, blindly appraising him. "I suppose not. Which is fortunate. Who are your friends?"

Hermod uttered some introductions.

Grimnir grunted a greeting, but Mist was preoccupied with Höd's companion, who, unlike the others, was dressed in modern clothing—jeans and a Greenpeace sweatshirt punctured by two ragged holes and caked with dried blood. Hermod realized now why she seemed so familiar.

"Hermod," Mist said in a choked voice, "I'd like you to meet my sister."

CHAPTER ELEVEN

L IKE A TRUSTY Scout leader, Henry Verdant ushered Hermod and his companions, along with Höd and Lilly, through a gap between the rocks, where a rickety ladder fashioned from sticks led down into a cramped tunnel.

"Dug by hand and stone," Henry said with pride, his face flickering in the uncanny light of bioluminescent torches stuck into the walls.

Hermod managed to summon a noise of appreciation. He remembered Nana saying how rare fire was in Helheim. "You people live down here?"

"Not this particular tunnel, no. This one's a staging area." Verdant went on to tell Hermod about the tunnel network: miles of underground warrens that served as hiding places, escape chutes, storage caches for the Iowans' crude weapons and tools, and places like this, which emerged at watch points near the road.

Hermod drew a fingernail along the wall. Sandy rock flaked away. "And you dug this whole thing yourselves?"

"Oh, no," Verdant said, waving off the notion. "A lot of it was done by others who came before us."

"There have always been escape attempts in Helheim," Höd said from the shadows. "Sometimes those who still have a desire to live and the will to do something about it manage to find one another and organize their efforts. But nobody has ever actually made it out, as far as I know. The hound gets them, and they end up being incorporated into the corpse gate. You're the exception, of course."

"Back then, Hel was willing to let me go," Hermod said. "I won't get a guarantee of safe passage this time."

"Still, it's fortunate our paths crossed," said Höd. "I think you can be of use to us."

Hermod didn't like Höd's phrasing. "Haven't we all had enough of being 'of use' to one another? Loki used you to kill Baldr, and now I'm being used by . . . I don't know by whom. By Odin, or the sibyl, or Hel maybe."

"I simply meant that I hoped you would stay and help us. I realize dropping in only to move on shortly thereafter is in your nature."

Verdant held up a hand. "Let's not put the cart before the horse, now. No offense, Mr. Höd, but we just took you and Lilly on, and I have to remind you, it wasn't a unanimous decision. I understand these newcomers are your kin, and I'm sure they're fine folk, but we'll need to talk over whether they can stay or not."

"Town meeting?" said Hermod.

Verdant answered firmly, "That's how we do things around here."

The Iowans filed through a slit in the tunnel, which

led to a larger chamber, leaving Hermod and his companions behind, along with Höd and Lilly.

"They seem like nice enough people," Grimnir said. "Hel's going to chew them like kibble with gravy."

"Quite possibly," agreed Höd.

Now that they were away from the Iowans, Hermod had so many questions for his brother he scarcely knew where to begin. He turned to Mist for help, but she and Lilly stood looking at each other intently, both with their arms stiffly at their sides, as if they were afraid to use them.

"You good?" Lilly asked Mist.

"Pretty much. You?"

"Considering everything? Yeah."

"Hug now?" Mist said.

"Yeah."

They held each other, weeping just a little.

Hermod turned back to Höd. He had thinned and whitened, like a forgotten garment hung out to dry, a necklace of purple bruises around his throat.

"These farmers are your resistance?" Hermod said.

"They're not farmers anymore. They're fighters now. I'll show you."

Höd led him through a twisting passage that opened onto a spacious chamber. "This is the Iowans' armory."

Hermod took in their cache of rocks, slings, bows carved of bone, and arrows of brittle-looking wood. Grimnir was right: Hel would annihilate these people.

"How many of these resistance cells are there?" he asked.

"I don't know, and neither do they," Höd said, leading the way back out of the chamber. "They work autonomously, harassing Hel and her soldiers. Mostly they just succeed in irritating Baldr, but that's something."

"What happened with you two? Despite your differences, you used to be so close."

"In Asgard, Baldr always shone," Höd said. "Here, it's dark. It turns out Baldr gives less light than he takes. He became smaller in Helheim, and meaner. But don't judge him too harshly. After a long time in Hel's realm, it is difficult not to wear away until you're nothing but a ghost woven from memory and resentment."

Henry Verdant met them in the corridor. "So, how about it, Mr. Hermod? Would you and your friends care to join forces with us?"

Really, Hermod would have preferred not to. "What about my dog?" he said, resigned.

Verdant smiled warmly. "So long as he doesn't bite the wrong people, he's welcome."

Using the femur of some animal, Verdant tapped a rhythm on the cavern wall. Within a few minutes, the resistance had assembled in the weapons cache room. There were about forty people in all.

Verdant cleared his throat. "Most of you know I was in a field artillery battery in France. Three whole days on the front line, mostly pushing horses through mud, until I was captured. I spent the rest of the war in the Langensalza POW camp. We had three objectives there: survive, escape, and sabotage. I know things aren't the same in Helheim as in that camp. For one thing, we're dead. As for escape, thousands and thousands have tried, and thousands and thousands have failed. But Mr. Höd has shared with me some new information, some new possibilities that promise hope. I've already talked it over with a few of you, and if you'll give Mr. Höd your attention, he'll tell you the rest."

Verdant moved aside, and after a moment Lilly guided Höd forward. Hermod had an uncomfortable flashback of Höd standing in the middle of Valhalla with a mistletoe spear in his hands, and from the look on Höd's face, he might have been having the same thought.

"I have been in Helheim a very long time," Höd began. "When I first came here, there was no Iowa. The continent in Midgard you came from wasn't even occupied by humans."

"Not even Indians?" said the little dead boy, Steven.

"Not even Indians," Höd said. "In the intervening time, billions of people have entered Helheim, but only Hermod ever left it alive." Hermod shifted uncomfortably. "The ship *Naglfar* has been under construction ever since things first started to die. The ship is made of death. Her hull is lined with the fingernails of the dead. Her boards are bones. Her sail is flesh. It's long been known that, in the time of Ragnarok, *Naglfar* will break free from her moorings. She will deliver Hel's dead army to the final battle and bring yet more destruction to the worlds. The details of this prophecy, however, are unclear. Some say the ship will set sail with Loki at the helm. Others say she will be steered by the giant Hymir. When a prophecy so lacks clarity, I see opportunity.

"We were aware that *Naglfar* was moored here in Helheim, but until recently her exact location remained a secret. Now we know she lies east of here, anchored on the banks of a certain unnamed tributary of the river Gjoll. We will go there. We will board the ship as galley slaves, and we will take her over. She will be our tool, not Hel's."

Hermod sighed. He'd been hoping to hear a *good* plan.

As the assembly broke up into smaller groups to discuss various logistical issues, Hermod drew Mist and Grimnir off into a secluded corner.

"What do you guys think?" Mist asked. "Suicide mission?"

"Obviously," Grimnir said. "Hel's army has actual weaponry and ammunition, the stuff she let them keep when they passed into her lands. How are forty farmers with Stone Age technology supposed to take the ship?"

"But it's not just farmers," Mist reminded him. "It's also two Aesir, not to mention you and me and Lilly."

"A few umbrellas don't make much difference in a hurricane, kid."

"Well, so what?" Mist said. "You're Einherjar. Isn't your whole existence about fighting a hopeless battle against overwhelming odds? Here's your chance."

"I'm supposed to fall in the clang and clatter of swords on the field of Vigrid. Not be chopped into pieces and used to patch holes in the corpse gate. That would hardly be the glorious death I've earned."

Mist turned to Hermod. "You're being awfully quiet. Say something."

Hermod ran a hand over the stubble on his jaw. "I think Grimnir's probably right, but not just because we'd have to overcome a force of arms. That's not the biggest thing we're facing here. It's what the sibyl told us about: the force of inevitability. The Ragnarok prophecy isn't a prediction of things that *could* happen. It's a description of the way things *will* happen. It's a map of time and occurrence. It's the way the universe is laid out. *That's* what we're up against."

"So, what, then? We give up? Let the farmers try to fix things while we sit back and—"

"No. I say we help them." Mist and Grimnir both looked at him with surprise. "The only hope we have of stopping Ragnarok is by attacking the links in the chain of events. The sibyl said the links were weakest in Helheim, so if we're going to strike, this is the best place to do it. And if we did manage to get control of the ship, we'd be severing a major link. That alone might be enough to avert the final catastrophe."

Grimnir rolled his eyes, but Mist stood on tiptoe and kissed Hermod on the cheek. The act left him with a sensation that was the closest thing to warmth he'd experienced since crossing over into these lands.

# # #

THE SABOTEURS set out on their long walk to the river Gjoll. The party consisted of Mist and her sister, Grimnir, Winston, and the two Aesir, but only three of the Iowans: Henry Verdant, his hulking twenty-year-old nephew, Ike, and Alice Kirkpatrick, Ellhead's librarian, a woman with silver streaks in her black hair and arms as tough and lean as strips of beef jerky. Höd and Henry had agreed that a group this large traveling across the plains of Helheim was already at great risk for attracting attention and that the rest of them would serve the cause better by engaging in diversionary tactics, like drawing Garm's pups into fruitless chases through the rock fields.

The Iowans had heard indications of other groups launching assaults on the corpse wall and on Hel's palace, but communication in Helheim was poor at best, and as far as any of the Iowans knew for sure, their operation was the only one under way.

"You and Höd are quite a team," Mist said to Lilly, falling into step with her sister.

"We have common goals," Lilly said, a little defensively.

Mist felt a glow. It had been a long time since she'd been able to needle her big sister about a boy.

"You actually seem tighter than I'd expect after only three months."

"Has it been only three months since we died?" Lilly said, surprised. "It seems like it's been so much longer than that. I don't think time works the same way here as it does back home. Anyway, I won't ask about you and Grimnir—I know walking sides of beef aren't your type. But what about Hermod?"

"Him?" Mist laughed at the absurdity of it. Perhaps a little too forcefully, she thought, catching Lilly's smirk. "Not even if he was the last god on earth. He's nothing but the kind of trouble I can't stand: flaky and distracted."

"I like it when he calls you 'Mist,'" said Lilly.

"It's my Valkyrie name," Mist protested.

"It sounds more like a stripper name."

"It should have been your name. You were always the fighter, first when we were kids and then later with all that rock-throwing you used to do at cops, sucking down tear gas. Me, I was the bookworm. When we got shot—"

"When we got shot," Lilly interrupted, "you tried to block me from more bullets."

"While you were trying to do the exact same thing for me."

"And now you're wondering why you became a Valkyrie while I got consigned to a crappy afterlife."

"Don't you wonder?" Mist asked.

"Sweetie, life's arbitrary and capricious and unfair. People are either born to a world with running hot water or they're born to a world where a mosquito kills them in their first month of life. People die rich and go to heaven or they die poor and go to hell. That's the way I've always seen it."

"And you're still an eat-the-rich kind of gal."

"You bet your ass I am," Lilly said. "This arrangement where Odin gets his dead and Hel gets hers? Nobody ever asked me what I thought about it. I didn't get a vote. So if all I can do is piss off some gods by screwing with their system, that's good enough for me." They walked along, vulnerable in the open plain. "What about you, Kath? What's your stake in all this?"

"I'm not as political as you. I just wanted you back. You, and a man I helped put here. That didn't work out."

Lilly made a sympathetic noise. "Sorry that got you stuck down here with me."

"I don't think we're stuck," Mist said.

"Maybe not. But assuming we get out of here, what then?"

"There's not much left to do at this point except try to save the world."

Lilly's shoes scuffed the dust. "Give me a pen and I'll sign your petition. And stop changing the subject. What's the deal with you and Hermod, seriously?"

# # #

THE SHIP first appeared on the horizon as a gray smudge with a skinny stick emerging from it, but as they drew closer to the river where it was docked, its immense scale became evident. Narrow and low to the waterline, *Naglfar* was long enough for a thousand oarsmen. She bobbed and creaked in the black waters. Dark, mottled scales clacked and rattled over her hull in the wind—the nails of the dead. A single mast made of femurs lashed together with sinew towered over the deck and supported a vast, square sail. Extending from the prow, a dragon-shaped figurehead reared up, wriggling human corpses impaled on its teeth.

Naglfar wasn't just a troop-transport ship. It was like a section of Helheim itself, a weapon of terror to bring death to the living lands.

Henry Verdant gathered the group behind the cover of a concrete-colored tree.

"I don't see any guards at all," Mist said. "No draugr, nothing."

"Just because you can't see something doesn't mean it's not there," Höd said.

The dead began to show up gradually, alone or in small groups, coming across the plain at their slow, relentless pace. These were neither draugr nor Hel's soldiers. They were hunters and gatherers and peasants and clerks and factory workers. Normal folk. When they arrived at the river's edge, leather-armored dead waiting at the ship drove them up the boarding ramp with whips and spears.

"This is good," Höd said. "We won't have to fight our way or sneak aboard. We can just let ourselves get press-ganged with the rest of the dead."

"I never figured getting on board would be the hard part," Grimnir said. "It's fighting our way through hundreds of Hel's troops that worries me."

"Overpowering them isn't part of the plan," Verdant reminded the party. He scratched a diagram in the dust with a stick. "We move to the back of the ship, trying not to attract any undue attention." He marked an X. "Then we gather here, at the tiller, and take out whoever's manning it. The Asgardians will handle the waves of troops who'll no doubt come for us then, while the rest of us founder the ship. We keep Hel's troops out of living territory. That's the mission."

Hermod looked down at Verdant's diagram with a skeptical frown. "Dead people are always so quick to suggest suicide missions. Höd, how many do you think you can clobber at a time with your stick?"

"As many as I need to. And you'll be ready with your sword."

Hermod shook his head. "Big talk, but it's not like we're Thor and Vidar."

The party left the cover of the tree and made their way to the riverbank, where they joined the procession of dead without attracting notice. The three Iowans took the lead position, with Lilly and Höd in line behind them, followed by Grimnir, Winston, and Hermod. Mist fell into place beside a decapitated man, whose head was fastened to his chest by straps around his forehead, cheeks, and chin.

"What befell you?" the man said after a few dozen paces. His speech was garbled from the straps limiting the mobility of his jaw.

"What do you mean?"

He waved vaguely toward his neck, from which emerged truncated vertebrae. "I murdered a duke in his sleep. Being highborn myself, I was granted the courtesy of the ax instead of the rope, for which I was very grateful, at the time. In retrospect, with hanging I would have suffered only a few moments of agony and I'd still have my head attached in the afterlife."

Mist couldn't think of anything to say to that.

"So," the man said again, "what befell you?"

"I was a murder victim."

He murmured his sympathy.

"Do you know why they need so many of us?" Mist asked him. "With Hel's troops already in place—"

"Her fighters are for fighting. But *Naglfar* needs bodies at the oars. That's where we shall be forced to serve."

The Iowans reached the boarding ramp and walked up to the rail, where a particularly beefy pair of dead fellows was stopping people for inspection before letting them on the ship. It was hard to tell by what criteria they were judging, but after a nervous few moments, Verdant, Ike, and Alice Kirkpatrick were given nods of permission, and they boarded without incident. Höd and Lilly climbed the ramp after them and were also let on board. But when Hermod tried to follow, one of the dead fellows put a hand on his chest.

"What do you think you're doing?"

"Getting set to sail," Hermod said jauntily.

Two more large men approached. Even dead, they projected an air of officious thuggery.

Squeezing past the dead separating her from Hermod and Grimnir, Mist hoped neither of them would do something stupid or impulsive. She looked up nervously at the ship. Having boarded, Lilly and Höd were no longer in sight.

One of the men leaned over Hermod and sniffed. "You smell funny," he said, wrinkling his nose. "You smell alive."

"I assure you, I'm quite dead," Hermod lied with indignation.

The man motioned the other guards closer. "What do you guys think?"

They all flared their nostrils, except for one of them, who had no nose and presumably admitted Hermod's life-affirming fumes through his exposed nasal cavity.

"Alive," pronounced the noseless one, and all the guards made noises of agreement.

The boarding of *Naglfar* had come to a stop, and Mist felt the press of the dead building up behind her. The decapitated man kept nudging her with his strap-on head. Mist elbowed him back and reached for her sword.

"We should go," Grimnir whispered to her.

"And leave Lilly and the others? No."

"We can't do them much good if we get ripped limb from limb," he retorted, but before Mist could formulate a response, an eerie, multivoiced, growling moan came from the ship.

"Draugr," Hermod yelled. He bear-hugged Mist and leaped off the ramp, absorbing the impact of landing with his own body. Grimnir and Winston dropped next to them.

The draugr came spilling over the ship's rail, clawing and gnashing at the dead scrambling to get out of their way. They bit the slower ones, tore their throats, plucked out eyes. Hermod doubted this was part of some planned attack. More likely, Hel's forces had simply lost control of their zombies. That was the problem with draugr: They made for a fearsome force, but they could just as easily turn on their commanders.

Mist madly swung her blade, but despite her efforts to scythe through all comers, the draugr kept pressing in closer, climbing over one another to snap their teeth near her face and reach in with raking fingers. Hands grasped her wrists, immobilizing her sword arm, but then Winston was there, biting her assailant's leg to pull the draugr off.

Mist struggled to make her way back up the ramp, to the ship, to help Lilly with whatever she was facing on board, but the crush of bodies boiling around her drew her farther away.

Then came a freight-train roar that gave even the draugr pause, and Mist glanced upriver to see a wall of water rushing forward, jumbled with chunks of ice and uprooted trees and tumbling dead. The wave slammed into her, smashing her breath away and lifting her up in a swell of water and debris. Rolling in the turbulence, her body cracked against tree limbs, against rocks and the bodies of the dead. As she struggled to stay on the surface, the current took her along the length of the ship and past it.

The ship strained against its mooring lines until they snapped, whipping around and striking dead, slicing them to pieces. The great sail billowed out, and the fingernails covering the hull clicked and clacked like a colony of scuttling crabs.

Naglfar set sail.

Mist fell beneath the current, dirt forcing its way into her tightly shut eyes. Her head collided so hard with some object that she was sure her skull would shatter like a flowerpot. Crushed, buried, battered.

The water popped her back to the top, and a hand grasped her flailing arm and pulled her onto a floating tree trunk. She lay there on her stomach, choking on water and mud. She was only dimly aware when somebody rolled her onto her side and pounded between her shoulder blades. After a while she was able to draw air into her tortured lungs. Some time later, she realized it was Hermod who was helping her. He cleaned out her eyes as best he could with water from his canteen.

They clung to the tree, carried by the floodwaters. Grimnir crouched down at one end, like the lookout on a ship's prow, while a miserable-looking Winston shook water and muck from his fur.

"What happened?" Mist managed to wheeze out.

"The prophecy says when the Midgard serpent stirs, *Naglfar* will set sail on the floodwaters," Hermod said, gazing upriver. "Guess the serpent's alarm clock went off."

"Lilly and Höd? The Iowans?"

"On their own now," Hermod said, daubing her forehead. Apparently she was bleeding. He patted her right leg, moving down from thigh to ankle, and then the left one. "Checking for broken bones," he explained, sounding defensive, when he caught a look from Grimnir. With a strip of cloth from his jacket, he buddy-taped her ring finger and pinky together.

"Guys, you wanna look at this?" Grimnir pointed ahead, but the gesture was unnecessary. The sky before them was a kaleidoscopic storm. Other worlds were visible in brief flashes through the fragments: enormous pines, mountains of frost, stalagmite-encrusted caverns, skyscrapers with snowdrifts piling up to the fifth floors.

"World's breaking apart," said Hermod. "I think this might be it."

The river spiraled into the crazy quilt, and Mist and Hermod clutched each other as the tree trunk rushed on.

CHAPTER TWELVE

LILLY CAST HER gaze down *Naglfar*'s long deck but, except for Höd, she saw no sign of her companions, lost in the chaos of the draugr skirmish on the riverbank. As Hel's troops struggled to leash the remaining loose draugr, Lilly tried to calm herself and get a grip on their tactical situation.

Hel's soldiers were well equipped: men in bronze helmets and ostrich plumes, a Confederate side by side with a Union soldier, a Nazi SS officer, and others dressed and outfitted in ways it would have taken a military historian to identify. Even if Lilly and Höd could find the Iowans, they had no chance of taking the ship.

A whip cracked over Lilly's head, and a man in a black wool peacoat stepped forward. His face was a mangled mess of welts, a rusty cargo hook embedded in his right eye. "All right, you worthless dead, man your posts. Malingerers get flayed and turned into sailcloth. You two," he barked, glaring at Lilly with his one good eye. "Why are you just standing there? Looking to get run up the mast?"

"We just boarded, sir," Lilly said, managing a reasonable tone of voice. "What are our posts, please?"

"The pumps," the man cried, gesticulating in any number of directions. "D'you think I want to sail all the way to Midgard with a cursed slurry 'round my ankles? Man the pumps or I'll have you as my own ration!"

"Aye, sir," Lilly said crisply, and she gripped Höd's arm and retreated as quickly as she could.

The other press-ganged crew members seemed no more sure of their assigned positions than did Lilly and Höd, and they gained little sympathy from the officers, who cracked their whips and struck any sailor unlucky enough to come within range.

Lilly hurried over to the pumps, devices fashioned from pelvic bones, and bent to the work.

"Who's at the helm?" Höd asked, close to her ear.

Lilly described the creature standing at the stern. Struggling to hold the tiller steady, he or she or it stood at least twenty feet tall, bulging with slabs of muscle, its head wreathed in thick, kelplike ropes of hair. Its bare chest was laid open, revealing ribs and lungs and a heart like a deflated football.

"A dead Jotun," Höd said. "A giant."

Some dozen draugr were arranged as a guard around the tillerman, straining against chain leashes bolted onto the deck. They snarled and bit at the air like junkyard Dobermans.

Höd scratched his chin in thought. "It might be harder than we thought to take control of the helm," he whispered.

"Gee, you think?" Lilly hissed at him. If only Kathy and Grimnir and Hermod had made it on board, their presence might have been enough to carry the day. Lilly could only hope they'd managed to survive the flood.

"Layabouts!" It was the whip-cracking sailor with the hook in his eye. "Didn't I order you gull-lovers to the oars? Thought you'd save your soft little hands from real labor?"

"You put us on the pumps," Lilly protested.

His whip snapped inches from her face, biting off a piece of the railing. "And I suppose I did that because I'm a dear pat of butter, wanting to make your miserable deaths easier. I suppose you think this hook goes all the way into my thinking brain? You don't like my thinking brain?"

"Just aim me in the right direction," Höd muttered. "I'll knock him right over the side."

"Sir, I apologize for this misunderstanding," Lilly said, forcing the words through gritted teeth. "We'll get to the oars right away."

Hookface slowly lowered the whip to his side. He smiled, making a faint sound as the hook grated against the bone of his eye socket. "Indeed, you will not, for I've got a better plan for you. Our journey's sure to be no fish run, and we're like to be battered by wind and storm before it's through."

He squinted up at the sail. Lilly followed his gaze. The broad expanse of cloth rippled and billowed in the wind, mottled with crudely stitched patches of yellow and tan and brown.

It's skin, Lilly realized with a swell of nausea. *They patch the sail with human skin.*

"I'll have these two clapped in irons and brought to knife," Hookface hollered. Men, whether dedicated crew or just press-ganged dead looking to curry favor with their overseers, came at Lilly and Höd.

Höd swooshed his stick around his head, smashing attackers and shattering bones, while Lilly managed to throw two attackers overboard. But in the end there were too many of them, and they pressed in until Lilly was down on the deck beside Höd, unable to move and barely able to breathe. Peering between the legs of the man holding her down, she watched Hookface clomp over to her. He held out his hand, and someone passed him a crude, bone-handled cleaver. The congealed blood on the blade was thick as jam.

He pressed the edge of the cleaver to Lilly's thigh, then yanked the hook out of his eye and placed the point near the cleaver's blade. "Fork and knife," he said, bursting into a coughing laugh. Then his single eye rolled up, showing the white, and he elevated into the air. Impaled, he wriggled on the end of a long pike, held aloft by the Jotun tillerman, who pointed an accusing finger at the men restraining Lilly and Höd.

"Enough of this horseplay," he bellowed. "We're on a schedule, if you please, and wind and current alone won't take us to Loki. Get on the oars, every one of you, before I mill you into flour for my biscuit. And as for you," the giant said to Hookface, "discipline begins at the top. You have to set an example for the men." With that, he slammed the end of his pike on the deck as though planting a flag, and Hookface screamed.

The men scurried away.

"Now what?" Höd said, brushing at his clothes.

Lilly fingered the hole in her jeans. "To the oars," she said. "For now."

She found Henry Verdant and Alice Kirkpatrick on a portside rowing bench.

"Where's your nephew?" she asked, taking a seat beside them.

Verdant shook his head and pulled on the oar.

"Draugr tore his head off," Alice Kirkpatrick said.

Which meant that somewhere, Ike Verdant was a chewed-up disembodied head and fully aware of it. Lilly managed to suppress a shudder.

"I don't think our friends made it aboard," Henry said, his back sagging under the labor of pulling the oar. "Our whole operation might be a bust."

"That's no kind of talk, Henry," Alice said. "You keep your spirits up, or I'll clock you over the head with this here paddle."

Chastened, Henry almost smiled.

# # #

THE RIVER Gjoll opened onto a black sea, and the ship passed out of Helheim. Where they'd come to, Lilly couldn't tell. She described the arrangement of stars in the sky to Höd, but it didn't help. "All the maps have changed since I was last in the world," he said.

Hookface remained atop the tillerman's pike. For a while a pair of ravens vexed him, landing on his shoulders and head and picking flesh from his ears. They stared down the deck with their glossy black eyes, and sometimes Lilly was sure they were staring at her.

# # #

THE SHIP slogged through dark caverns in the lower roots of the World Tree, her sail lying slack against the mast. Water fell from the cave ceiling in a steady, icy rain. The oars dipped into the black river, and the only other sounds were the crack of the overseers' whips and nails shivering against the hull.

Knives of pain gouged Lilly's back and shoulders as she pulled on the oar. Höd rowed beside her without complaint. In the yellow light of the lanterns, his face was strangely beautiful, the lines of his cheeks less severe, and the dark hollows of his eyes soothing. She supposed being a god of things dark and hidden meant that he was now in his natural place.

Hel's loyal dead paced the deck, brandishing their weapons and growing more restless as the journey wore on. In her work as a professional agitator, Lilly had often found herself in similar situations, getting keyed up with anxiety and impatience. Soldiers in this state were dangerous, like springs too tightly coiled. Anything might set them off.

The subterranean river opened into a small lake with sharp geological formations rising from the water, and the Jotun tillerman steered the ship toward a precarious arrangement of three massive, spade-shaped rocks. The order was given to ship the oars, and the tillerman let momentum carry *Naglfar* around to the other side of the little island.

A giant easily exceeding *Naglfar*'s length lay bent backward over the rocks, a sharp point jutting into the small of his back. Blue ropes that looked like intestines secured him by wrist and ankle. The giant's skin was translucent, tinged with orange and yellow, as though fires burned beneath his flesh.

A woman equally as large knelt at his side. She might have been lovely once, but now bony wrists emerged from the sleeves of her threadbare gown as she held a cup over her companion's face. The cup caught oily venom that dripped from the fangs of a serpent coiled around a massive stalactite above them.

"I must empty the cup now," said the giantess.

The giant's face screwed up in pain and anger. "You lie! You always lie! It can't possibly be full yet!"

She peered into the cup. "But it is, husband. It nearly brims with venom. I shall be but a moment."

"No! Don't—"

She rose slowly and leaned off the edge of the rocks to overturn the cup. Venom oozed out in sticky strands. Meanwhile, the bound giant howled as venom from the serpent's fangs fell into his face. He bucked and thrashed, sending tremors through the rocks. Waves smashed against the ship's hull.

"Curse you, bitch! You do this on purpose! Curse you to torment for all eternity!"

"It is already so, my dear husband," the giantess said placidly.

The overseers and the armed men watched the scene play out with expressions of uncertainty. Even the Jotun tillerman, standing now at the ship's rail, seemed disquieted.

"I know that voice," Höd whispered. "That's Loki."

"Oh, look," the giantess said. "My cup is full again."

"That's impossible! You can't have caught more than three drops!"

Lilly was inclined to agree. The venom fell slowly, and the cup was the size of a wine barrel, but the giantess once again left her husband's side to empty the cup. Loki watched in wide-eyed horror as a bead of venom formed on one of the serpent's fangs and stretched in a long string down to his cheek. He arched his back and bucked when it made contact. Rocks shook loose from the cavern ceiling. On the ship, the armed men took shelter under their shields, but the rowers were defenseless. A cantaloupe-size boulder smashed the skull of a man two benches in front of Lilly.

"The cup!" Loki shrieked. "Bring back the cup!"

"It is emptying," the giantess assured him, staring into the cup's depths.

"It *hurts*!"

"I know, my sweet candle, I know. Best not to dwell. Tell me a tale to take your mind off it. One of your funny stories, perhaps about how you changed yourself into a mare to mate with a stallion and gave birth to eight-legged Sleipnir. Or how you disguised yourself as an old woman and tricked Höd into killing Baldr with a mistletoe spear, thus ensuring the death of all that lives in the nine worlds, including, of course, myself. That one is so funny. You are so funny, my husband."

Loki thrashed and the world shook. "I didn't mean to hurt anyone," he cried. "It was all supposed to be a laugh! Oh, please, bring back the cup!"

"In a moment, my love. I am still emptying it and laughing at your jokes."

"We can't let him on the ship," Höd said as Loki's spasms sent a wall of water bursting over the rail. "Once he takes the helm, he'll steer us to the final battle."

One of the whip-bearers looked back menacingly, and Lilly swallowed her response.

The giantess finally returned to Loki's side, but she didn't place the cup under the venom drip.

"What are you waiting for?" Loki demanded, twisting his neck to avoid another glistening drop.

The giantess upturned the cup and squinted at it. "I think it's cracked," she said. "Yes, right here, do you see? There's a crack as big as Ginnungagap." She pushed the cup toward Loki's face.

"You bitch! Just catch the drip, will you?"

She moved the cup aside and a globule of venom fell into Loki's eye.

"Yes, definitely a leak."

Loki shook with pain, and the cavern shook with him. Huge chunks of the ceiling plummeted into the lake, sending drenching waves over the ship's deck. Stalactites fell like bombs, one of them crushing a pair of overseers and three benches of rowers. The Jotun tillerman uselessly threw his arms up over his head as a boulder smashed him down.

Loki howled and thrashed, his bonds stretching like elastic bands. Höd dragged Lilly beneath their bench, and they huddled there with Henry Verdant and Alice Kirkpatrick.

At last the tremor ended, the deep-earth rumbling and Loki's screams replaced by the soft sloshing of water against the ship's hull and the moans of the injured. Lilly disentangled herself from Höd and peered out through the dust-clouded air. The sail hung in shreds, and the bodies of rowers and armed dead littered the deck. Only one of the tillerman's arms was visible beneath a slab of cavern ceiling, the fingers scrabbling uselessly.

On the island, Loki rose shakily to his feet and cast away the shredded remains of his bonds. Wincing when his head hit the stalactite the serpent was wound around, he tore the serpent apart with his bare hands and tossed the segments in the water.

"You have been very cruel to me, Sigyn," he said, stretching his back and arms. His joints popped like gunshots. "I am feeling cross."

Sigyn brushed pebbles from her skirts and hair. "I will not deny it, husband. Over the years, your torment became my only entertainment. I'm sure you can understand the appeal."

"Indeed. And I would find it amusing myself, were I not the victim of the jape."

"But, of course, I was only fulfilling my part in things," Sigyn said, meeting his fiery gaze. "Had I not, you would still be bound by your son's entrails, and those events you helped put in motion with Baldr's murder would be unable to play out to their conclusion."

"Then you feel I owe you thanks for thousands of years of mockery and torture?"

"Yes," Sigyn said. "It is my due."

Loki bowed low at the waist. "You have my sincere gratitude, my love. Well played." His high-arched eyebrows went up as he took in his surroundings and noticed the ship.

"Ah, my transport! Hello!"

He waved genially at the disarray on the deck. Some of the dead waved back, but Höd dipped his head to avoid recognition.

"Come with me, dear?" Loki asked, wading into the lake.

"No, I think I'll stay here to be buried alive and then burned to a crisp, along with the rest of the World Tree, as is inevitable. I don't suppose that gives you any pause?"

"Some," Loki admitted. "I might have had a less cruel jailer, but never one so lovely. But I must deliver this boat of Hel's to the battlefield. And then I will fight the Aesir to the death."

"Go, then, husband, with my curses for a painful ending upon your back."

Loki cackled. "And may you burn and suffocate, in that order. Farewell, my love."

"Farewell, my light," Sigyn said, wiping away a tear with her sleeve.

"We're never going to get a better chance than this," Lilly said to Höd and the Iowans. "We take the ship now or whatever-happens-after-death trying."

She didn't wait to see if her comrades agreed. Instead, she rose to her feet. Cupping her hands to her mouth, she shouted, "To the tiller! Take it!"

There was a moment when all sound seemed to die, except for the echo of her voice reverberating through the cavern. Then others took up her cry. Her command was repeated in a dozen languages, with war whoops and ululations. The dead rose from their benches, and though many were hacked and stabbed by Hel's soldiers, they moved forward in a surge.

Reducing himself in size, Loki climbed on the deck. He towered over the melee and laughed.

"Oh, good," Höd said. "I was hoping for a chance to kill that horsefucker." He snapped his oar, picked up a long, sharp length of it, and ran down the deck toward the sounds of Loki.

This wouldn't be an uprising, a hijacking, or an insurgency, Lilly realized. It would be a battle between gods. Lilly picked up a spear from a fallen soldier and took off after Höd.

CHAPTER THIRTEEN

MUSPELLHEIM IS A world of fire and smoke and soot. Buffeted by updrafts and explosions of molten rock, Munin and I beat our wings hard to keep our course. A sea of orange crackles and oozes below us. Flaming meteors rain from above. Munin counts the meteors as we fly. He keeps track of the temperatures and commits the numbers to memory. My brother does this because that's how his brain is wired. For once, I envy him, because reducing his discomfort to mere statistics provides him distraction, while I have no choice but to dwell on the heat of my burning feathers and meditate on its significance and reason out its consequences. That's how *I'm* wired.

The fire giant Surt is very proud of his realm. You can tell by the way he stands on the lip of a volcanic crater, hands on his hips, his chest bulging like a tectonic plate. No place in the nine worlds is as lovely as Muspellheim. Other places have fire, yes, but their flames are weak and not as orange as the flames of Muspellheim.

Surt stands guard against incursions by the Aesir,

whom he considers his lifelong enemies, always ready to make war on his people and take their lands. He has been standing on the lip of his volcano for a very long time, but not once, ever, has a god of Asgard even flirted with the notion of coming to a place where a tankard of beer would evaporate in a matter of seconds. It is with a mixture of alarm and pride, then, that Surt spots Vidar and Vali scaling his volcano.

His first instinct is to squash them with his flaming foot. But then he reconsiders. First he should find out what they want. Then he can crush them into little crispy motes of carbon dust.

Vidar and Vali have come especially outfitted for this occasion. They wear suits of dwarven craft, made of metal that resists even the heat of Muspellheim, hammered cunningly thin and flexible. In their hoods are built windows of clear crystal so that the Aesir may see their way without their eyes bursting into boiling orbs of meat and liquid.

Munin and I fly circles around the smoking crater as the two gods struggle to the summit and come to stand before Surt. From his vantage, Vidar can barely see over the tops of Surt's toes, and Vali not even that, yet it is Vali who speaks first.

"I hate this place," he says, in a whining snarl. "This is the worst place ever!"

Surt, expecting something more along the lines of a declaration of war, is momentarily dumbstruck. Around him, mountains crumble and splash into the molten sea. Gaseous plumes explode on the horizon. Who in his right mind could hate Muspellheim?

More evidence that the Aesir are not like other people.

"I squash gods," he says. Heat blasts from his mouth, and my tail feathers catch fire. Munin cackles with laughter at me, but then his tail ignites as well.

Vidar bows his head and he lays his hand on Vali's shoulder, and the child-size god is almost driven to his knees. Vali aims a kick at Vidar, but the silent god stays out of his range. After glaring through his crystal window at his older brother, Vali turns and addresses Surt's foot with an obviously memorized speech, delivered in a high-pitched singsong: "Great Surt, we sons of Odin humbly ask your forgiveness for coming uninvited to your kingdom. We beg you to consider the direness of the hour."

Surt crosses his arms with a haughty sniff that almost sucks us into his nostrils.

"Surely you have noticed how the worlds have fallen under siege from warfare and sickness and disaster," continues Vali. "Surely you have seen that Ragnarok is upon us."

Surt nods, even though he noticed no such thing from the comfort of his realm.

"Then why have you not prepared?" Vali asks. "Why are the sons of Muspellheim not assembled in their ranks? Why do their thunderous war chants not make the other worlds shudder down to their very foundations? Why does Muspellheim lie dormant?"

The words come from Vali's mouth, but Vidar has crafted them as expertly as any dwarf could craft metal. They could not be better designed to insult Surt to his core.

"I am always ready for war," Surt bellows. "Raise

arms against me, and you shall see the preparations of Muspellheim put into action. Never let it be said that Ragnarok comes as a surprise to me. I *am* Ragnarok."

Surt exaggerates. He has no better claim to sole credit for Ragnarok than the Midgard serpent, or Loki, or the sky-eating wolves. But certainly he has a great part to play in it. The sibyl's prophecy says that Surt will go marauding into Asgard, bringing down the rainbow bridge and setting the world aflame with his fiery sword.

"If you are ready for the last battle," Vali says with a sigh, growing weary of having to recite his lines, "then where is your sword?"

Surt fails to hide his dismay. He has never needed a weapon. Indeed, his body *is* a weapon. The surface of his skin is hotter than a bolt of lightning. Lava flows in his veins. What does Surt need with a sword?

Except that the sibyl's prophecy mentions his sword. So he must have a sword.

"Fear not, great Surt," Vali intones. "We have a gift for you."

Many people think that Munin and I have seen so much that we're impossible to impress, but that's not so. Hermod, for example, impresses us regularly. For someone with so few perceptible advantages, he has the potential to achieve things others of the Aesir would not even consider, and that is why so many of our hopes are pinned on him. We would never tell him this, of course. For one, we are under no obligation to speak plainly to anyone but Odin. For another, it would simply scare him to death.

We are impressed now by the sword Vidar produces from a pouch in his metal suit. It appears at first no larger than a pocket comb. But then he unfolds it, and the blade is as long as a surfboard, and Vidar struggles to bear it.

"Take it," Vali says to Surt. "It folds out more." And Surt unfolds the blade until it's sixty feet long and six feet wide. The sword is clearly the work of the dwarf Dvalin, who also constructed the boat of Frey, which can transport the whole host of Asgard or be folded like a cloth and stuffed in a pocket.

Surt looks at his sword, somewhat puzzled and disappointed, until Vali instructs him to dip the blade into the volcano. Surt does so, and the blade ignites, glowing white hot and sending off brilliant bursts of plasma. He sweeps it around his head in a shrieking circle, and the resulting rush of air sends Munin tumbling into me. We claw at each other until we regain stable flight.

"Do you like it?" Vali asks Surt.

"Oh, yes," Surt says, unabashedly pleased. "Very much so. Thank you!"

"Then marshal your troops and prepare to meet your ancient enemies on the plain of Vigrid."

Vali turns to Vidar with a pout that means, *Is there anything else? Can I go kill something now?*

Satisfied, Vidar begins his descent down the mountain, with Vali soon overtaking him in his haste.

Surt looks happily at his sword. He smiles. Whirlwinds of blue gas flash in his teeth.

CHAPTER FOURTEEN

HERMOD LAY FACEDOWN in the sand, listening to the quiet slap of waves against the shore. He was in pain, but at least he was warm. Gradually he became aware of Winston's tongue lapping the back of his ear. Hermod groaned and lifted his face from the sand. He wiped blood from his nose and hissed as he withdrew a pencil-length sliver of wood from his thigh.

They had ridden the flood for days, it seemed, through rapids and falls, out of Helheim and down the rivers between worlds. Hermod had steered them with nothing more than a broken branch for oar and rudder, exhausted and navigating solely by strength and instinct.

Reluctantly rising to his feet, he saw Mist a few yards off, splayed out on her back. She was moaning weakly, but at least she was moving. He went to her, and after trading mutual inquiries into each other's condition and receiving only mildly reassuring answers, Hermod offered his hand and helped her up.

"Where are we?"

Hermod took in his surroundings. A vast plain of charcoal waters melted into a starless black sky, and, looming in the distance, a mountainous black column curved up away from the horizon. Thick atmosphere obscured the column in a haze, but the shape of it was still recognizable as the twisted trunk of a tree. Overhead, knots of branches and tendrils in the sky gave off a faint, lime-colored glow of bioluminescence. Sweet aromas of plant life and decay clogged the air. Hermod felt like an ant in an overgrown garden.

"We're at the bottom of the World Tree," he said. "Down at the roots."

Mist shook her head, as if trying to jiggle her thoughts into more sensible order. "Where's Grimnir?"

Hermod spotted Mist's thug a few yards off. Draped over the remains of their shattered tree-raft, he waved off their assistance. "Leeme alone," he said. "I'm dreaming. I'm in San Francisco. I'm going to see a professional lady of my acquaintance."

"But you're awake," Mist observed.

"Impossible. I smell Chinese food."

"It's a hallucination. You probably cracked your head when we— Wait a minute. I smell it too."

Hermod sniffed and got a strong whiff of grease and garlic and ginger. A few feet away—resting against a Jotun boot the size of a bathtub, pottery shards with elvish markings, a garden gnome, and other jetsam— chow mein noodles spilled from a plastic grocery bag. The noodles were waterlogged and inedible, but the sack also contained a sealed Tupperware dish with kung pao chicken. Only after Hermod and his companions fell upon it and devoured its contents in a brutal feeding frenzy did they begin to address the question of how the Chinese food had gotten there.

"For that matter, how'd we get here?" Mist asked, licking grease off her fingers.

Hermod gazed forlornly into the empty container. "If the Midgard serpent stirred and the world's seams are splitting apart, then the rivers in Helheim and a lot of other places must have broken their banks in the flood, and since all rivers run down to the bottom of the world eventually, we washed up here with the rest of the junk."

Hermod watched Mist's face as she worked out the grim calculus of his suppositions. The serpent's thrashing could have caused tsunamis to wash over every continent on Midgard. Without any check on the wolves, they would have grown large enough to complete their destiny and eat the sun and moon. And they'd seen *Naglfar* set sail with their own eyes. The ship would deliver Hel's handpicked draugr and armed dead to do battle with the gods. Ragnarok was humming along just fine.

"I should be with the boys in Valhalla," Grimnir said, without his usual bluster. "I'm supposed to be gearing up for a fight, not mucking around in the sludge at the bottom of the world. Maybe Radgrid went off the deep end a little bit, but she had the right idea: Somebody's gotta be there at the end to bring the fight to the giants and monsters, and I'm supposed to be one of those somebodies."

"If we make our way back to Midgard," Mist said, "I'll send you to Valhalla."

Grimnir was silent for a while. Then, "Thanks, but that's a mighty big if," he said.

Hermod suggested they search the shoreline for more food. Indeed, Grimnir found some soggy but still-plump berries from a bush that grew only in Alfheim, but Hermod warned him against eating them. He'd once dined in Alfheim and ended up as a love slave to a beautiful but abusive mistress for three hundred years. So, reluctantly, they left the berries behind and stepped around the detritus of nine worlds toward the prodigious tree trunk rising in the distance.

Hermod instantly recognized the stabbing whinny that flew across the water and rose into something like a lunatic shriek. There was no mistaking its source: Sleipnir.

The horse thundered over the lake's surface, gunmetal foam spraying from his eight hooves. He took the shore as though attacking it and reared up on the hindmost of his eight legs, releasing another harsh, laughing cry.

Grimnir and Mist both had reached for their swords, and Hermod had to put a hand on Winston to still his growling.

"Easy, everyone," he said. "I know this horse."

Despite his words, Hermod felt no ease in the presence of the horse he'd long ago ridden to Helheim and back. Sleipnir was powerful and unpredictable and too similar to Loki, the horse's father—or mother, as Loki had taken on the form of a mare and given birth to Sleipnir before returning to his male form. In any case, other than Odin and Hermod, no god would even venture close enough to Sleipnir to get within range of his gnashing teeth, let alone to ride him.

Hermod slowly approached the horse and reached

up to stroke his neck. Sleipnir had grown since Hermod had last ridden him.

"Fancy meeting you here, boy," Hermod murmured. "Did you wash up with the rest of us?" The horse shivered and snorted but allowed Hermod to continue petting him. Raking his fingers through Sleipnir's mane, Hermod brushed against a flat stone tied in place with a leather thong. He stood on tiptoes to unfasten it.

The runes etched into the stone were tiny, the language ancient, and the hand familiar. After impatient prompting, Hermod translated it for his companions, relating the meaning of the words if not their actual tone, which was dry and cold as the arctic wind yet thrumming with simplicity and magic.

Hermod cleared his throat. "*My son*—I assume he means me—*difficult are the tasks set before you, and once more I lend you Sleipnir to see that they are done. Go to the well where I left my greatest treasure and reclaim it.*" Hermod silently read that bit over again, wondering if he was mistranslating. After all, these runes were to his Asgardian language as Aramaic was to modern English. But repeated readings did not alter their meaning.

The letter ended with an admonition not to foul things up as badly as he had the last time. Skepticism and disappointment were evident in every carven stroke.

"You stopped reading," Mist informed him.

Hermod coughed. "Sorry. He goes on to say that he would write more but he's very busy right now. He wishes me nothing but success."

"*Greatest treasure?* What's all that about?" Grimnir asked.

Hermod tucked the stone in his jacket. "He means for me to go get his eye."

# # #

SLEIPNIR SCUTTLED along the ground like a spider, efficiently crawling over debris and uneven terrain. Barebacked, he was large enough to carry the entire company, with Hermod in front, where he could guide the horse with one hand entwined in his mane. Mist rode behind him, and Grimnir behind her. Winston ran alongside for a while, but the malamute couldn't keep the pace for long. It was left to Grimnir to carry the dog awkwardly in his arms, until Mist fashioned a harness and basket carrier from elf rope and PVC pipe they found in the flood wash.

After what seemed like a day's journey, the great tree trunk still loomed ahead, dominating the entire span of the horizon and rising so high that it curved backward over their heads. The tree and the ground were really the same thing, the entire universe being made of the tree's very substance.

Sleipnir folded his legs and let the riders dismount. While Mist and Grimnir stretched their sore muscles and Winston ran around in pursuit of his own tail, Hermod approached a water-filled cavity in the ground, no more than a dozen yards across, like a bullet hole in the world's body. He stared into its infinite darkness and contemplated Odin's instruction to him: Reclaim the treasure.

"You look green," Mist said.

"So do you. It's the light down here."

"That's not what I mean. You look haunted."

"Again, so do you. It's this place."

"We're really down in the bowels, aren't we? Tell me again why we want Odin's eyeball?"

"Odin's been trying to find wisdom almost since his creation," Hermod told her. "Mimir was one of his best sources. He just came into the world with his head full of runes and knowledge. We traded Mimir to our rival tribe of gods, the Vanir, to end a war, but they didn't like him. Talked too much, they said. So they sent us back Mimir's head, which Odin cast down here at the bottom of the world.

"Later, the Norns gave Odin some glimpses into shadow, and what he saw in those shadows was death. Baldr's death, to be particular, and with that, Ragnarok. But these were only shadows, and Odin wanted more. So he turned again to Mimir, who'd been steeping in the well, absorbing whatever the worlds told him. Mimir agreed to trade a draft from the well for Odin's right eye, and once Odin got his drink, he saw how the worlds would die. He saw all the battles and the terrors, and he returned to Asgard to put together the Einherjar and to prepare. But his eye stayed behind, sunk at the bottom of the well. It's been sitting there all this time, soaking in wisdom."

Hermod felt a rare touch of awe. This was the very place where his father had stood and plucked out his own eye. Such a benign word, *pluck*. To grasp one's eye with thumb and fingers, to steel oneself and yank. To endure the literally blinding agony and keep pulling until blood vessels and nerves stretched to the point of snapping. And then to remain conscious in order to claim one's prize.

"Mimir, show yourself," Hermod called out. "I've come to talk."

Nothing happened for several minutes. Hermod stared into the well, trying to see below the surface. Mist kept quiet, and even Grimnir refrained from making comment.

The water held still.

Hermod found a flat, round stone by the shore and tried to skip it across the water, but the well claimed it the instant it touched the surface, and it sank without a splash.

Moments later there was a disturbance, the water bubbling like gloppy soup. Fearing an explosive geyser, Hermod drew Mist and Grimnir back. He didn't know what would happen if the water made contact with their skin. Maybe it would make them smarter. Maybe it would drive them to wear tinfoil hats.

A cloud of fizzing foam erupted from the depths, and when the bubbles cleared, a face covered in barnacles and muck bobbed to the surface. A few patches of mushroom-white flesh showed through a slimy green and black beard. Lips the color of snails opened and closed with great fish gulps. The eyes fluttered open, and the face floated quietly in the water.

"Greetings, Hermod," said Mimir, cordially enough.

How should one return the salutation of a severed head bobbing in a pond? Since Mimir was still of the Aesir, and Hermod had come seeking favor, courtesy was required. But the customary compliments about the host's hospitality would ring false here.

"How's the water?"

Mimir treated the question seriously. "Noisy," he said after a time. "The voices clamor for attention, and I cannot give them all a fair hearing."

"Somebody once told me that wisdom is about learning which voices to listen to and which to ignore."

"Do you follow that advice?" Mimir asked.

"I try to."

"I haven't that luxury," Mimir said with regret. "All waters flow here, to settle and stagnate. You should hear the things they tell me."

Hermod had never been overly fond of oracles, and he really didn't want to hear about all the things Mimir had been told over the millennia. He didn't have time, and his experience with the sibyl had already been more than enough.

"Mimir, I've come to retrieve my father's eye."

Mimir blinked in confusion. "Your father's eye? Do I have your father's eye?"

"He sacrificed it to you for a drink from your well. Don't you remember?"

"Was this recently? I'm sorry, but my waters have grown turbulent, and nothing is clear anymore. Why ever would I have wanted his eye, I wonder." Mimir was speaking to himself now, muttering about crowded waters and misplaced things, about once possessing a rune for happiness and something else about a catfish. Then the fog seemed to clear and he focused on Hermod again. "Oh, yes, I do remember Odin's eye. Vidar reminded me."

Hermod started. "My brother was here? When?"

A ripple of water rolled over Mimir's face. "Not so

long ago, I think. He was in the company of another brother of yours, a child. Quite mad, that one."

He had to be talking about Vali, which struck Hermod as strange since so few could stand to be in Vali's presence, Vidar least of all. Odin had fathered Vali to kill Höd in revenge for Baldr's death, a job Vali had accomplished before he was even a full day out of the womb. Hermod couldn't imagine being born to a single purpose—to kill your brother—and having fulfilled that purpose before learning your first word. It had left Vali stunted. He'd never grown beyond his terrible twos and had settled for a life of infantilism and random violence.

"What did they want here?" asked Hermod.

"The same thing you want, except they were more insistent. Vali did the talking. He has a violent mind. They each dove to the bottom of the well, but the eye wouldn't go with them. Vali was very angry, and Vidar even more so. Only he didn't express it in words. He was silent. And frightening."

"Did they say what they wanted with the eye? Did Odin send them for it?"

"What does anyone want with an eye?" Mimir said. "They want to see. As for who sent them, they didn't say."

Hermod felt as though he was on the verge of falling for a trap, though he wasn't clear on its nature, its purpose, or its consequences. This was a very familiar feeling to him, and he almost felt comforted by it.

"Just to be clear," Hermod said, "the eye is still at the bottom of the well?"

Mimir misunderstood the question. "I wouldn't

say 'still.' It shivers sometimes. I don't think it has ever liked it there at the bottom."

"It doesn't 'like' it there? You mean the eye's alive? It's conscious?"

"The *world* is conscious, Hermod."

Mist brought her toes to the edge of the well. "Just how deep is this hole, anyway?"

Grimnir's face broke into a challenging smile.

"Hermod's a god; he can hold his breath a long time. Ain't that right, boss?"

Hermod recalled all the times he'd nearly drowned. The worst was when he'd gotten caught in a flash flood in a Jotunheim box canyon. Pressed down in a sludge of frozen mud, his empty lungs burning, he had so desperately craved release that he'd called out in silent agony for someone, anyone, to deliver him. He'd understood then, for the first time, why men so desperately clung to gods who didn't care for them in return.

He stared into the impenetrable blackness of Mimir's well.

"Odin took only one drink," Mimir said absently. "It did not go down easily. When he recovered his voice, he used it to scream."

Mist shook her head. "I don't like this. It may be the eye of Odin, but it's still just a normal-size eye, right? How are you supposed to find it in the dark mud, with who-knows-what lurking down there?"

Hermod gave her a smile that he hoped was reassuring. "Possessing Odin's eye is too good an advantage to pass up," he said. "We should at least give it a shot. And it's like Grimnir said: I'm Aesir. I should be fine."

Mist gave him a dubious frown, but she didn't offer further protest. Hermod rather wished she had.

Well, then.

He stripped down to his boxers. "What?" he said, catching a strange look from Mist.

She blinked and looked at her feet. "Nothing. Just be careful."

"Right. Okay." He jumped into the well and treaded the water. It felt like icy pudding. There was no rush of voices in his head. No wisdom. No insanity. Not yet. He glanced back to Mist and detected warnings and cautions and exhortations trapped unspoken behind the strained line of her pressed lips. He gave her a small here-goes-nothing wave, took a deep breath, and dove beneath the surface.

There were worlds down below. Cities and continents and oceans turned beneath him, as though he were observing a planet from high orbit, only it was more than just one world. A mosaic of countless worlds braided and dovetailed. Mountains and rock formations and canyons and plains and fields covered the surface of the World Tree's roots.

Great, Hermod thought, *I go looking for an eye, and instead I get grand visions.* Did these visions constitute wisdom? Not if he couldn't glean any useful meaning from them, they didn't.

Maybe he wasn't wise enough to receive wisdom.

He kicked his legs and swam to greater depths. He'd hoped that, in this environment, water wouldn't act like water, but he felt stabbing pains in his ears as the pressure increased, and squeezing his nose and clenching his jaw gave no relief. Down he went, toward the worlds at the bottom of the well.

He paddled toward a continent where a sea of lava spilled into a sea of ice, pushing out great gouts of steam. He had a good feeling about this location. It was the sort of place Odin tended to favor: fire and ice, with destruction at the interface.

He tried and failed to ignore his desperate need to breathe. Even at great depths it would take more than a few minutes to drown him, but spots wavered in his vision, and hideous clamps of pain squeezed his head. He wanted to return to the surface, get away from the pressure, breathe. He wanted to quit. He wasn't supposed to be here, down at the bottom of everything. This was no place for living creatures. But going where no one was supposed to go was what he always did. It was his purpose. Wanderer, seam-walker, interloper. Nobody else could do this. So he put his pain aside and went deeper.

A marvelous model-train world spread out before him, with miniature glaciers cutting tiny chasms, and tiny waves battering the shore. Were there little civilizations at arm's reach, too tiny to see? What would happen if he brought down his foot? Was this how his kin always felt? Huge and powerful, truly like gods?

Not even Odin sees the world as his toy, said a watery voice.

Hermod spun around, looking for the source of the voice but finding none.

You cannot find me. You cannot know me.

Who are you? thought Hermod.

Your kind credits the All-Father with having created sky and earth from the corpse of his father, but he is just a piece of it, and a small piece at that.

Mimir, is that you?

Look at what is revealed to you.

You mean Dinky Town down there? I've been looking.

You look, but do you see?

So far, this disembodied voice was irritating Hermod about as much as conversations with the all-knowing usually did. He should have expected that swimming in the well of wisdom would only aggravate him.

What is it I'm supposed to see?

Down here in the thickness of Yggdrasil's deepest waters, one can see everything.

I am Hermod, son of Odin, late of Asgard. I have come here with the permission of this well's keeper, and I am running out of patience and breath. Who are you?

I am what you seek, if what you seek is what you came here for.

I came seeking after the eye of Odin. Are you it?

That may be what you want, but it is not what you need.

Nice dodge. You are Odin's eye, aren't you?

And there was silence, which Hermod took as a sure sign that he was right.

He floated past a range of sharp crags blanketed in snow, similar to ones he'd climbed in Jotunheim or that in Midgard would be sparsely dotted with Buddhist monasteries and climbers' camps. Illusion, certainly, covering plain, mucky lake bottom. He came to a stop and reached down to grab a handful of whatever it was below. Mountains crumbled in his grip.

Long ago, when the Aesir had battled their rival tribe, the Vanir, much had been destroyed in the collateral damage. Hermod knew what a falling mountain looked like. It looked just like this.

He opened his palm and watched pebbles, grit, and dust drift away in the currents.

Now you have earned a new name, the voice said. *Hermod, Destroyer.*

It's not real, Hermod thought. *It's just a vision.*

The voice sighed, impatient. *It is a vision, but it is a vision of what's real, or at least another way of looking at it. The world as metaphor, and the metaphor literalized, if that helps you understand it.*

With his lungs crying out for air, his head imploding, and the last specks of a mountain in his hand, Hermod didn't feel like struggling with the mysteries of existence.

Did I just kill a whole lot of people? he asked.

I am not sure. I couldn't see that well from my vantage. Does it matter? Are you not a god?

Hermod looked down at the wreckage he had created. Stone, earth, and snow lay in clumps around the runnels his fingers had dug. And floating in a lake of molten rock was an eye, the iris storm-cloud gray, glinting with lightning.

Hermod picked it up. Its weight astonished him.

Father? he asked.

His eye, merely. And obviously.

Did I just kill a lot of people down there?

I can't see the mountains if I'm staring at you. Turn me around.

Hermod did as he was told.

After an unbearably long time, the eye said, *This part of the world was uninhabited. You owe no compensation.*

Hermod nearly sobbed with relief. He closed his fingers around the eye and kicked toward the surface.

When we get back to land, Hermod thought at the eye, *you're going to cooperate with me and dispense all the wisdom you have. You're going to be a regular wisdom vending machine, understand?*

The eye did not respond. It sat cold and dense in his fist.

After dragging himself ashore, Hermod sat on the beach, filling his lungs with air. Mist hovered over him, catching her own breath after a tirade about how long he'd been underwater (much longer than it had seemed to him, apparently) and how only Grimnir's muscle power had prevented her from diving in to retrieve his corpse. The eyeball felt like a partially frozen brussels sprout in his hand, slimy and cold and slowly thawing.

"Got it," he wheezed, loosening his grip to show his prize. In the open air, its color was a sad yellow, with a cataract film over the iris. He had to hold it away from Winston, who tried to sniff it.

Are you awake? Hermod thought at the eye.

The eye silently glistened.

He asked the question again, this time aloud. The lack of response didn't surprise him.

"So," Grimnir said. "The eye of Odin. There it is."

"Yeah."

"Do you feel wiser?"

"I feel like crap. And not any smarter."

"Maybe it's not enough just to have the eye," Grimnir suggested. "Maybe you have to yank out your own eye and shove Odin's eye in the socket."

"Great idea. You first."

Grimnir demurred.

Hermod stepped to the edge of the lake, where Mimir's brow, nose, and chin stood out in the black water like the raw white of a cut tree root.

"Now what?" Hermod called to the head. "What do I do with it?"

Mimir let out a long, hollow sigh. "Much the same question Odin asked after taking his draft. He had gained knowledge of the worlds' end, but what ought he to do with that knowledge?"

"What did you tell him?"

"The same thing I shall tell you, walker of in-between places: Seeing isn't everything."

"That's what passes for wisdom these days?"

With great weariness, Mimir closed his eyes and sank into the waters. A few bubbles broke the surface, and then the well was quiet.

"Guess that settles it," Grimnir said. "You'll have to pull out your own eye."

Hermod wrapped the eye in his handkerchief and tucked it in his jacket, against his belly. The chill leached into his skin.

CHAPTER FIFTEEN

MUNIN AND I circle three thousand feet over calm Pacific waters, above the delicate ring of the Enewetak Islands. Munin has been quite generous in sharing the history of the atoll and its people with me, and I reward him by pecking his neck in midflight to make him shut up, but not before I've learned about Operation Hardtack, in which the United States conducted thirty-five nuclear detonations in the South Pacific before calling a halt to the tests in 1958. The island was rendered uninhabitable, the soil and lagoon irradiated. Later, at great cost, the islands were cleaned up and the people returned—only to be evacuated again last year for the resumption of nuclear tests. As Ragnarok approaches, the bonds of kinship among men break, including those codified in nuclear nonproliferation treaties.

Down below, a small flotilla of Navy vessels is sprinkled one hundred miles off the atoll's western edge. "USS *John S. McCain,* Arleigh Burke–class destroyer," Munin says. "USS *Gary,* Oliver Hazard

Perry—class frigate. USS *Ronald Reagan*, Nimitz-class supercarrier."

While Munin goes about naming every single ship in the group—a feat that he will no doubt follow up by reciting the name of every single crew member—I'm more interested in the reason the ships are here: a barge about the size of a family restaurant, to which is moored, at a depth of two thousand feet, a thirty-megaton bomb.

The ships have charts and calculations that help them keep a safe distance from their monster, but there are other monsters in the deep. The greatest of all is a son of Loki: Jörmungandr, the Midgard serpent. It lies on the seafloor, its hide camouflaged with crags and volcanoes. Whenever it twitches in its sleep, tidal waves kill hundreds of thousands. It opened its great red eye once, and fish took to land and evolved lungs and legs, just to get away from it.

When the men of Midgard detonate their bomb, there is very little drama at first. No fireball, hardly any noise. But a moment later, a dome of spray rises a third of a kilometer in the air, and a gas bubble of indigestion bursts through the dome, sending a surge of saltwater jets almost four thousand feet up, chasing Munin and me skyward.

Below, the Midgard serpent remains sleeping in the poison currents. It takes a lot to rouse such a serpent from its slumber. But then there is a voice in the gurgle and rush of water. A soft voice, motherly and soothing, but also insistent. It is the same voice that long ago extracted the oath that failed to protect Baldr.

"Time to wake up," the voice coos. "You have

work to do. Wake up, Jörmungandr, and fulfill your destiny."

The oceans fill with the groans of whales, and the Midgard serpent stirs, slowly rising from its ancient sleep.

CHAPTER SIXTEEN

HERMOD NAVIGATED SLEIP-nir through a long, twisting network of seams that finally led back to Venice, California, Midgard. The streets were flooded up to six blocks inland. Offshore, chunks of ice bobbed in the swells, a sight novel enough to draw people out with their cameras, risking the waves in dinghies and Zodiacs. Ragnarok was gawk-worthy. When Mist spotted news vans broadcasting from the highest ground with their telescoping antennae raised into the soggy sky, she gave Hermod a nudge. They'd have to be particularly careful to avoid being seen. Mist didn't even want to think about the chaos that would ensue if Channel 5 caught a glimpse of an eight-legged horse crab-walking through Venice.

On the other hand, there was plenty of spectacle to keep all the news outfits occupied. An earthquake, maybe several, had struck while they were away. Venice had become a geological jigsaw puzzle. Places of low elevation had been thrust upward by earthquakes. The remains of the boutiques on Abbot Kinney clutched precariously to the now-sloping street, while the hills north of Mar Vista had melted in mud slides.

"God, look at that," Mist said, peering through the opening of the alley Sleipnir crept down. Amid a jumble of snapped telephone poles, the corpse of a forty-foot-long gray whale lay trapped in the lines. Pigeons and rats and gulls and crows squabbled over the remains.

The party dismounted to get a closer look, leaving Sleipnir in the alley. Grimnir's boot heels crunched over buckled sidewalk as he walked beside Mist. "Now what?"

"Now you go home," she said.

"To my Boston flat? I'm sure NorseCODE stopped paying rent on it once Radgrid realized I'd gone AWOL."

"No, I mean *home*. For you. Valhalla."

He stopped, giving Mist a suspicious look.

"I failed to rescue Adrian Hoover," Mist said. "I failed to save Lilly. Odin's eye isn't talking to Hermod. The world is dying, and I don't think there's anything more we can do about it here. But maybe if you go back to Asgard, back with your Einherjar buddies, you can tilt the balance in our favor."

Grimnir walked on, mulling. "Thanks, but someone still has to watch over you." He gestured toward Hermod, walking a few yards ahead with Winston. "You've fallen in with a bad crowd."

"You've already done your part, trying to raise me right," Mist said. She tried to keep her tone light. "You taught me to fight with a sword and hot-wire a car. You didn't turn me over to Radgrid. You helped me find Hermod. And I dragged you to Helheim.

You, a warrior who earned heaven. You deserve to be in Asgard, and I want you to go."

"Come with me," Grimnir urged.

Mist smiled. She shook her head. "Heaven's not my home, Grim. I have to stay here. Maybe there's a food bank or something I can volunteer at. You know, while you're swinging your sword, I can roll bandages."

Grimnir scratched his boot heel on the pavement. He sniffed and wiped his sleeve across his nose.

Hermod turned back and approached them. Mist could tell from the look on his face that he'd overheard.

"What about you?" Grimnir said. "Our side could use another god. Glory and adrenaline, and what finer end could you ask for?"

Hermod seemed touched by the invitation. "Thanks, but I'm staying. Midgard's the closest thing I have to a home."

Mist held out her hand. "Give me your lighter, Grim."

"Kid . . ."

"I'm still your boss, Grimnir, and you swore an oath to me. I know you swore other oaths, but this is the one you chose to honor above all others. Now you get your reward. I'm a Valkyrie, and I'm sending you to Valhalla. Give me your lighter."

The one seam Mist had been empowered to open was that between Midgard and Valhalla. She flicked the Zippo and dialed the flame to its full height. Just as Radgrid had taught her, she traced a rune in the air, over and over, until it blazed a trail of light. It grew bright red, then orange, then yellow, and when she killed the flame, the rune hung in the air, cycling through all the colors of the rainbow.

Men who had seen Bifrost often described it as a rainbow bridge, and Mist supposed that was as good a description as any. The arch of light rose from the ground and curved up to the clouds, and within the confines of its shape swirled eddies of energetic color, the colors of the rainbow and other colors that weren't quite in the rainbow.

Grimnir engulfed Mist in a sudden embrace. She emerged from it out of breath but intact.

"You be careful," she admonished him.

"I won't be careful, but I'll be fine. You, however . . ."

"I'll be fine too."

Grimnir gave a brief salute to Hermod, and Hermod returned it. Then Grimnir stepped up to the arch and began to climb. He grunted with effort to maintain grip but made slow, inexorable progress. After several minutes, he faded into the shimmer and was gone. The bridge dimmed and vanished soon thereafter.

Winston beat his wagging tail against Mist's leg as she quietly wept.

# # #

THAT NIGHT, Hermod and Mist made camp onstage at the Hollywood Bowl. The graceful curve of the concrete concert shell provided some shelter from the wind. Mud slides had rendered the hills impassable to wheeled vehicles, and after a day of trying to remain out of public view on an eight-legged horse, Hermod was happy to have found some privacy. He tried to imagine the seats filled with a dancing, cheering audience, an image that belonged to a different world in a different time. A dead kudu, escaped from the storm-battered zoo, would provide an ample supper, and Hermod and Mist even risked attracting unwanted company by building a fire to roast it on. The cries of hyenas pierced the dark like lunatic ghosts and were answered by the roar of big cats.

Tucked under Hermod's jacket, Odin's eye grew increasingly heavy, as if it were resisting Hermod's efforts to drag it through Midgard. It had remained silent since its removal from Mimir's well, and only its uncanny weight convinced Hermod that it was anything more than a dead orb of sclera and humors.

Mist stared into the fire. She'd probably said fewer than a hundred words since Grimnir had departed.

"All told, this isn't so bad," Hermod said, turning a slab of kudu flank on his makeshift spit. "I remember when the Neanderthals were dying out. Scarce game, dwindling resources, competition from your species . . . Now, *that* was a rough time." Dripping kudu grease hissed in the flames. "I didn't think Homo sapiens would hang on either, but you lot managed just fine. You're more stubborn in your own way than we Aesir."

Mist stood up. "Hermod?"

"Yeah?"

She walked over to him. "Shut up."

"Oh, okay. Sorry."

Tugging gently on his wrist, she pulled him to the ground.

"Oh," he said. "Are we going to . . . I mean, do you want to—"

"No," she said.

"Oh, right, I didn't think—"

She curled up close, which was very nice.

"Let's just consider this our first date," she said, yawning.

The kudu meat burned to a crisp. Later, they ate it anyway.

\# \# \#

THE MORNING broke frigid and wet, with eddies of frost swirling up the hills. Mist lay nestled in Hermod's arms. Not wanting to wake her, he tried to ignore his madly itching nose and focused instead on the slow, steady rhythm of her breathing. This was a nice place to hide from the world, in this little pocket of warmth, with food in his belly, with a woman who maybe liked him a little bit. It wasn't that far removed from his end-of-the-world fantasy, and he was content to stay here awhile.

Winston ruined it with a sharp bark, and Mist started awake. A few dozen feet away, in the third-row seats, sat Vali, manic eyes gleaming. He'd grown since Hermod had last seen him. He now had the appearance of a grubby-faced three- or four-year-old, with a tangle of dirty-blond hair falling over his eyes. He bounced in his seat and swung his legs.

Sitting beside him, Vidar gave off the impression of a calm, snow-covered mountainside at rest before an avalanche.

Vali pointed at Winston with a chubby finger. "Stupid dog! You be quiet!" Which naturally set Winston off into a fresh barrage of throaty barks.

Mist put an arm around Winston's neck, trying to

shush him. Hermod's vision passed over the scabbard belted to Vidar's hip. Nausea corkscrewed down his belly. There was something about that sword. . . . He swallowed.

"What a pleasure to receive a visit from my brothers."

"We were looking for you," said Vali. "Vidar figured you'd be on a hill above the ice and you'd make a fire, and guess what?" He glanced around the bowl, fidgeting. Vali was a god sired to mete out justice, but it was a poorly controlled, hyperactive brand of justice. He sang a little la-la song and then jumped to his feet. Hermod and Mist stood as well.

"Do you have Daddy's eye?"

Hermod weighed his possible responses. He decided to go with a bald-faced lie.

"No. Last I heard, it's still at the bottom of Mimir's Well."

"We already looked there," Vali said, picking his nose. "I swam and swam and swam, all the way to the bottom of the stinky well, and then Vidar swam and stayed under while I threw rocks at Mimir's head, and when Vidar came up he didn't have the eye because he couldn't find it."

"Wish I could help you," Hermod said. "Want something to eat? I've got some kudu here if you don't mind it well done."

"Yay!" Vali clapped his hands and jumped up and down, and for a moment Hermod thought maybe he could get out of this encounter losing nothing more than a few pounds of antelope meat. But then Vidar came to his feet, rising ever higher in a way that made Hermod wonder if he would continue on, taller than the treetops, higher than the clouds. Hermod blinked, and then Vidar was no taller than a man.

Vidar drew his sword. His blade wavered like a heat mirage, disobeying the laws of optics such that it was visible from all angles at once. Hermod recognized the sword now. It was the same one he'd seen in the dwarves' workshop below the scrap yard.

"The eye is under your jacket," Vidar said. Hurricane forces raged behind his voice, tremendous energies contained in his bare whisper. Mist staggered, but Hermod held himself steady. He would not be intimidated. Had Vidar ridden to Helheim and back? Had he stood before the queen of that realm, whom even Odin feared? No. Hermod had done those things. He would not fear his brother.

"Our father's eye lay steeping in the well of wisdom for thousands of generations," Vidar said. "Did it reveal its wisdom to you?"

Hermod thought of the toy world at the bottom of Mimir's Well and how he'd crushed a mountain with an effortless movement of his hand. What was he supposed to have learned, other than that, under the right circumstances, he could be as destructive as any god?

"I really don't know," he told Vidar.

"It is not everyone's fate to be the recipient of knowledge," Vidar said. "Had I hung on the World Tree for nine days like Father, I might have gained nothing more than an acquaintanceship with pain."

"I'm not giving you the eye, Vidar."

"You cannot stop me from taking it." Vidar spoke the truth. Hermod would not be able to beat him in combat, not even if he somehow took Vidar's magic sword out of the equation.

Vidar moved the sword, and Hermod had to look away.

"You've never been a thief, Vidar. If you want the eye, what are you willing to give me in return?"

"My pledge that I will not harm you. Nor your companion."

"Then it sounds like what you're offering me is a nicely gilded threat. Will you at least grant me answers to some questions? Getting the eye wasn't easy, and you could do me the courtesy of telling me why it's so valuable."

"True wisdom is the ability to see the world as it is," Vidar said. "That's a useful skill if one wishes to adapt the world to a particular purpose."

"The sibyl says you're among the few who survive Ragnarok and that the world that rises from the ashes will be yours to rule."

Vidar dipped his head, which Hermod took as an admission. "Ragnarok must happen, but it is not such a bad thing. The world that comes after will be a good one."

Hermod remembered the battle against the Vanir, the Aesir's rival gods. Their home of Vanaheim had been every bit the paradise Asgard was, possibly even more beautiful. But when the war was over, every living thing there had been killed. Every man, woman, creature, and blossom. Only twigs and scorched rocks were left, all beyond recovery. A truce was declared, and the gods walled off that dead world and renamed it Helheim.

"Ragnarok isn't something that happens," Hermod

said. "Ragnarok is something we do, and when it's over, it'll make Helheim look like a kitchen garden. You'll preside, but your new green world will be fertilized by corpses."

Vidar vaulted the distance between them, and his elbow connected with Hermod's jaw. Hermod's head snapped back and he flew into the concert shell with cement-cracking force. Hearing footfalls crunch over rubble, he scrabbled to his feet, just in time to duck and roll as Vidar's blade swung over his head. There was a sound like an ax biting wood, and, floating in the air where Vidar's sword had sliced, a ragged black line wavered and flapped like a torn sail in the wind. Through the thin seam, Hermod caught a glimpse of a timber palace among ocean waves. Air shrieked through the seam, threatening to pull Hermod off his feet, a sensation much like being drawn into the vacuum of a wolf monster's open maw.

"Hermod! Here!" Mist tossed him his sword in a tumbling, underhand arc that sailed over Vidar's shoulder, and, grateful though Hermod was, he knew Vidar's blade would cut through his own sword like a razor through cheese. Besides, he wished Mist would concentrate on her own problems: Vali danced circles around her, giggling, trying to get past her saber. Mist looked grim and courageous and so mortally fragile.

Hermod lifted a fragment of concrete and hurled it at Vidar. It exploded in a puff of powder upon impact, leaving a short length of rebar emerging from Vidar's neck. His face drawn in pain, Vidar silently withdrew it and tossed it aside. It landed with a ringing clang at Hermod's feet. A fountain of blood spurted from Vidar's wound.

"Your fighting skills have improved, Hermod."

Vidar raised his sword high overhead in an executioner's posture. When he brought it down, there was again the colossal sound of chopping wood, and a wide rent appeared in the air. Hermod felt salt spray on his cheeks. Black swells broke against white towers, and with dread Hermod recognized the place he was seeing through the seam: his mother's home.

Drawn by the seam's gravity, he stumbled into Vidar's sword and felt the blade slide into his shoulder. He struggled feebly as Vidar removed Odin's eye from under his jacket, and there was a colorless moment before he fell out of the world.

Waves washed over him. Lightning split the sky. His blood mingled with seawater.

From the other side of the seam, Hermod saw Vali leap high, his pudgy hands reaching for Mist's throat. Despite his agony, Hermod tried to get up. There was a scream—not Mist's—as Sleipnir rushed forward and raked Vali's face with his tail. Rearing up, the horse hammered Vidar with six of his hooves, giving Mist time to mount. She held on, clenching her teeth with effort as Sleipnir surged forward and leaped through the fissure. Winston followed, landing in the water beside Hermod.

Mist spilled off the horse and reached into Hermod's bag. On the other side of the seam, a bloodied Vidar recovered from Sleipnir's battering and marched ahead. Hermod was in no condition to fight him. Merely remaining conscious was taking all his effort. The world was fractured, and there was something wrong with Mist's hand. It was giving off sparks.

No, Hermod realized, it wasn't her hand that was sparking. It was the last of the black-market grenades. As Vidar thrust his sword through the seam, Mist lobbed the paper-wrapped bomb.

The world shuddered weakly, and Hermod could no longer see the Hollywood Bowl, or Vidar, or anything other than a white flash.

CHAPTER SEVENTEEN

GRIMNIR STRODE ACROSS the field of blood and smiled at the sight of the fat orange sun glinting off Valhalla's roof of shields. At least the sun was still shining somewhere. Corpses littered the field—throats slashed, bellies torn open, some of them still gripping swords. Servants and slaves picked their way through the carnage with baskets, collecting arms and legs and matching them up with the torsos they belonged to. Grimnir waded through the butchery, blood-wet grass streaking his shins as he stepped over the bodies.

Things crawled and slithered unseen in the grass, but no rat or beetle dared nibble on the fallen here. Grimnir paused over the body of a young warrior with blue tattoos swirling across his chest. His throat had been cut open, but restoration was already in progress. Frayed tendons and muscle fibers reknit. Missing flesh re-formed. The lips of his throat wound reached to meet and seal the gap.

Grimnir watched similar scenes happening all over the field. Intestines retracted into split bellies. Limbs re-formed attachments of muscle and bone.

The tattooed warrior gasped and sat up. "Where is he?"

"Where's who?" Grimnir asked.

"He calls himself Wani of the Salmon Clan, but I call him Smells Like Wet Dog." The man was breathing steadily now, color returning to his face.

"He's the one who slit your throat?"

The warrior rubbed his healed wound. "He got lucky. If I hadn't tripped on a rock—"

"I get lucky every time," said another warrior, clad in tree-bark armor and an elaborate headdress of bright bird feathers.

Grimnir moved off and left the two behind to settle their differences. All around him, the other warriors were stirring, readjusting their armor and clothing. Some joined in small groups to brag about their feats of combat. The more experienced fighters criticized the technique of the newer ones, and there was much mockery.

It was good to be home.

Later, inside the hall, with the sounds of laughter ringing to the rafters and the smells of spilled beer and roasting meat, Grimnir felt a knot of tension loosen in his neck. He only wished he could have convinced Mist to join him. She was a good, brave kid, and he would have enjoyed partying away the last days of the world with her. He'd hated leaving her in the company of Hermod, even though he'd managed finally to gain some respect for the flaky Aesir. But Mist had made her choice, and he had to respect that too. Now it was time for Grimnir to make sure he was ready to fight and die with his Einherjar buddies. And that would require some drinking.

The nightly feast was in full swing, the fighters carousing in a babble of languages. It didn't take Grimnir long before he found himself seven drinks up in a healthy arm-wrestling contest. His current opponent was a pumpkin-headed anarchist in a Che Guevara T-shirt.

"I hear we're going over the top tomorrow," the anarchist said, grimacing with effort.

"Enh, they've been saying that for a hundred centuries. I'll believe it when I hear the horn."

Grimnir's blithe dismissal was insincere. Unlike most of the other Einherjar, he'd recently been out in the world. He'd seen decay and winter, and he knew things would be happening soon. What would the Einherjar's reaction be if they knew it too? Would their enthusiasm falter?

"Enh," he said again, slamming the anarchist's arm to the table.

Another man slid into his opponent's place, one whose face Grimnir recognized. "Tang Xiang," Grimnir said with pleasure. "Lose any limbs lately?" Shaven-headed, with fine wrinkles at the corners of his eyes, Tang Xiang returned Grimnir's greeting with a quiet nod. Grimnir took no offense at his friend's reserve; a master from the Shaolin temple at Fukien, Tang Xiang had always expressed himself better with the sweep of his curved broadsword than with words. The man was phenomenally skilled, but in ways so opposite to Grimnir's combat style that Grimnir could only admire him the way he admired Sinatra.

Tang put his elbow on the table and opened his hand. Grimnir grasped it, and they began the contest. Grimnir dwarfed the man, but he already felt the strain in his muscles, while Tang remained implacably still.

"You have been working for the Valkyrie Radgrid, I understand."

Grimnir grunted. "That's right."

"I've been making the acquaintance of some of the fighters she's been recruiting into our ranks. I must say, I do not entirely approve of her methods."

"There're a lot of doors in and out of Asgard. Not everyone has to come over the traditional way. But what do you think about the fighters themselves?"

"I question their loyalty," Tang said, direct as a sword thrust. Grimnir's arm tipped back, and he recovered barely in time to avoid losing the match.

"What are you talking about? I've personally faced each and every one of Radgrid's recruits, and I'm telling you, those guys are as solid as anyone."

"I have no reservations about their martial prowess," Tang said evenly, forcing Grimnir's arm backward again. "As I said, it is their intentions I question. I have heard things. Whispered conferences. Things said in moments of drunken indiscretion. I have noticed whose eyes will not meet mine squarely when I speak about the final battle. I have a sense that these men you helped bring to Asgard will not be fighting on our side."

Grimnir's arm bent nearly to the table. He ground his teeth and forced Tang Xiang's arm to vertical. "That's stupid," he said. "If they're not on our side, whose side are they on?"

"The answer to that should be obvious. It is whoever stands to profit most from Ragnarok." With that, Tang took a deep breath and slammed Grimnir's arm down. He offered a small, unenthusiastic bow and removed himself from the table without waiting for Grimnir to honor his victory by fetching him a drink.

Grimnir spent the next few hours in a dark cloud that not even wrestling or drinking could alleviate. Why did Tang Xiang have to spoil his homecoming? And why should Grimnir give a goat's shit what the little Shaolin thought? Everybody had a crackpot theory about something or other. Tang's accusations sounded just like the sort of thing Hermod would say.

But Hermod wasn't always wrong.

Something absurdly large bumped into Grimnir's shoulder. He staggered back, spilling beer from his cup.

"Whoa, dude, sorry," came a voice from above. Grimnir peered up into a broad, sunburned face framed with curly blond locks. Below it swelled a muscular body, easily twice Grimnir's width, dressed in a yellow T-shirt, floral-print Jams, and rubber flip-flops.

"No problem," Grimnir muttered, anxious to move on. He'd never liked Thor's son Magni, nor his brother Modi, whose bulky presence moved behind Grimnir. Like their father in his youth, they spent a great deal of time on Midgard, but Grimnir had always managed to avoid running into them. Just his luck to see them now.

"You're Grum-Ear, right? The dude who works with that Valkyrie hottie?" Magni smiled lasciviously.

Grimnir wanted to give him a quick, noncommittal response and keep moving, but such behavior wouldn't do here, especially not when it came to discourse with Aesir.

"The name's Grimnir. And, yeah, I work for Radgrid."

"Right on," said Modi, grabbing four beer tankards from a passing slave and downing them all in rapid succession. He belched fetid breath and let the tankards crash to the floor. He was wearing a pair of wraparound mirror shades, a smear of heavy-duty suntan lotion across the bridge of his nose.

"Cool party, huh?" said Modi.

"Right on," said Magni.

Grimnir now remembered that he did not merely dislike Magni and Modi but that, in fact, he hated them. And to be asked a second time since arriving in Valhalla about his association with Radgrid—well, it was weird.

Claiming the need to pee, he bid the brothers farewell and fled the hall.

Grimnir kept some private rooms near the servant quarters on one of the city's lower slopes, and as he made his way there, the contrast between the revelry in Valhalla and the subdued atmosphere beyond its timbers could not have been more stark.

His breath clouded when he entered his rooms, the fire in the hearth dead despite the fact that he'd hired a man to keep it stoked at all times. It was hard to get good help in these late days. He himself hadn't turned out to be such a faithful servant to Radgrid—a source of shame but not regret. Mist needed him more. And, in the end, he'd come to believe in her cause over any others.

Feeling along the wall to the woodpile, he stewed over Tang Xiang's accusations. Who stood to profit from Ragnarok? The obvious answer was, anyone who survived to inherit the new world that was coming after. According to that old bat sibyl, that meant Baldr and Höd, Vidar and Vali, and those two faux-surfer hodads, Magni and Modi. That was six gods right there who had reason to discourage anyone from fighting against the monsters and giants at the end. Some of them might even be willing to help Ragnarok along, to speed the ascent of the survivors. That was certainly what Grimnir would do, if he were an Aesir prophesied to rule after Ragnarok. And he'd go a step further by promising afterlife favors to anyone who supported him now, even if he had no way of assuring those persons' survival.

With no shortage of people who might try to game the system, Grimnir hadn't really left Mist behind to tilt at windmills. He'd left her to fight a damned conspiracy.

How fast, he wondered, could he get back across the rainbow bridge? If he grabbed a fresh horse while Valhalla partied, he might be able to find Mist before Hermod had a chance to drag her off on his next series of disasters.

"Grimnir."

He drew his dagger and turned around to be struck by a flashlight beam. Even in the glare, he recognized Radgrid's silhouette.

"Bright," he said, blinking.

"My apologies." She redirected the beam to the stone wall, casting the room in a cone of lemon-colored light. Her hair glinted like burnished copper, framing her icicle-white face. "I don't mean to trespass," she said, "but I'd heard you were seen leaving Valhalla, and I thought I might find you here."

She's going to ask me for a progress report, thought Grimnir. She'd want to know if he'd ever managed to track down her little renegade Valkyrie. She'd eventually get around to asking about Hermod too. And she'd use the interview as an opportunity to find out if Grimnir knew about the Ragnarok conspiracy, of which he was now as certain as he was about his own shoe size.

I know nothing, I suspect nothing, don't make a face, don't make a face, think about your shoe size, don't make a face.

Radgrid's expression changed subtly, growing cooler.

Dammit, thought Grimnir. He must have made a face.

"Fourteen triple-E," he said.

He charged her like a bull elephant, lunging to the side just in time to avoid Radgrid's side-thrust kick to his knee. He whipped his dagger around and struck for her neck, but she was too fast, and his blade made only a shallow nick in her arm. Rather than dance with her, he moved around and dove through the door.

He was not surprised to find Modi and Magni waiting for him outside.

Grimnir ran. He knew he had no chance of besting the brothers in combat, even though most of their great feats of strength were probably exaggerated, but he might have a chance of reaching the rainbow bridge if he could lose them in the labyrinthine markets near Höd's fallen-down old hall. Like most of the Aesir, Magni and Modi seldom came near this part of the city, but Grimnir knew its every stable and back alley.

He scaled the timber wall of a slave house and crept along its roof, listening for sounds of the brothers' clumsy pursuit.

"Dude, Radgrid's removed all her protections. If you die outside Valhalla, you'll be totally dead," one of the brothers called. "Come on out and we'll let you live."

Leaping between rooftops, Grimnir made his way to the trades district, where hammers striking anvils rang from the workshops. The roofs were too far apart to leap across here, and he was forced to ground. His boots splashed in stinking waste as he ran down the tanners' lane, and he didn't slow as he raced through a market specializing in Alfheim pornography. In his haste, he knocked over a cart of explicitly carved stones but kept on going. He wasn't far from the tall grassland between the city and the bridge, and if he kept low, he doubted those two lumbering clods would catch him.

An arrow pierced his back. Grimnir fell with a shocked scream.

He rolled onto his shoulder and tried in vain to reach the arrow while Radgrid slowly approached, another arrow nocked in her bow. Every movement sent spikes of pain shooting through his entire body, down to the tips of his toes. He drew his sword.

"Do your friends have the eye?" Radgrid said.

Leaning on his sword for support, Grimnir forced himself to his feet. He struggled for breath. "Even if I knew what you were talking about, I wouldn't tell you."

She loosed her arrow, and Grimnir's blade sang

when he knocked the shaft from the air. The effort cost him. He blinked sweat from his eyes.

Radgrid nocked another arrow.

"What did they promise you, Radgrid? The chance to be some godling's lap bunny?"

She loosed the arrow, and Grimnir swatted at it. The broken shaft scratched his cheek. His knees felt like water.

"I will be no one's concubine," she said. "Instead, I will be a goddess myself, given a world all my own."

"How nice for you. Who's arranging this little promotion? It's totally out of Magni and Modi's league. Vidar, then? Come on, you're going to kill me anyway. Consider filling me in on things my severance pay."

Radgrid nocked another arrow.

"How high up the chain of command does this go? Is it Frigg? Odin himself?"

She loosed the arrow. It glanced off his sword and lodged below his collarbone, and he roared at the drilling pain.

She nocked another arrow and pulled back on the string.

"Swords, you bitch. Let's finish this with swords."

The Valkyrie stood motionless for a moment, and then she slowly relieved the tension on her bow. "As you wish, Grimnir."

Modi and Magni stepped from the alley behind her, red-faced and breathing hard. Their sword blades resembled chain saws. Radgrid put down her bow and drew her own sword, a long, lethal needle.

With two arrows jutting from his body, Grimnir grinned. "You wanna wait for your two thugs to catch their breath, or should we just launch right into it?"

"You can't win, Grimnir. It's hopeless."

Grimnir coughed. He tasted blood. "Is that supposed to discourage me? I'm Einherjar. Hopeless fights are my specialty."

"It didn't have to be this way," Radgrid said, with what seemed like genuine regret. "Why didn't you bring Mist to me instead of allying yourself with her and Hermod? Your higher oath was to me."

"The simple truth is, I like her better." He raised his sword as high as he could, and with a cry of rage and pain, he surged forward.

He dodged Radgrid's first thrust and rammed his shoulder into her, knocking her back into Magni. With the two of them busy untangling themselves, Grimnir went for Modi, driving his blade halfway through his skull. The god collapsed with a soft squeak, his brains leaking from his crushed head, but Grimnir could not dislodge his sword. He heard Magni's footsteps thundering behind him.

Ah, well, thought Grimnir. *I've been a dead man for centuries anyway.* And, hey, he'd killed Modi, who was supposed to have survived Ragnarok. So much for the prophecy, then.

He regretted only that he wouldn't be able to tell Mist about it. She would have found it encouraging.

CHAPTER EIGHTEEN

THERE WAS NOISE and there was pain. The noise was the ringing buzz of a misshapen gong that wouldn't let the little bones in Mist's ears stop vibrating. The pain was a deep bone ache, as though she'd been beaten with pillows stuffed with lead shot. Both were courtesy of the shock wave from the grenade she'd tossed through the seam before it had sealed, with her and Hermod on one side of it and Vidar on the other.

Most of Vidar, anyway. His singed hand and forearm lay a few feet away, fingers still gripping his sword. Mist made a point of not looking in that direction. The severed arm was a grisly sight, but the weird blade was downright objectionable.

Mist and Hermod and Winston had fetched up on a sharp knuckle of rock in a small bay ringed by crumbled masonry. Lightning flashed in the indigo sky, but no report of thunder followed. The scent of warm bread hung on the air.

A mild wind rustled Sleipnir's mane. Mist cautiously patted the horse's neck, grateful for his help in the timely evacuation from the Hollywood Bowl. Now she just needed to figure out how to hoist Hermod onto Sleipnir's back so they could get out of here before Vidar came after them. Hermod's wound didn't look too gruesome, just a clean slit in his shoulder a few inches long, but he was in bad shape. Mist drew a healing rune around the wound in Sharpie pen, but it didn't seem to help. Hermod murmured feverishly. The words Mist could pick out were limited to *wolves* and *eye* and *coffee*.

Rhythmic splashing wafted through the fog, accompanied by the hollow drumming of wood bumping against wood: a rowboat.

Hermod continued to babble. Would he suffocate if she stuffed his jacket in his mouth to shut him up?

"Put the eye in the hole," Hermod groaned. "Oh, the hole in me is so big."

The sounds of rowing paused. Mist held her breath, but it was useless. Hermod moaned softly, Winston panted wetly, and Sleipnir rumbled with a distinctly unhorselike growl.

Mist pried Vidar's fingers from his sword, kicked his arm into the water, and struggled against nausea while she stowed the sword in Hermod's duffel. She drew her own sword and crouched low as the graceful prow of a boat approached the rock.

Long white oars rose out of the water to be stowed aboard the boat, and then a figure gracefully lifted itself over the gunwales and settled on the ground. Mist found herself huddling before a woman dressed in a swan-white gown, her golden hair gleaming even in the dim light. Splattered with muck and blood, Mist said, "This man is under my protection."

The woman raised a slender hand in a gesture of placation. "Be at ease, Lady Valkyrie. I have no intent to harm him. He is, after all, the son of Frigg."

Hermod groaned.

Mist kept her sword drawn as she watched the woman kneel to examine Hermod's wound. "This is more than an injury of the flesh," she said. "What caused it?"

"Something sharp," Mist snapped. She took a breath to calm herself. "Can you help him?"

"He needs Frigg's medicine, and soon, or I think he will die."

Mist managed to hide her surprise. She'd thought this woman *was* Frigg, but evidently not, unless Aesir goddesses referred to themselves in the third person, like professional athletes.

Hermod was deadweight, and with Mist taking him by the armpits and Frigg's lady taking his legs, they struggled to lower him into the boat.

"The waters are shallow," the lady said, eyeing Sleipnir. "You can follow me on the All-Father's horse, and we will make best speed."

Mist despised the idea of leaving Hermod in this stranger's care, but Hermod was no longer moving, and his breathing had become labored.

"Lady, if you hurt him, I will kill you. Understand?"

The woman nodded serenely.

Sleipnir clopped behind the boat, following it down an inlet into a marsh, where the low-hanging fog thinned to reveal an amalgam structure that was part timber hall, part gigantic gingerbread cottage, part modern suburban tract house, and part membranous tent shaped like a uterus. Home. Motherhood.

Long piers of white stone formed a narrow channel that led through arched openings, into the building. Once through the arch, the lady guided the boat to a dock where more ladies in white gently lifted Hermod from the boat and placed him on a stretcher of woven boughs, cushioned with grass. As they bore him down a walkway bordered on each side by running water, Mist followed, Winston's nails clicking on a floor that was exactly the same linoleum she'd grown up with in her grandmother's kitchen. Was Frigg's house conforming to Mist's expectations of home?

The ladies left Sleipnir behind with more of Frigg's attendants, who argued quietly over who should attempt to feed him.

Pathways and bridges crossed a network of pools and rivulets and waterfalls. Here and there were platforms of stone, little island-rooms, equipped with looms and beds and cauldrons hanging over cooking fires.

"Can we hurry it up?" Mist asked when she could no longer stand the funereal pace of the wordless procession. One of the women turned her head and gave Mist a dignified smile. Everything about Frigg's matrons was calm, controlled, and very Stepford Wife.

They passed beneath a timber archway and into a spacious, enclosed grotto. Water trickled down rough walls threaded with flower-dotted vines. In the center of the room rose a splendid bed of gnarled wood, dressed with white pillows and piles of fleece, bright as sunlit clouds. Mist concentrated on the bed, because she was terrified of looking directly at the figure dominating the room: Hermod's mother.

Frigg stood before the hearth, stirring an enormous kettle with a paddle. Mist attempted a greeting that caught in her throat, and Frigg smiled gently, her cheeks touched with pink, her blue eyes like a warm bath, and Mist wanted to fall into her abundant bosom and hear lullabies.

"Ma'am," Mist managed.

"Thank you for bringing my son home," Frigg said as the ladies transferred him to the bed.

"He's badly hurt," Mist said. "It was a special sword. It can cut through—"

"We can talk of this later. First I shall attend to Hermod. You must go with my ladies and rest. They will bathe and feed you and return you to your full strength."

"I'd rather stay here, ma'am. If that's all right . . ."

"I am mother to healing and renewal, daughter. Let me care for Hermod's needs while my ladies care for yours."

Mist allowed herself to be led off by one of the ladies, stealing a backward glance at Hermod's white, clammy face. Frigg sprinkled something into her cauldron and stirred. The air smelled like earth and spring rain, and Mist couldn't understand why she'd felt any misgivings at having arrived here and leaving Hermod in Frigg's care.

All was well in the house of Frigg.

The lady brought Mist to a room where a clean white robe and furs awaited on a bench, and Mist nearly wept when she saw the wooden tub brimming with steaming water. Beside it on a small table rested a board stacked with meat and cheeses and fruit.

"Will this do, Lady Valkyrie?"

Oh, sweet Jesus, yes, thought Mist.

The lady withdrew, and Mist shrugged off her coat.

# # #

HERMOD AWOKE in a cocoon of warmth and safety. Soft fur blankets pressed down on him with comforting weight, and the air smelled of cinnamon. He was dimly aware of something wrong with his right shoulder, but he wouldn't have to worry about it as long as he kept his eyes shut. He could deal with it later. Better yet, someone else could deal with it. Nothing could touch him as long as he kept his eyes shut.

"Hermod," someone said. For some reason, he associated the voice with the color green. It was gentle but strong, like a towering pine tree, boughs swaying in the breeze.

"Hermod, wake up."

And now he was completely and utterly alert, but he kept his eyes shut and listened. His mother's voice was pleasant but deeply frightening.

"Open your eyes, Hermod."

Hermod obeyed.

His mother's face, leaning over him and smiling, was lovely, of course. Not youthful, but ageless. She put a cool hand on his forehead. "How are you feeling?"

"Frightened," he said.

"Of what?"

"Of you."

She shook her head as though he'd uttered some charming bit of childish nonsense.

"Eat this."

A spoonful of soup came toward his mouth. He slurped it and felt a spreading warmth. He would gladly starve for a thousand years if he knew at the end of it there'd be his mother's soup.

"More, please?"

"Sit up." Frigg fluffed his pillows and fed him another spoonful. "You came to me badly hurt, Hermod. What happened to you?"

"Did I come here alone?"

"You were with a Valkyrie. And a very loyal dog. He would not leave your side."

Winston rose up and put his paws on the bed, panting and slobbering on the furs.

"Good dog. Where's the Valkyrie?"

"My servants are seeing to her needs, as I will see to yours. What happened to you?" she asked again.

Could he lie to his mother? Not quite. Perhaps, though, he could try evasion. "Things have gotten absolutely mad in Midgard," he said. "It's an age of wolves over there. And my need to poke my nose where it doesn't belong is still stronger than my sword arm."

"You've always been one to keep your own counsel," Frigg said, her smile sad. "I suppose there's even less chance you'll tell me what you have been doing since your brother's funeral."

She meant Baldr's funeral; it was the last time he'd seen his mother. Since then, glaciers had advanced and receded over Midgard more than once.

"Are we going to be coy, Mother? Everyone else seems to know what I'm doing and where I'm doing it. Surely you do as well."

"I didn't say I didn't know," Frigg said with reproach. "I said that you wouldn't tell me. The difference between the two is as vast as Ginnungagap. Why will you not trust me, Hermod? Am I not your mother?"

There was such genuine sorrow in Frigg's face. How could one not love her, not want to make her happy? She was not just Hermod's mother; she was motherhood itself. She was life budding from fertile soil after the long winter. She was life in the womb.

Hermod understood that if he didn't take an oath to help her bring about the destruction of worlds—and mean it—he would not leave here alive. Maybe it was the dip in Mimir's Well that had given him this insight. Maybe it was his brief possession of Odin's eye. More likely, it was the thousands of years he'd had to think about things, culminating in a point at which he could no longer deny obvious conclusions.

"At least tell me why you had Baldr murdered."

"It was necessary," she said, offering him another spoonful of soup. Hermod declined it. "Fate stretches before us and after us as a chain of linked events. For there to be Ragnarok, Baldr must die. For Baldr to die, there must be Ragnarok."

"That's the part that makes no sense to me. Why must there be Ragnarok? Why did you have to tell Loki about Baldr's weakness to mistletoe?"

"How long has it been winter, Hermod?"

"Three winters. No summer between."

"It has been winter much longer than that. It has

been winter since the first shoots of grass pushed up from the earth. From its very first moment, the world has been dying, just as an infant's first breath makes certain its last. I am life in renewal, and I crave the new green world to come after Ragnarok. To rail against the end is merely preserving a corpse."

"So, Ragnarok is an act of euthanasia. And once it's over, you and Vidar and whomever else you've drawn to your side can preside over the reanimated corpse."

"We see things differently, Hermod."

He leaned back against the pillows and closed his eyes. He was so tired. "Why did you send me to Hel to ransom Baldr? Was that just cover, so Odin wouldn't suspect?"

"No. It was my genuine hope that you would win Baldr's life back. Baldr had to die, but that didn't mean I wanted him to spend his death with Hel. Do you not think I love my children?"

"Did you love Höd less?"

Frigg didn't answer, but Hermod felt a change in the air pressure, like a storm building. He shrugged and instantly regretted having done so. His arm had started to ache and burn.

"I assume you love everyone and everything," he said, "but you'll eat your own young if it serves your purpose. What are your plans for me now?"

"No harm will come to you as long as you remain with me."

No harm, as long as he stayed in bed and ate soup. As long as he sat back and let the world die.

"I'm sorry," Hermod said. He sprang from the bed and punched his mother in the throat. She sank to her knees and emitted a choked whistle. Frigg's power didn't rely on muscle, nor was she some special-effects magician who could shoot purple lightning from her fingers. She could speak to life and convince it to do her bidding, but in the short term, Hermod had her number. Frigg clutched her throat and gawped like a fish.

Winston, demonstrating discretion, kept his distance from Frigg and Hermod both. He didn't even bark.

With only one fully usable arm, Hermod went about the slow business of dragging Frigg's hands behind her back and tying them to the bedpost with the linens.

He wept as he did so. Frigg was intent on the greatest mass murder of all time, but it was impossible to watch his mother struggle for breath and not despair.

He wiped tears from his eyes and gagged her.

# # #

MIST AWOKE in the bath when a grating screech struck her in the head like a rusty spear, the sound of a million diamonds scraping against a million windows. She pressed her hands to her ears, tighter and tighter. Chunks of ceiling fell about her, and she looked up to see lightning draw cracks in the sky. If the bolts were accompanied by thunder, she couldn't hear it. There was just the continually rising scream that, despite its colossal power, sounded like a giant chicken.

The rust-red cock will raise the dead in Helheim, the sibyl had said, *and the golden cock Gullinkambi will crow to the gods.*

Her head still buzzing, Mist shot from the steaming bathwater and put on her clothes, which were now soft, mended, and smelled like spring flowers. Damn Frigg and her hot bath and nourishing food and Stepford matrons. While Mist had been lounging in the tub, Hermod had been left alone and vulnerable. Had Mist been so fatigued that she'd fallen for it, or had Frigg's house cast an enchantment of fog over her?

She crossed the narrow bridge that connected her room to a network of stone walkways and found the household in chaos. The rooster's cry had shattered calm and physical structure alike. Crushed stone and splintered timber lay everywhere. With the house in shambles, she couldn't retrace her steps back to Hermod.

She heard a group of attendants coming her way and ducked into a small alcove. Casks and baskets of grain lined one wall, and set into the other was a wooden door. Over the sound of rain coming in through the gaps in the ceiling, Mist eavesdropped on the ladies in the hall.

"He attacked Mother?" one of them was saying, incredulous. "Is she harmed?"

"Not as badly as he'll be when we find him. The Valkyrie has left her room too."

"Find her and kill her."

My, but these Stepford matrons were mean. Mist moved farther into the alcove as more ladies approached. She barely had time to hide behind a stack of barrels before three of the matrons poked their heads in and shone torchlight into the corners. Mist held her breath until they withdrew.

There was still too much activity in the outer corridor for her to dare venturing into it, so she went for the little door on the other side of the alcove. Cautiously, she cracked it open. On the other side, two ladies lay dead beneath a fallen beam. They weren't dressed like the others, instead outfitted in chain-mail vests over their gowns and armed with swords.

Guards.

And what, Mist wondered, were they guarding?

Before her ran two rows of pens at least the length of a football field, with a corridor between them. She stepped deeper into the vast room. In one pen, a gorgeous chestnut foal lay motionless on a bed of straw. In another, three leopard cubs cuddled in a heap, absolutely still. They didn't look dead. They looked switched off.

All the pens housed inert babies. It was a veritable zoo of them. In one of the pens, the babies were human.

A noise at her back, and Mist spun around.

"Oh, hey, it's you," Hermod said. His right arm hung in a sling, and his face was clean, the bruises from the drubbing Vidar had given him faded. Winston wagged his tail at Hermod's side. "We have to get out of here. This is my mother's house."

"I know," Mist said. "I met her."

His eyes widened. "Did she do anything to you?"

"She gave me a bath and did my laundry."

"That's just like her."

Mist handed him his duffel. "Careful with this. Vidar's sword is inside."

Hermod grimaced as he took the bag from her.

They hurried between the pens, looking for a way

out of the stable that didn't involve going back into the heavily trafficked corridor. Winston ran ahead and sniffed the door on the far end of the stable. He barked impatiently.

Hermod pushed the door open a crack and issued a low whistle.

"What is it?"

He opened the door wider and stepped through. Mist followed him into a cavernous room of maps and drawings and saw what had impressed him. In green ink, drawn directly on the walls and on the floor and on the ceiling, was a depiction of a world gone mad with life: a naked man and a woman provided scale, dwarfed by forty-foot blades of grass and daisies the size of roller-coaster loops. Jumbo-jet dragonflies buzzed through the air between flies and moths and bees the size of Volkswagens. Trees soared above, vanishing in foreshortened perspective. Behemoth melons sprung from the ground. There were seas too, packed with a dizzying array of fish and whales and squid and snails and forests of kelp.

Written over the whole of it in a precise hand were runes that Mist didn't know and geometric patterns that suggested a crossbreeding of abstract art and an attempt to illustrate space-time.

"I think this is Frigg's blueprint," Hermod said. "This is what she wants built in the aftermath. And those animals in the pens are like a DNA repository to populate her new world."

"Too bad the current world has to meet the wrecking ball first."

Hermod shrugged. "I guess there are worse reasons to destroy everybody and everything."

"But if she and Vidar are acting to artificially encourage Ragnarok, then there should be something we can do to halt it."

"It stands to reason. Except we're so far out of our league. Frigg's ability to manipulate the very substance of the universe is unequaled. She proved that a long time ago, with her spell to protect Baldr."

"But she's not invincible," Mist insisted. "After all, Baldr *did* die."

"Only because Frigg wanted him to. She intentionally left a loophole by neglecting to get an oath from mistletoe. Then she had Loki exploit that loophole to trick Höd into killing Baldr."

Mist shook her head as she walked down the length of the wall, awestruck not so much by Frigg's power as by her thoroughness. She'd suborned Vidar and Loki. She'd arranged the murder of Baldr and set Höd up as the fall guy. She'd taken steps to see to it that her influence would be perpetuated in the new world to follow Ragnarok. And what sickened Mist most of all was that Frigg was no doubt comfortable in the thought that all this was being done for a greater good.

Not all the drawings were gargantuan versions of familiar life forms. There were also terrestrial creatures that looked like jellyfish with fur, and glowing globes with corkscrew tails, and things that looked like mounds of baby bunnies, only with more eyes. Frigg's Earth 2.0 would be fecund and strange.

Mist was gaping at a many-torsoed centaurlike animal and almost missed noticing the door it was drawn upon. What manner of creatures would she find on the other side, she wondered? With her hand on the pommel of her saber, she cracked open the door.

Vast darkness lay beyond the threshold, like an endlessly deep hole in all directions. Though Mist braced herself against the doorjamb, the emptiness pulled her in. Her grip slipped and she flew forward, nothing below her feet, air rushing out of her lungs, like an astronaut blown through an airlock into space. She felt the atomic bonds of her body break apart into disconnected particles as her thoughts lost clarity and shattered like a mirror. With her last shred of unraveling awareness, she perceived a kind of revelation, an understanding of the true absence that had existed before the creation of the universe. This was the wisdom of gods.

And then Hermod was beside her, falling into the vortex, and she decided, no, they would not lose to Frigg this way. They would not be disappeared. She threw herself back and, with a silent cry of effort, slammed the door shut. She sank to her knees and clutched Hermod.

"Hey, careful," Hermod whispered. "We almost fell there."

It was moments before Mist could speak again. "There's nothing on the other side," she said, shivering.

"I know. That's why you need to be careful."

"I mean there's nothing. Not like there's not anything, but like . . . Oh, holy shit. There's *nothing* on the other side." She clutched him tight, desperate to feel his comforting solidity.

"I know," he said, rubbing warmth into her shoulders. "We've almost fallen inside monster wolves.

There's some of that nothing inside them. Or they're like a portal to nothing. It's upsetting, I know."

She and Hermod held on to each other.

"There's nothing in Vidar's sword too," squawked a voice. Mist turned to see a pair of ravens hopping on the floor.

"That was a close shave," one of them said. "If you hadn't caught yourselves before you fell in, you'd have been so completely erased that no one would have even remembered you'd ever existed. Because, well, you'd have never existed."

"I would have remembered," said the other raven. "I've got a mind like a steel trap. And I'm talking about dwarf steel. A lot of people think elf steel is the best steel there is, but in terms of hardness, elasticity, ductility, tensile strength, and uncanniness, you really can't beat dwarf steel."

"Also, Munin and I have the advantage of being partly made of nothing ourselves," said the first. "We're a bit like Vidar's sword in that sense. It's made of seven impossible things, the seventh being nothing. Nothing is great stuff. Nothing cuts through anything."

"Talking birds?" Mist asked Hermod.

"Hugin and Munin. Thought and Memory. Another source of Odin's wisdom," Hermod said. He made quotation-mark gestures with his fingers when he said "wisdom."

Mist's head felt empty, her body bloodless. "Terrific. Maybe they can tell us this: Why does Frigg have a room full of nothing?"

Hugin cocked his head sideways. "All the something she's planning to build has to go somewhere.

And you don't think she'll be content to make a single new world, do you? Or even nine? She'll be making hundreds of worlds, thousands, all teeming with life. It's selfish, in a way, you trying to stop her, putting the needs of you and your sad little dying worlds ahead of the endless possibility of the new."

"It wouldn't bother me so much if there weren't already people living on the old ones," Mist shot back.

"Don't let the bird bait you," Hermod said. "The ravens don't want Ragnarok to happen any more than we do. They may be hyperniscient pests, but they want to live, and ours is the universe they live in. If it gets flushed away, they go with it, just like the rest of us."

Munin pecked at a drawing of a fat worm on the wall, but Hugin grew still, fixing Hermod with his black mirror eyes.

"Losing possession of the Sword of Seven was not a good move on Vidar's part," the raven said. "Because the sword cuts through anything, it can be used to make new seams in the World Tree. Vidar needs the sword to make sure that the destruction of one world will spill over into the others. It's like a domino effect, but for one domino to topple the others, the barriers between the dominoes have to be removed. Odin's eye is what shows Vidar where to make the cuts, to slice those barriers out of the way."

"So Vidar's got the eye," Mist said, "but we've got the sword. As long as Vidar doesn't have both, we're okay?"

"Vidar's not that stupid," Hugin said. "The nothing in the Sword of Seven is a tricky substance to work with, but there's no shortage of nothing."

"In addition to the Sword of Seven," Munin piped in, "he commissioned an Ax of Seven, a Spear of Seven, a Hammer of Seven, a Crude Bludgeon of Seven . . . His backup arsenal of Seven is quite extensive."

Hermod rubbed his face. He looked as drained as Mist felt. "I get the picture. What do I do about Vidar?"

"We," Mist reminded him. "What do *we* do about Vidar?"

Munin shat on a rendering of a coral reef.

"It's a mistake to think that you can solve all problems by wrestling Vidar," Hugin said. "First, you're no match for him. Second, he's already set Ragnarok in motion. He's freed Fenrir and armed the fire giant Surt. He's cut seams in the World Tree to make sure that the destruction of one root will bleed into the others. If you have any hope of improving affairs, you have to address Vidar's work, not just Vidar himself. And you might begin by addressing the part you're personally responsible for. You're the one who set the sky-eating pups from Ironwood loose. It's probably too little, too late, but you could try to do something about that. It'd be better than nothing."

"See, Hermod?" Mist said with great cheer. "You're better than nothing!"

CHAPTER NINETEEN

FINDING THE WAY back to Midgard proved frustrating. If there were seams forming direct pathways between Los Angeles and Frigg's domain, Hermod couldn't locate them. The days of fruitless travel wore at his endurance as Sleipnir galloped on, splashing through the marshlands of Frigg's domain. Winston, by contrast, seemed happy enough, leaning from his harness like a dog in a pickup truck.

"Hugin said that Vidar was using the Sword of Seven to open up new seams," Mist said, launching another volley in an argument they'd been having on and off for the last several days.

"But that's Vidar. It's his sword. And he's Vidar. I don't know how the damned blade works. Also, Hugin said Vidar needed Odin's eye to wield the sword properly, to show him where to cut. I could make a slice in the World Tree and end up opening a pathway right to the bottom of the Atlantic Ocean. Or to the core of a star."

"Vidar didn't have the eye yet when he *started* using the sword."

"It's Vidar's sword," Hermod said again. "And he's Vidar."

They'd had this same conversation at least a dozen times and always ended up here, with Hermod feeling correct but unsatisfied and Mist left stewing behind him. Times were desperate and drastic risk-taking was past due. But the memory of collapsing an entire mountain range at the bottom of Mimir's Well with a careless movement of his hand was still fresh in his memory. Blindly slashing about with the Sword of Seven just didn't seem smart. That was the sort of thing gods did, real gods with real power. Not people like Hermod. Unfortunately, he was the one with the sword.

He sighed and brought Sleipnir to a stop on a soggy spit of land. "Fine, then, I'll give it a try. But don't blame me if I end up slicing a canyon through the middle of Paris."

"Assuming there still is a Paris, I won't hold you responsible," Mist assured him.

They climbed down from Sleipnir, and Hermod unsheathed the sword. The moment he laid eyes on the blade, sickness spiraled in his head and stomach. How was he supposed to use a weapon he couldn't even bear to look at?

Ignoring the sounds of Mist retching behind him and Winston's whimpers, he fixed his focus on the blade and would not allow himself to look away.

He looked away.

"Dammit!"

He sucked down a deep breath, held it, and slowly exhaled. Bending at the knees, he rooted himself in the ground with a solid stance. He squared and relaxed his shoulders. The blade wasn't as featureless as he'd thought; a pattern of finely etched lines swirled in the steel, like a topographic map in motion. The whorls and eddies swam before him, faster and more turbulent, causing him physical pain, like thin metal wires piercing his skin and worming into his head. It required all his concentration to maintain his grip on the sword and keep looking at it.

For a sliver of a moment, the pattern almost made sense, was almost even familiar. It *was* a map, charting the folded convolutions of the nine worlds.

I can see it, he thought with sudden jubilation. *I understand it!*

And then, just as quickly, the sickness returned. His hands jerked involuntarily, the tip of the blade making a small incision in the air before him. His vision shattered, and the world broke up into chaos.

Hermod dropped the sword and fell to his knees, panting.

He'd really done it this time, he thought. He'd screwed up the universe.

But when he looked up, the little seam he'd cut had sealed itself, and the dark marshlands around him appeared to have returned to normal.

He got shakily to his feet and helped Mist to hers.

"And that," he rasped, shaking his finger in Mist's face, "is why you don't fuck around with someone else's dwarf sword!"

In the end, they relied on Hermod's talent for finding natural seams and on Sleipnir's reckless speed to get them back to Los Angeles.

They emerged at night, not far from Pier Avenue, at the remains of the café where they'd consulted the sibyl. It seemed like such a long time ago. Shattered bricks and crumbled mortar lay at their feet, along with charred paperback books, coffee mugs broken into ceramic fragments, jumbled and burned tables and chairs, shards of window glass. Hermod picked up an intact coffee mug from a black slush of sodden ash. The coffee inside was frozen solid. With disappointment, he poked the bakery case with the toe of his boot. "I'd kill for a muffin," he said, to no one in particular.

The clouds had cleared to reveal a sharp, full moon, bright enough to hurt his eyes. He peered up at it. He'd been walking the lands of Midgard long enough to have seen the continents change shape. He'd seen forests become deserts, and seas become valleys. Even the moon hadn't been a constant, meteor impacts changing its face over the years. But it was still there. The wolves hadn't yet eaten it, and Hermod forced himself to take some comfort from that. Things weren't hopeless. And he didn't have to bear the burden of Ragnarok alone. It felt good to have allies after so many years of wandering in solitude. He had the Valkyrie, and the best dog in the world, and a fierce, eight-legged mount, and a sword that made him ill.

"All right," he said, clapping his hands. "This moping isn't doing us any good. You think our enemies are sitting around, all downcast and sulking? If we're going to pull this out, we have to be at least as committed as they are."

"I swear, if you tell me it all comes down to who wants it more, I'm going to take you out at the knees," Mist said. But she said it with a smirk, and when her smirk grew into a brief moment of genuine laughter, it felt like a ray of sunshine warming Hermod's face.

"I can't find any honey." Stepping from behind a mound of rubble, the sibyl picked through the wreckage. Her outfit had changed since their last encounter, her yellow rain pants and purple Vikings cap exchanged for a skirt of greasy animal skin. Necklaces of small bones and bird feathers hung over her breasts.

"Getting honey was so hard in the old days," she said. "It took a genius just to figure out we could eat the stuff and a million stings before someone discovered that smoke would make the bees sleep. I remember my clan's shaman dying of anaphylactic shock. We assumed he was possessed by spirits. I wasn't happy about taking over for him, but then I realized the office came with the best cuts of meat and all the honey I wanted. These days the honey comes in little plastic bears. But now it's all come down to this, after millions of years of progress and innovation. An age of wolves 'til the world goes down."

Grinning a gummy smile, she cocked her head to the side. "Oh, they're finally here."

Hermod heard the howl a moment later, a rising hornlike note that spoke directly to his spine. Other voices joined in, forming dissonant chords with squeaks filling the spaces. Four wolves came lumbering around the corner. They'd grown to the size of trash Dumpsters, shaking the ground with paws as big as manhole covers. Pebbles in the debris field vibrated.

Hermod unsheathed the Sword of Seven. He

steeled himself against the sight of the blade but still staggered, feeling the ground slip beneath his feet. The wolves weren't immune to the sword's effects either. Their growls faltered, much to Hermod's satisfaction.

Okay, then. This would at least be a fight. *Glory and adrenaline, and what finer end could you ask for?*

"Mush," Hermod said.

The wolves leaped at him. Hermod darted in a quick diagonal, blocking their path to Mist, but one of them vaulted overhead in a gray and white blur and was upon Mist before Hermod could react. He moved to help her, but another wolf blocked his path. Snarling, it lunged at him but kept beyond the range of his sword. Hermod knew he wouldn't survive long if he played elk to the wolves' hunting pack, so he leaped high in the air, swinging his sword in a circle around his head with an air-cutting whoosh, and came down with the blade's edge across the wolf's neck. Its head separated cleanly, blood and foam spilling over its speckled, lolling tongue and mixing with ash and asphalt.

Hermod moved again to help Mist, but two wolves intercepted him, eyes drawn to slits, teeth gleaming.

"You don't scare us," the pair snarled in a joined voice. "You're just like everything else in the worlds: fuel for Ragnarok. Come burn in our bellies." They stretched their jaws, and Hermod felt the now-familiar tug of wind and gravity. Whirls of soot whistled through the air, spiraling into the wolves' gullets.

Hermod charged, but the wolves moved too quickly for him. He found himself facing one wolf, with the other at his back. The attack came from the rear. Dropping to the ground and rolling toward the assault, he barely avoided being bitten in two. He aimed a cut at the wolf's legs but missed, and now he was on his back, even more vulnerable. Slaver splashed on his face, hot as blood. His arms burned with fatigue, the sword heavy as he made fast thrusts to keep the wolves at bay. He was tired, fading, and he knew he couldn't keep his defense up much longer. Through blurred, tunneling vision, he saw teeth and tongues and yawning chasms of nothing. With a great sobbing wail of exertion, he rose to his feet and swung in a blind arc. A piercing yelp gave him hope that he'd landed a blow. On reflex, he spun and thrust out the sword and heard another yelp. Not stopping to see what, if any, damage he'd inflicted, he ran a few steps and would have run farther, but his legs finally gave out and spilled him into the rubble. His sword clattered away.

Panting, Hermod craned his neck to look up, expecting to see the wolves coming at him at full speed. Instead, both cowered a few yards away, mewling. One bled from its head, the other from its chest. The third surviving wolf made hesitant attacks at Sleipnir, who was situated between the wolf and Mist.

Hermod crawled across the wreckage to retrieve his sword, which had fallen only a couple of arms' lengths away, and stood on weak legs. The wolves bowed their backs, heads and tails lowered in ambivalent displays of aggression tempered by fear.

Hermod liked being feared. It was a new experience. He took a step toward the monsters.

That's all they were: monsters to kill. And he was a god, wielding a mighty weapon.

Something massive fell from the sky, landing between the wolves and Hermod with shuddering impact. A towering bulk loomed before him, with a snout the length of a full-grown man and teeth like hatchet blades.

Hermod looked up into Fenrir's black-rimmed blue eyes.

"You won't hurt the young ones," Fenrir said. His voice was chocolate.

Hermod ran at him, but instantly something hit him in the chest with the force of a cannonball, and he was on his back again, squeezed against the ground by a paw five feet across. All the air escaped Hermod's lungs, and he could draw in no breath to replace it.

"You won't hurt me either," said Fenrir with no malice. "I do not know what your doom is, but it does not involve my death."

Debris dug into Hermod's back. He felt a rib crack. Dimly, he heard Winston's barking. He wished Mist would tell the stupid dog to go hide somewhere. He wished she would go with the dog.

"You will have learned by now that you can manipulate the small details of events, but things that were meant to happen must happen," Fenrir said. "I will eat Odin, because I must. Vidar will kill me, because he must. And my pups will eat the moon and the sun, because the world demands it. There is nothing that can be done to change it."

Hermod still held the Sword of Seven in his hand, but moving to use it against Fenrir wasn't a thought. He couldn't even summon a moan of pain.

Fenrir twisted his head around to address the three

wolves, putting even more pressure on Hermod's tortured chest. "This is no time to lick your wounds, children. Your hour has arrived." The whimpering ceased.

The wolves sprang into the sky. They sailed higher and higher, blood from their wounds raining down in dime-size splotches, moonlight gleaming off their white fur.

When Fenrir finally removed his paw from Hermod's chest, the relief was offset by deep stabbing pains in his ribs. Mist dropped to his side, resting her hands lightly on his chest. "Stay down," she said, as Hermod tried to control the agonizing spasms of his lungs.

"It will be over soon," Fenrir soothed, stepping back. "A flash of burning pain, and then rest and sleep for all."

"You mean death, and worse. Annihilation." Mist said this matter-of-factly, not inviting argument. And Fenrir offered none.

"The worlds are quite old," he said. "Forests cannot live when old growth casts new buds in shade. Unlike others, I seek no profit from Ragnarok. I am prepared to die. If I can accept this, why can't you?"

"Because I'm not a slave," spat Mist. "Not to prophecies, not to sibyls, not to Norns, and you don't have to be either. Nobody does."

Fenrir made a chuckling rumble, deep in his throat. "Oh, little morsel, Odin built the very ground you walk upon, and even he must answer the call of Fate. Nobody's life can be wound into endless thread."

Mist stood. "If you're so sure about your assumptions, then test them. Try opting out of the game.

Don't show up to the battlefield. Don't attack Odin. When Vidar faces you, run away. Don't play along. What have you got to lose?"

"Watch" was all Fenrir said.

Hermod's gaze fell upon the moon. A faint halo had formed around the disc.

"Help me up," he begged Mist. He sucked in a breath of pain as she pulled him to his feet as gingerly as she could. He would not witness his defeat lying on the ground, at least.

She supported him with an arm around his waist, and he drew her in close, while the moon's edge grew ragged and indistinct behind the expanding nimbus, like a lump of dissolving chalk. Soon there was just a dusty, globular cloud in the sky with a few winking particles. Then that, too, faded.

"It is done," Fenrir said. "The serpent will grapple with Thor and stain the sky and earth with his poison. Loki will deliver *Naglfar* with its crew of dead to the plain of Vigrid, there to be joined by gods and giants and elves and dwarves and men to do battle. Surt will lead the sons of Muspellheim and scorch the earth, and Loki will do battle with Heimdall the bridge guardian. I will devour Odin, just as my pups devoured the moon, as they shall soon devour the sun. The nine worlds will die in fire and ice, and what comes after is not my concern."

Hermod raised his sword to Fenrir, but the wolf took no apparent notice, leaping to the sky and vanishing into the moonless night. Hermod and Mist clutched each other, watching the stars wheel in the sky, ever faster.

CHAPTER TWENTY

VIDAR HAS COME to a place in Midgard. Once this was a San Fernando Valley shopping center, a vast field of asphalt rimmed by stores as large as the halls of Valhalla. The shelves were stocked with nine different kinds of peanut butter and thirty different kinds of frozen pizza, and basketball shoes and lawn mowers and picture books and laser-guided table saws. There was also a movie theater here, a tae kwon do school, and a yogurt shop.

Now the shopping center is a charred sprawl. News crews film the looting.

Hovering above, Munin and I watch Vidar. His right arm terminates a few inches below his elbow in a bloody, bandaged stump. He seems to be measuring something, but we can't see what he sees, because now he sees with Odin's eye. It bulges from the socket, ill-fitting. His cheek is plastered with dried gore.

Vidar has a scythe. It's quite obviously dwarfcraft. The snath, gracefully carved from a single piece of wood, is as long as Vidar is tall. The blade, like the Sword of Seven, is made of the roots of mountains, the breath of fish, the beards of women, the footfalls of cats, the sinews of bears, the spittle of birds, and nothing.

Satisfied with his calculations, Vidar nods, and without fanfare or posing, he sweeps the scythe before him. For a one-armed swing, it's pretty powerful. There is no thunder, no big bang, no flash of blinding light. Just a web of seams and worlds spilling through them.

He nods again. The final battlefield now stands ready for battle.

CHAPTER TWENTY-ONE

THE STARS RACED overhead, as though time had sped up. Hermod wondered if age would finally catch hold of him now in a big dose of Dorian Gray, but when he put his hands to his face, expecting to feel rugose flesh and mummy dust, his cheeks felt the same as always.

"The stars' accelerated motion is due to conservation of momentum," Mist was explaining. "The loss of the moon's mass translates to a four-hundred-percent increase in Midgard's spin, for a six-hour day. Now that the moon's been eaten, earth will prematurely pull away from the sun, beyond the capacity of the world to sustain life. But that's many thousands of years off."

"You sound like Munin."

"Hey," Mist said, offended. "You don't have to be a raven to figure this stuff out. I took a little astronomy in college. You want to check my numbers?"

"I believe you, Professor. But none of it matters. If we don't stop Ragnarok, the universe won't last 'til next Wednesday, let alone thousands of years from now."

They had taken refuge on the roof of a parking garage off the Third Street Promenade in Santa Monica. The air smelled of tear gas. The pops and cracks of gunfire and the sizzle of Tasers reverberated up from the shops and cafés, which had erupted into full-scale riot since the moon disappeared. Hermod couldn't even imagine what people were fighting over. Perhaps the rising wall of pre-Ragnarok chaos had simply broken through the dam.

Winston munched on a stingray he'd found near the stairwell. Sleipnir, left downstairs to forage, had hopefully found a fallen tree or car to eat.

"I'm going to look at my sword again," Hermod warned Mist. She nodded and turned away. Hermod had been forcing himself to gaze into the blade runes, hoping to make sense of them before the nothingness and impossibilities built into the sword overtook him.

He unsheathed the Sword of Seven, just a few inches, and looked at the blade with almost-shut eyes. These were runes in the language that Odin had learned after hanging on the World Tree for nine days. They were a guide of some kind, an explanation, or a map of the tree itself, charting all the intricate nooks and crannies in its skin. Frigg and Vidar needed a way to connect disasters across worlds so that the moon eaten in Midgard would also result in its loss in Asgard and in all the other worlds. If he could only figure the map out, maybe he could predict Vidar's next move and somehow stop him. . . .

Darkness closed in on the edges of Hermod's perception—not just tunnel vision but encroaching oblivion. He looked away and sheathed the sword. It was no good. He needed Odin's eye.

"Hermod, look!"

"I don't want to."

"No, *look*," Mist insisted. "In the sky."

Hermod followed the direction of Mist's gaze to where a massive black object approached, perhaps a hundred feet over the beach. He thought it was a zeppelin at first, but as it grew closer he recognized the dark, pearly hull, and the square sail, and the great dragon figurehead.

"That's *Naglfar*," Hermod said.

"Lilly and Höd and the Iowans," Mist said. "We have to get up there."

"How? You have a jet pack you've been holding out on me?"

"Maybe we can bring the ship down to us—" But before Mist could complete her suggestion, a gunshot sounded, and a small crater materialized in the cement wall behind them. Hermod threw himself on top of Mist as more shots whizzed by. They crawled behind a big SUV for cover.

"Who's after us this time?" Mist shouted over the noise of bullets crashing into the wall.

Hermod reached up and broke the side mirror off the SUV, then crawled forward, taking care to stay behind the engine block. He angled the mirror to get a look at the shooter. A woman in a white leather coat stood at the top of the stairwell with a rifle. Tall and broad-shouldered, her red hair bright in the gloom, she silently directed large, well-muscled men to take positions around the roof.

"It's Radgrid," Mist said, looking over Hermod's

shoulder at the reflection in the mirror. "I guess NorseCODE finally caught up with me."

"You don't think Grimnir—"

"No, I don't. He had plenty of opportunity to sell us out, and he never did."

"Mist," Radgrid called. "Come out, please. I need to speak to you." More shots rang, and the SUV's front tires burst.

"Is this about my performance review?" Mist called back. Crouching between cars, she and Hermod moved toward the other end of the roof.

"We can discuss your unexcused absences later. Right now I want to talk to you about some of your associates."

They hid behind a minivan, listening to Radgrid's thugs prowling over glass and gravel.

"Surrender to me, Mist, and I will spare your life."

Mist looked at Hermod and rolled her eyes.

A huge, bearded man came around the rear of the van, rifle pointed at them. Hermod hurled a stone at his chest and the man flew back in a spray of blood, firing his gun in the air.

"Fine, then. Open up," Radgrid shouted. "Shoot everything!"

Bullets ripped through the air, shattering glass, puncturing metal and rubber. Shots passed close enough to shave Hermod's stubble. *Maybe this is it,* he thought. *Maybe I die on the eve of Ragnarok, just before everything goes down the big toilet.* Covering Mist with his body, he was sorry he never got to spend time with her on a white-sand beach.

Over the clatter and roar of the gunfire, Hermod heard the distinct drumming of Sleipnir's hooves. He dared peer up, and there the horse was, eyes blazing in the parking-lot aisle. Winston crouched, barking, beneath the horse.

Hermod grabbed Mist's arm. "Come on!"

He hoisted Mist onto Sleipnir's back and stuffed Winston into the harness, then leaped behind the horse's withers. Steam curling from flared nostrils, Sleipnir trotted to the far end of the roof and turned himself around. Bullets shattered car windshields and punctured steel.

"Hold on tight," Hermod warned Mist. Leaning forward, he whispered encouragement in Sleipnir's ear.

Sleipnir took off with a shock, jolting the riders back, his muscles compressing and releasing in a thundering rush. Sparks danced from his hooves. Cement cracked beneath him. Radgrid's men fell away as Sleipnir ran them down. Bare inches from the edge of the roof, he took a great galloping leap into the sky.

Hermod twisted around and looked down. Radgrid fired off shots from the roof, but soon they were out of her range, a hundred feet up, two hundred, the whole city block beneath them, people running, black smoke, ocean swells flooding the streets. Then, a wider expanse as Sleipnir climbed ever higher, his eight legs moving like the oars of a ship.

As they drew close to *Naglfar*, Hermod realized he'd misjudged the ship's size and thus its altitude. It was much larger than he'd thought. Perhaps it had grown.

Sleipnir came even with the keel, and then the horse's hooves struck the hull. He galloped up at a sheer vertical. His mane cut into Hermod's palms as Hermod gripped two handfuls of hair to keep from falling. Mist squeezed Hermod's waist, while Winston cried, dangling from his harness. Sleipnir charged up the side of the ship, a froth streaming from his mouth. The horse landed on the deck with an explosion of splintering planks. He reared up and shrieked, his front hooves slashing the air.

The ship was awash in full-scale combat. Hermod couldn't quite discern who was fighting whom. The majority of the conflict seemed to be between soldiers and unarmed dead, and the soldiers were outnumbered. They desperately hacked away at the swarming masses that kept coming at them. The mutineers pried weapons loose from the soldiers' grips, gouged eyes, smothered the soldiers with overwhelming force.

"It's a revolt," Mist shouted over the din. "Let's help out!"

Hermod would have been glad to oblige, but it was easier enthused than done. An Ottoman Janissary in an ostrich-plumed hat aimed his rifle of brass and oiled wood at Hermod, but before the man could work the complex firing mechanism, Sleipnir rushed forward and bit his face. The Janissary fell, but a Zulu wrested the gun from him and took aim to fire. Hermod unsheathed the Sword of Seven and cut the Zulu in half.

Some of the fighters ran from the sight of the blade, while others were gripped with dry heaves. But for the most part, Hel's army was comprised of soldiers at least as hearty as their counterpart Einherjar, and most of the fighters pressed on with their attack.

The direction of the conflict shifted and started to swirl around Sleipnir like a whirlpool. The soldiers and mutineers both saw Sleipnir as a threat, or as a weapon to claim for their side, and Hermod and Mist could only struggle to remain mounted as the horse kicked and bit and whipped his tail at the attackers.

Hermod felt something zing past his ear and craned his neck around to see a man in desert camouflage gear firing an M16. Three meaty thunks, and Sleipnir bucked, screaming. Blood welled up from a trio of sloppy bullet holes in his neck. The man held his ground, firing, as Sleipnir ran him down.

"We're making things worse," Mist shouted, hacking away at a soldier wearing a George Custer mustache, while kicking at a woman in a postal-clerk uniform. Armed dead and press-ganged galley slaves were becoming an undifferentiated swirl.

Hermod yanked on Sleipnir's mane, trying to get him to reverse direction and head for the stern, where they might be able to fight for control of the helm, but the horse was in a rage, storming through anyone in his path and leaving a wake of wrecked bodies.

A high voice rose above the clamor: "Leave the horse alone!"

Hermod sought out the speaker, and he and Mist found her at the same time. Lilly Castillo stood upon a pile of corpses, her face scratched and bleeding, her blood-greased fingers gripping a long spear with a diamond-shaped point. Beside her, wielding a trident and a Chinese hook sword, respectively, stood the Iowans, Henry Verdant and Alice Kirkpatrick, grinning fiercely in their blood-splattered clothes.

A red-coated soldier sprang up and aimed a

curve-handled pistol at Lilly. Alice Kirkpatrick ripped his throat open.

"Lilly!" Mist shouted, waving her arms at her sister, while Hermod looked about for Höd.

"Take the helm" was Lilly's only acknowledgment.

Blood flowed freely from the bullet wounds in Sleipnir's neck, making Hermod's hands slippery as he tugged with all his might on the horse's mane to get him to turn around. Whether in response to Hermod's exhortations or acting on his own, Sleipnir spun around and spider-scuttled sideways down the length of the ship.

Hermod chanced to look down, over the rail. They were no longer in Midgard, but where they'd arrived, he couldn't say. A few miles toward the horizon rose stately pillars of trees, perhaps a thousand feet tall, their boughs consumed in flame. Hermod had never seen such trees anywhere outside the forests of Jotunheim. But there were also black mountains pocked with cave openings of the kind native to Svartalfheim. The Asgardian hall of Valhalla was down there, its roof caved in. A shopping mall with a Home Depot and a Costco smoked below.

Vidar must have sliced seams into the tissue of the World Tree, and the worlds had spilled out of their confines. Now they butted against one another like a puzzle of ill-matched pieces. At the very center of the parking lot was a vast asphalt field. A shopping-mall parking lot, then, would serve as Vigrid, the pivot point of Ragnarok.

The ship sailed over the armed force gathered on the nearer end of the parking lot. The armor of the

Einherjar glinted in reflected flames, but their numbers seemed scant, thinly distributed over the field.
Arrows flew past the ship—some of those Einherjar
were damned mighty archers, Hermod thought—but
the few that hit the hull did no harm, and *Naglfar*
sailed on toward the opposing army on the other end
of the lot. This was a much larger force, made up of
giants. Some were as beautiful as any god, resplen-
dent in mirror-bright gold armor, and some were
shambling grotesqueries with mouths like basking
sharks or skin covered in mud and turf. Rocks and
snow avalanched down the backs of the frost giants
as they drummed their chests, and when they threw
their heads back and shouted war cries, Hermod felt
the shrieking cold wind even at this altitude.

Towering over them all, a swirling mass of flame,
too bright to look at directly, rocked the earth with
every step. This had to be Surt, holding a sword big
enough to sever mountains from their roots.

It was too much. It was laughable. Compared to
the giants, the Einherjar were a Cub Scout troop.
They wouldn't die bravely. They would be rendered
into grease and dust and ash. Hermod at long last
truly grasped the concept of a futile battle. The world
was over. It just didn't know it yet.

His sore ribs complaining, he raised himself off
Sleipnir's back to gaze across the length of the ship's
deck, past the heads of the soldiers and mutineers. At
the stern, perhaps fifty yards away, Loki manned the
tiller. His posture was relaxed, like a weekend sailor
steering his yacht, and he looked out over the carnage
on the deck with smug satisfaction.

"Loki!" Hermod shouted. "You fucking hermaphrodite! I'm coming for you!"

Loki's eyes locked on Hermod's, and he laughed with malicious glee.

"Hold on," Hermod warned Mist. He raised the Sword of Seven high over his head and kicked his heels into Sleipnir's sides, urging him into a charge. The deck cleared, the fight forgotten, combatants breaking off to get out of the way, and Sleipnir growled, a noise like that of no horse or any other animal in Hermod's experience. With great pleasure, Hermod saw Loki's expression shift into a frightened grimace.

In a bid to slow Sleipnir's charge, Loki gave the tiller a harsh tug. The bow lurched up. Bodies fell and tumbled down the inclined deck past Sleipnir's legs, but the horse continued up the steep grade, gaining speed.

Loki was scarcely two dozen yards away now, and Hermod whirled the sword around, building momentum for his final strike. Hot rain fell from the interdimensional incisions he made in the air.

Draugr threw themselves at Sleipnir, but most were crushed to pulp beneath his hooves or fell to Hermod's and Mist's swords. Some managed to claw their way up Sleipnir's sides, using Mist's and Hermod's bodies for hand- and footholds. Fingers raked Hermod's face. Draugr hung on his arms and legs like heavy parasites, dragging him off Sleipnir's back. Smashing to the deck, he swung the sword back and forth, trying to drive away the draugr. Limbs flew, heads separated from bodies, but the full force of the draugr squad was on him, and they were fearless. No matter how many he cut down, replacements crawled through the gory mess he made. One bit into his shoulder, another into his calf.

So this is how I die, thought Hermod. *Flesh-eating zombies. Of all the ways to go.*

He kicked a draugr in the face, smashed the face of another with his elbow, drove the sword's hilt into another's chin, and now, afforded some small freedom of movement, swept his blade around in a 360-degree arc that split torsos from legs and sliced a wind-sucking hole in the air.

The draugr kept coming.

With the rowers completely involved in the melee, the ship was being propelled only by the sail. If *Naglfar* lost her sail, and therefore her forward momentum, would she fall?

Hermod drove through the draugr mob, fighting his way to the mast. The Sword of Seven slid through bodies, parting the air with thunder cracks, and when Hermod had gained a yard of clear path, he jumped to the mast of Jotun bones and started climbing. The sail battered him, crackling and flapping in the wind, smashing him against the mast. He kept climbing, draugr coming up after him, like a treed bear with hounds snapping at his feet.

Reaching the crossbeam—a single giant femur—Hermod sliced through the thick bone, and it fell away from the mast. The sail went with it, tangling in Hermod's legs.

His bones sang like a hammered steel rod when he crashed to the deck. He could take punishment, but, damn, he was getting tired of pain. Groaning, he struggled to free himself from the sail, now wrapped around him like a shroud.

Draugr hands gripped his wrists and tried to pry his fingers away from his sword. He held on but could do nothing as they lifted him from the deck, carrying him like a battering ram and rushing to the side of the ship, where, without ceremony, they pitched him over.

Tumbling and falling, he heard Loki's laughter.

CHAPTER TWENTY-TWO

ERMOD LANDED DEAD center on the painted wheelchair of a handicapped parking space. He felt as if his every bone had shattered to pieces the size of teeth, all the fluids in his body bursting out like a broken water balloon.

Spitting a gob of blood, he lifted his head to see *Naglfar* listing over the battlefield, not more than twenty or thirty feet off the tarmac. Einherjar on the ground tossed spears and shot arrows at the ship, but they had no more effect than toothpicks flung at a rhinoceros.

Hermod dragged himself to his feet. He spat some more blood. With limited relief, he realized he'd fallen onto the Asgard side of the battle line. The Einherjar around him were as motley a crew as Hel's fighters on the ship had been, though better fed and better equipped. The man closest to him wore camouflage pants, combat boots, Mickey Mouse ears, and nothing else. *It's a Small World* was tattooed in script across his bare chest. He rather casually pointed his sword at Hermod and took a drag off a massive joint.

"Buddy, you landed on the wrong side of this parking lot. There's five hundred of us been waiting to kill guys like you."

"I'm Hermod, son of Odin," Hermod said. "Fuck off."

He scanned the faces of the men around him, hoping to spot Grimnir and, to a lesser extent, his Aesir kin, but the battlefield was vast, the parking lot stretching into other worlds through cracks in the World Tree. Hermod could sense living wood beneath the thin layer of asphalt at his feet.

Naglfar limped across the gap between the two armies, and Hermod kept waiting to see Sleipnir leaping to the ground, away from Loki and Hel's fighters and the draugr. Admittedly, that would bring Mist onto the scene of the final battle, but then at least she'd be close by. But the ship continued angling down toward the ranks of trolls and giants, listing farther to starboard until it had almost completely tipped over. Dead were leaping off the deck and sliding down the dangling rigging. Hermod sprinted away from the Einherjar front line into the no-man's-land between the two armies.

The ship struck the ground bow-first, the hull collapsing behind it in a slow implosion of bone and cartilage. The fingernail scales flew like confetti, and the great mast toppled. Dust and debris billowed across the battlefield, and a bleeding Loki limped out from the cloud, towering over the battlefield.

# # #

AFTER THE draugr had tossed Hermod over the side of the ship, Mist grabbed two fistfuls of

Sleipnir's mane and urged him to the rail. The horse took several galloping steps but then jerked to a stop, almost throwing Mist over his head. "What are you doing?" Mist shouted. "Leap over! We're going after him! Hurtle, damn you!" She couldn't survive the fall on her own. She needed Sleipnir to make the jump, and even then all she could do was hope for the best. But Hermod was down there. She wouldn't let him face death by gravity or monster all by himself.

"Mist! Over here!" Lilly was upslope on the leaning deck. Her face bled from multiple scratches, and there was an ugly clot of blood and hair on her forehead. She made vicious thrusts with her broken spear at the draugr and Hel soldiers crowding her. Fierce as Lilly was, she'd soon be ripped apart like a live chicken tossed into a pen of starving hyenas. But Hermod needed Mist too. He was an Aesir, but despite whatever combination of courage or foolishness drove him, he was out of his league down there on that battlefield. And yeah, dammit, she loved him. Maybe loved him. Sort of loved him.

"Get me to Lilly," Mist commanded, despairing. Sleipnir bolted up the deck, sure-footed as a mountain goat. The soldiers in Sleipnir's path held their ground against his advance, one of them scoring a hit on the horse's flank with a poleax, but Sleipnir broke the man with a mule kick, raked his tail across another man's eyes, and bit off the leg of another.

"Get on!" Mist ordered Lilly, leaning out with her hand extended. Once Lilly was seated behind her, Mist ignored the slices Sleipnir's hair was making in her fingers and grabbed hard to steer him back to the rail.

"Where are you going? The fight's up there," Lilly yelled in her ear, pointing toward the ship's stern.

"Hermod got tossed over the side. I'm going after him."

"No, we have to crash the goddamned ship before it delivers Hel's army."

"Jesus, Lilly, did you hear me? I said Hermod went over."

Mist expected Lilly to yell back, to grab her and shake her and scream in her face. Instead, she spoke softly in Mist's ear, and even above the screams on the deck and the ring of steel and the crack of gunfire, Mist heard her.

"Okay, babe, I'm sorry. Do what you have to do. But let me off the pony first. I need to help sabotage the bad guys' shit." She ran a gentle hand through Mist's hair.

"Better hop off, then, Lilly. I'm gonna think global and act local and help Hermod."

But Sleipnir had other ideas. Wheeling around, he plowed through Hel's fighters and draugr to get to the helm. In a pounding charge, he flew up the deck but then came to a sudden, splintering halt. Mist and Lilly barely managed to stay mounted. Jostled in his harness, Winston whimpered.

"What the hell is wrong with Glue Factory?" Lilly barked, but Mist saw why he'd put on the brakes. Loki's face was tilted up to the sky, as though he were enjoying sun and spray. Höd stood before him, one of his arms drooping, clearly dislocated. He leaned on a spear shaft, about a foot of which had been sheared off, leaving exposed raw wood and a sharp, ragged point.

"Help me guide my aim once more, Loki," he said, "and I will gladly throw another dart."

Loki chortled. "Sorry, dear, no. I have some tasks left that require me to live a bit longer. But you're a son of Odin, are you not? Surely you can throw a stick without my help. Haven't you developed a dog's sense of smell to compensate for—"

Höd hurled his stick.

The point punched into Loki's right shoulder, and Loki howled and staggered back, falling against the tiller. The deck lurched sharply downward.

"Now! This is it! Take it down!" Henry Verdant rushed past Sleipnir's legs, a blood-slicked bayonet in his hands. Loki swatted him away with the back of his hand, but Alice Kirkpatrick retrieved Henry's bayonet and took up the charge in his place. Höd demanded another dart to throw, while a mass of press-ganged dead surged forward, swarming over Loki like a pack of dogs. The trickster god was strong, but he began to sag, and with his weight on the tiller, the ship dropped with him.

The dragon figurehead splintered like windblown straw when it hit the ground. The corpses impaled on its teeth collapsed into jelly, and then the shock wave of impact traveled through the deck. Amid ear-gouging cracks as the ship's ribs and boards fractured, bodies flew, helpless as fallen leaves in a storm.

# # #

A ROAR encompassed the entire bowl of the sky, and Hermod looked up to see the Midgard serpent rise from the horizon like a mushroom cloud. Covered in brown and green and black scales, its skin reflected oil-slick rainbows. The serpent glared down at the earth, its eyes filmed over with yellow cataracts. It flared its great translucent, mucus-colored ruff and released a blast of poisonous air that drove giants and Einherjar alike to their knees, retching.

Hermod hurried toward the serpent, his throat burning. Thor was prophesied to die fighting the serpent, but he was also supposed to kill it. What if Hermod could kill the serpent instead? Wouldn't that be removing a huge link from the event chain? Could it be enough to shove Ragnarok off the rails? Of course, Hermod fully realized he wasn't Thor. He couldn't subdue Jörmungandr any more than he could wrestle a tornado to the ground.

With the sound of shattering rock, Thor rumbled past in his goat cart, every vein and muscle fiber in his arms carved in high relief as he held his hammer aloft. He was monumentally huge, like a formation of earth, but Jörmungandr dwarfed him.

"Thor, wait! Stop!" Hermod bellowed, but Thor paid him no mind. Hermod ran after him.

Another thought occurred to him: Removing a domino from the sequence didn't necessarily mean defeating any of the Aesir's enemies. Killing Thor would also be removing a domino, wouldn't it? But could Hermod kill his own brother? Even if it meant averting Ragnarok?

He sprinted hard. He had a clear shot at Thor's head. If he threw the Sword of Seven . . . But Thor made it a moot point. He launched himself from his cart, flying like a missile into the upper reaches of the clouds, where the serpent's head was obscured behind a haze of its own poison.

The serpent's cries cut through claps of thunder, and then it wobbled like a gigantic spinning top losing its energy. It sank in an achingly slow descent, falling in a coil upon the Home Depot and the rest of the shopping center and into the distant mountains and seas of the cracked-apart worlds. Its skin burst open, spreading steaming toxins across the field. Those whom it washed over screamed, their skin burning, peeling, hanging in sheets.

Thor crawled out from between the coils, hammerless. His face was disfigured, the texture of cottage cheese. Blood gushed from his nose. He groaned, and Hermod saw that all his teeth had fallen out.

Hermod reached his brother's side. Thor's chest rose with thin, agonized breaths. Tiny pin drops of blood beaded on his skin. And after a series of bone-fracturing convulsions, Thor died.

# # #

THE SHIP came down around Mist, wood and bone and fingernails. Winston spilled from his harness and fell the last few feet, and Mist was almost thrown from Sleipnir's back when the horse hit the ground. "Move," she commanded the dog and the horse, urging them clear of the falling wreckage.

On the ground, Hel's soldiers continued to clash with mutinous dead, and Mist tried to see through the clatter to spot Lilly and Höd, but she saw no sign of them.

"Miss Castillo!"

Instinctively, Mist reached for her sword, but it had gone missing in the crash.

Henry Verdant ran over the rubble, grasping hands

with Alice Kirkpatrick. The two were dirty and bloody, but Mist let out a gasp of relief to see that they were intact.

"Have you seen my sister?" Mist asked.

"She and Höd went after Loki," Alice said, waving out over the parking lot. The battle boiled with humans and monsters and frost-covered figures the size of buildings.

"We're going to try to link up with the Einherjar," Henry said. He'd secured an assault rifle for himself. "Join us?"

Mist turned to go with them, but then, across a pile of smashed and overturned cars, she saw a flash of red hair heading into Costco: Radgrid.

"I'll try to find you later," she said to the Iowans. "There's something I have to do first."

Henry gave her a puzzled look but then flashed her a quick salute. "We all have to do what we can. You take care, Miss Castillo."

"You too, Henry. Look after him, Alice."

"I will," Alice said with a nod and a brief smile. "You tried hard, Miss Castillo. Never forget that."

Mist gently pulled on Sleipnir's mane to guide him toward the Costco.

The store had been trashed by looters and wrecked by the battle. Conduit and wires dangled from the ceiling above a floor strewn with glass and plaster and concrete.

Quietly, as if he understood the necessity for stealth, Sleipnir crept down the aisles. Even Winston stepped carefully, and so Radgrid was unaware when they came up from behind her.

She was in the barbecue department, standing

before a laptop computer resting on a grill. The case was etched with runes, the screen divided into windows showing live feeds from the battle. Mist hung back in the aisle to watch and listen. "Thrúdi, it's Radgrid. Heimdall is beating Loki. Bring your squad around and help him out. . . . I don't care how, shoot the Aesir in the head, whatever. Just distract him so Loki can bring him down. Radgrid out."

So she'd come inside the store to coordinate the operations of her Valkyries and private warriors in relative peace and quiet. She'd apparently found a half-gallon can of peaches in heavy syrup and was daintily nibbling a glistening slice from the end of a fork.

Mist drew in a long breath. She could no longer do anything for Adrian Hoover. She couldn't overthrow Hel and free all her prisoners. She couldn't stop Frigg and Vidar from bringing about Ragnarok. But she could kill Radgrid.

A massive figure appeared in a window on Radgrid's laptop screen, leaning his broad face into what was probably a rune-enhanced camera. He wore matte-black armor and a horned helmet, of all things.

"I just thought I'd let you know that Thor is dead," he said. "My father is dead."

Radgrid barely grunted in response. "Just a sec," she said, clicking on another window. "Hrist, what's the status of Frey? Surt should have burned him by now. . . . No? Do whatever it takes to pin Frey down. Radgrid out. Okay, Modi, what now?"

"Weren't you even listening? My father is dead."

"Yes, I heard," Radgrid snapped. "You knew Thor

wouldn't survive the battle, and he didn't. That means things are progressing as they should. Except for you, who should be out there looking for Mist."

"Yeah, about that—how much longer am I supposed to do your dirty work?"

"Until Frigg lifts her charm," Radgrid said. "And not a moment before."

Modi's voice blared over the computer speakers. "Listen, do you not get that I am a *god*? When this is all over, I'm going to be one of the most powerful beings in existence! I mean, fuck, I'm one of the most powerful beings in existence right now! And you've got me running errands. Following cars for you, killing nobodies like Grimnir, bringing you coffee—"

Grimnir?

Mist jumped from Sleipnir's back to the floor. Radgrid spun around and drew her silver sword. "Ah, Mist— No, I'll call you Kathy. You don't deserve the honor of—"

Mist didn't let her finish the sentence. Unarmed, she rushed Radgrid, knowing it was hopeless but not caring, so long as she got to finish out with violence. A very fitting tribute to Grimnir. Radgrid's blade came at her face, and Mist went down into a baseball slide, taking out Radgrid's knees. The laptop and peaches clattered to the floor.

"I guess sometimes people do get the death they deserve," said Mist, grunting as she used the can of peaches to bash in Radgrid's skull.

# # #

OUTSIDE, THE battle stormed on. Tyr grasped Hel's dog, Garm, by the throat, but he was tiring, with Garm's jaws snapping only inches from his face. Frey burned alive beneath a carpet of flame laid down by Surt. Vali, laughing with blood in his teeth, was fighting anyone within reach, be they frost giant or Einherjar. He stood on a pile of dismembered corpses.

The sibyl's prophecy said Vali would survive Ragnarok. If Hermod killed him, then, the prophecy should be broken.

He beat a path to Vali and struggled up the mound of bodies, blood-slicked arms and legs shifting beneath him. Vali saw him coming and hopped up and down, clapping his hands. "Oh, yay, it's Hermod! I'm going to kill you with all my might. I'm going to rip open your belly and pull out all your tubes, and then I'm going to wrap the tubes around your neck, and I'm going to tie a really good knot, and I'm going to squeeze and squeeze and— Oh."

Hermod loomed over him. He brought down the Sword of Seven with an overhand chop, but Vali ducked and pranced down the slope of limbs. He scampered away like a gingerbread man, laughing over his shoulder about how the sibyl said he got to live, how Vidar was going to give him his own land to rule over, with cows and pigs and sheep and otters.

Hermod slid down the limbs to give chase, but his attention was drawn elsewhere. The clang of weapons dampened, the combatants nearby lowering their swords and spears and cudgels as Fenrir and Odin approached each other.

Fenrir had grown even more colossal, crushing cars and shopping carts with every step. His low growl rumbled through the ground and shook Hermod's belly.

In his full armor and helm, Odin strode forward, horrible and spectacular. His beard shone white like a snow-clad mountaintop, and in his empty eye socket, Hermod recognized the nothing it contained.

Odin lifted his spear and broke into a run. Fenrir crouched down and passed his tongue over his teeth.

Last chance, thought Hermod. He knew he couldn't defeat Fenrir, even with a sword made of nothing, for Fenrir was more nothing still. But maybe he could interpose himself between Fenrir and Odin in a bid to distract the wolf, even if just for a second, and give Odin some scant advantage.

Odin fast closed the distance to the wolf, and Hermod ran, sped on by thoughts of beer and the taste of roast beef and the pleasure of walking and of loyal dogs and Mist and a world filled with everything he'd ever loved.

Fenrir opened his mouth and expanded, both the shape of a wolf and a shapeless expanse of emptiness at the same time. He was a great hole made of wolf, and Odin fell inside him and was gone.

Dumbstruck, Hermod could only stare at the empty space where Odin had stood. A great cry rang out: delight from the giants and the trolls and Hel's fighters, rage and sorrow from the Einherjar. The cries were muted, colder somehow than they should be. A certain quality of sound that Hermod hadn't been conscious of before, some kind of background music to the universe, had died along with Odin. The world had lost its first and greatest magician, and

NORSE CODE \ 279

in his place, there was nothing. Hermod sank to his knees.

Then Vidar was there, wearing a funny boot. It was made of scraps of things, weaves and mail and strips of material that glittered like diamond, and other material that drank all light. More dwarf tech. He placed his booted foot on Fenrir's bottom jaw, and either he grew to Fenrir's size, or Fenrir shrank to Vidar's, or size lost its meaning. Bracing Fenrir's lower jaw with his boot and grasping the wolf's upper jaw with his one arm, he pulled the monster apart. Fenrir unraveled like the sleeve of a sweater, the threads coalescing into a black whirlwind that thinned and spread across the sky, like ink in water, killing the last daylight, bringing out the stars, which winked in the smoky air, only to fade moments later. The sun leached into shadow.

Footfalls crunched on the gravel, and Hermod looked up to see Vidar's face staring down at him. His brother's cheek was a gluey mess of blood and other fluids. And there was something strange about his eyes. The left one was his. The right one was Odin's.

"Things are going swimmingly for you today," Hermod said.

Vidar surveyed the battlefield. Most of the combatants had fallen. A few Einherjar stood in a cluster, back to back, shaking with fatigue or fear as frost giants lumbered toward them. Surt towered over the Home Depot with magma dripping from his sword. Flames roared in the sky behind him. The corpses were piled high enough to challenge the height of the corpse gate in Helheim.

"There is nothing left for you to do, Hermod. The

sibyl's song has been sung." Vidar's voice was rough from disuse but not unpleasant. He seemed more tired than victorious. "Must you fight me still?"

"I'm the great nuisance of Asgard," Hermod said, rising to his feet. "Getting in the way is what I do."

"But the prophecy has been fulfilled. The gods are dead, and the moon is gone. Soon the sun will be eaten as well. Can't you see that there is nothing left to be done?"

"I guess I don't see the things you see, Vidar."

Vidar closed his own eye, bowing his head in acknowledgment. Odin's eye remained open, watching.

He unslung a folded object of some kind from his back, snapping it open to reveal a scythe with a blade containing the same substance as the Sword of Seven.

Without another word, Vidar swung the scythe in a one-handed horizontal arc. Hermod leaped back and thrust his sword out to deflect the blow. The two blades made contact with a blinding flash, sending jolts of breathtaking pain down Hermod's optic nerves. He staggered and swept his sword back and forth, just hoping to keep Vidar at a distance until he could blink the dazzling colors from his vision. Vidar went at him again, and Hermod felt the blade whisper through the fabric of his shirt and leave a cold chill across his belly. Another millimeter and it would have disemboweled him. Their blades struck again with another flash, the pain driving Hermod to his knees, and then the scythe was coming down on him. He rolled away, but not quite in time, and the scythe cut through three fingers of his right hand.

Hermod found himself staring at his own sword after it clattered to the asphalt, his fingers lying beside it like small, dead animals. Then the pain hit, and he cried out and made a desperate grab for the sword with his left hand.

"Enough," Vidar said quietly, kicking the sword. It spun away, out of Hermod's reach. "Look around you, brother. The war is over. You suffer now only to keep the world's corpse alive. Enough." He raised the scythe and twisted his waist, a spring ready to uncoil. Hermod tried to stand, to fight back, to not make it easy, to die on his feet, but there was no more strength in his legs, and he was grateful again for never having known how he was supposed to die. If he'd been aware that he was fated to perish in a parking lot, gravel digging into his knees, he might have indulged in an even more meaningless life.

"I shall name something for you in the next world," Vidar said.

A hammering of hooves, a movement of grimy white bulk, and Sleipnir slammed into Vidar's chest. Vidar fell back with enough force to shatter the ground. He rolled and regained his feet, a pair of bloody puddles on his chest where Sleipnir's hooves had struck. Riderless, Sleipnir turned and came in for another charge. Vidar was ready with the scythe, waiting. Hermod despaired at the thought of seeing Sleipnir beheaded. He forced himself over to his fallen sword and picked it up.

When he next looked toward Vidar, he saw with horror that Mist was racing up behind him. With Vidar's attention on Sleipnir, he didn't hear her coming. She brought her saber down through Vidar's shoulder. Bone splintered, the sound of a snapping broomstick, and Vidar's arm hung by only a thin strip of flesh. He opened his mouth in a silent scream, walked three steps, and then crumpled, just as Sleipnir sailed over Mist's head.

Mist thrust her sword through Vidar's chest, but Vidar was still moving, so she yanked the sword free and went in for another thrust. Then a third. A fourth. A fifth.

Vidar made a sound, a whistling gargle. His eye closed. Odin's eye remained open, seeing what Vidar no longer could.

# # #

HERMOD DIDN'T look away from Odin's eye until Mist gently took his forearm. "Hermod, your hand—"

"I'm fine," he said, too pained to laugh at the absurdity of his own assertion.

She cut away fabric from Vidar's shirt for a bandage and wrapped it around the bleeding stumps of Hermod's fingers.

"If Vidar's dead, does that mean we stopped Ragnarok?" she asked him.

Flames towered around them, feeding on the corpses. Black smoke boiled like oil in a cauldron, rising into the matte-black sky. Shadows crawled across the face of the sun. The fight was over, but the aftermath was eating the worlds. Killing Vidar had removed a domino, but it was as the sibyl said: The last one was still toppling.

Hermod could think of only one thing to do.

He bent over Vidar. With the thumb and index finger of his ruined hand, he plucked Odin's eye from Vidar's socket. It was apparently unattached by nerves or blood vessels or any connections of the flesh. But it was heavy with its own gravity.

"Hermod," Mist said with alarm, "you're not going to—"

Hermod reached up to his face with his good hand. He slipped a finger under his eyelid and grabbed his eyeball. The pain was already immense, but he pulled, screaming, the veins and arteries and optic nerve and muscle resisting, stretching, and he pulled until they ripped and snapped, ball-peen hammers and augers and metal screws driving into his head. To pass out now would be a waste, so he remained conscious. He plugged Odin's eye into his now-empty socket and screamed some more.

# # #

THE WORLD was a tree. Hermod had always known this, had even walked among its exposed roots, but now he saw the tree in its entirety. He towered before it as he had done before the toy mountain ranges at the bottom of Mimir's Well.

He saw how soil and crust and the ocean formed a thin skin over the tree's deeper substance, the living wood. The trunk was riddled with cracks, more seams than he'd ever imagined, some natural, some freshly cut. He saw the seams as clearly as lines drawn on a map, so tightly knotted that he could reach out his hand and watch it pass through three different worlds.

The roots of Jotunheim and Svartalfheim were burning in full conflagration. Alfheim and Niflheim and Nidavellir had collapsed into piles of ash. Helheim and Asgard were broken to chips and dust.

Flames licked at the edges of Midgard, growing hotter. Up the trunk, in a crook where the limbs branched out, was Vigrid, the battlefield where he now stood. Higher up still were more branches and other worlds, whose identity and nature he didn't know. Above it all, the sun hung, glowing black with rot or a cancer. He followed the sticky black threads of rot to their source, a small sliver of the remains of Asgard: Frigg's home of Fensalir, and her closet of nothing.

There was a small part of the tree that had become separated from the rest. The terrain looked familiar— valleys and mountains of Alfheim that Hermod had once enjoyed hiking across but that now burned lifeless. On impulse, he reached out and took hold of the chunk of dead world and hung it in the sky.

"I just made a moon," Hermod said to himself. It seemed easy.

He knew what he had to do now. He turned to Mist. Runes danced over her skin, like living tattoos. They were in his own hands, too, and in the blood seeping through his bandage. They were in Sleipnir's flanks, and in Vidar's body, and in the soil, and in the sky. The runes were everywhere, and they were very interesting. They wanted to tell him things. They wanted to reveal their secrets to him, and he wanted to stand there and read them forever.

But wisdom was knowing when to stop listening to the voices.

He sucked in a breath. Seeing how the worlds were arranged was one thing. Having the confidence to do the right thing with the Sword of Seven was completely another.

"Do whatever you're going to do without regret," Mist said.

"Right." He wanted to kiss her. Runes crawled over her lips, and he liked what they said. But there was no time.

He saw where the root of Midgard joined others. Then he raised the sword over his head and chopped down, through the wood, severing Midgard from the rest of the World Tree.

The ground dropped out beneath Hermod's feet, and then Midgard fell and fell, leaving the other worlds behind.

CHAPTER TWENTY-THREE

A WEEK LATER, when the tides receded, Mist and Hermod stood on the debris-strewn beach. Blocks of ice bobbed in the black sea, but the thaw was already noticeable. Sleipnir trotted in the surf, with Winston running behind him, nipping at his hooves.

Mist stepped back from the driftwood boat she'd built. It wasn't seaworthy, but it wouldn't have to sail far. "What do you think?"

Hermod stared at it for a very long time. Then he looked at her with his mismatched eyes, Odin's gray iris glittering in the predawn light. He still spoke and acted like his old self, and he mostly looked the same—in need of a shave, and with his fingers wrapped in dirty bandages—but Hermod had changed.

"It's a good-looking funeral boat," Hermod said. "I think Grimnir would have liked it."

They'd learned the details of Grimnir's fate from a Chinese Shaolin Einherjar, one of the few Einherjar who'd held on a while after the battle. He'd told them that Grimnir had died bravely, on his feet. He said that he'd have been happy with his ending.

Mist doused the boat with a can of lighter fluid. She wished she could give Grimnir a proper burial, but this would have to do. His body, like so much else, had been lost with the worlds of the World Tree Yggdrasil.

"I just hope it'll catch fire."

"I'll make sure it does," Hermod said, and Mist looked at him nervously.

"So, you're some kind of fire god now too?"

"What? No, I just mean I've got another can of lighter fluid in my bag that I stole from those looters. I figured it might come in handy."

Mist smiled. Not everything had changed.

"Hush now," she said, touching the flame of Grimnir's Zippo to the fuel-soaked wood. The fire did a weak ghost dance, and Mist feared the boat wouldn't catch. But then the flames took hold with surprising strength. Within a few moments, Grimnir's funeral ship blazed on the beach, sending up twirls of tiny orange stars. For the first time in longer than Mist could remember, she felt warm.

She held Hermod's hand and whispered part of a prayer she'd learned on her grandmother's lap: "All streams flow into the sea, yet the sea is never full. To the place the streams come from, there they return again."

"That's a good one," Hermod said.

They remained on the beach until the waves came in. Cold seawater met the fire, and the boat breathed steam into the morning.

# # #

RIDING BEHIND Hermod on Sleipnir, Mist spotted a frost giant cowering in the shadows of an alley. She felt sorry for it and was glad when Hermod rode on without comment. Through the cracks that Almost-Ragnarok had wrought, giants and trolls and elves and dwarves and living dead had entered Midgard, and now that Hermod had cordoned the human world off from the rest of the dying universe, humankind would have to share their world with these refugees from faraway places.

News reports from across the globe were grim. Hundreds of thousands had died in battle and disaster, and more would die in its aftermath. But humanity had been facing war and famine and all manner of natural disaster since its very beginnings. Most had perceived Ragnarok as windstorm, hurricane, tsunami, and flood, as tremors that had torn earth apart and bled flame and magma. They had seen a monstrous serpent, or maybe it was just a tornado.

But many knew the truth. The veils had fallen, and they'd seen gods. This was not the first time. Man had known gods before but had forgotten them or consigned them to story. Maybe this time, with their footprints still in evidence, they wouldn't forget.

No, the world was not the same. But, Mist thought, looking up at the round lump of silver in the sky—Hermod's moon—at least it was still alive.

Mist and Hermod rode to a park in Pasadena, where Lilly and Höd and the Iowans had established a command center, from where they were organizing grass-roots relief efforts.

"Saint Lilly of the Molotov cocktail, and her companion, Friar Grumpy," Hermod said affectionately.

"They do sort of resemble a band of outlaw folk heroes, don't they?" Mist said, dismounting Sleipnir.

Lilly came over. "Did you give Grimnir his grand send-off?"

"Not so grand," Mist said, moving off with Lilly. "But it was traditional. He would have liked that part of it."

"Well, I managed to score a couple cases of beer. We can give ourselves epic hangovers in his honor."

"Beer?" Mist said, touched. "How did you ever—"

"Feh, black markets are my favorite kind of shopping. I even got some roast beef. I know how much Grimnir liked bloody meat."

"For a dead sister," Mist said, "you're not half bad."

Lilly smiled, looking off into the distance. "I feel too alive to be dead. But I guess dead is what we still are. Which is weird. Can we die again? I mean, *die* die, for good? With Valhalla and Helheim gone, do we go anywhere afterward?"

"I kind of like not knowing," Mist said. "It's more open-ended this way."

They walked together through the park, not talking. Mist just enjoyed the feel of solid ground beneath her feet, the sensation of her own pulse.

"Hermod and I are leaving," she said.

Lilly sat on the playground swings. "Yeah?"

"Yeah," Mist said. "Adrian Hoover's family was in New Jersey when Grim and I abducted him. If they survived, I need to see them in person. I can't repay my debt to them, but I owe it to them to let them know what happened to their son. Whether they believe me or not."

Lilly nodded. "I guess saving the world doesn't get you off the hook for everything that happened before."

"I think that's one of the reasons Vidar and Frigg were so set on starting a new world. New beginnings are attractive."

"But we're not gods," Lilly said.

Mist sat on the swing next to Lilly's. "Nope. We're responsible."

Side by side, they swung for a while.

# # #

"ARE YOU going to keep that thing in your head?" Höd asked.

Hermod had built a small fire in one of the park's barbecue grills. He wished he had something to throw on it. Some chicken, or hamburgers, or even one of those chemical-filled hot dog things. What did a god have to do to get a decent meal around here, anyway?

"Hermod," Höd said, interrupting Hermod's musings. "The eye. Are you going to keep it?"

Hermod sighed. "It was showing me more than I wanted to see at first. But I'm getting used to it now. Which scares me." He looked into the flames. "I'm going to pull it out."

"May I ask why?"

The question surprised Hermod. He'd thought Höd would be pleased to hear that he didn't want to hold on to Odin's vision.

"Our history is too full of seers and of our so-called betters using wisdom as an excuse to tie puppet strings to us all," Hermod said. "The eye is a remnant of a time when we Aesir, whatever we are, chose to play at being gods."

Shadows made depthless caverns beneath Höd's

brow. "How would you destroy it? Throw it into the ocean? Bury it in the earth? Cast it into a volcano?"

"Pluck it out of my skull before it does damage," Hermod said. "Then cleave it with Vidar's sword."

"It's no longer Vidar's sword," Höd said mildly. "Just as it's no longer Father's eye. Both are yours. You refashioned the world after your own design, Hermod, as decidedly as any god to emerge from fire and ice. Can discarding your tools ever change that?"

Hermod didn't answer. He walked away, and a few minutes later he found Mist, sitting alone on the swings. He stood before her and held out his hand.

She took it and smiled. There was a look in her eye.

"Oh," he said. "Is this a second date? Do you want . . . Are we going to—"

"Shut up," she said. "You know we are."

"Right here? In the playground?"

She put her hands on his shoulders, and he let her push him to the ground, and for a while the world was very strange, but only in a nice way.

# # #

MUNIN AND I circle above the playground, observing the two Aesir and their companions. Hermod and Höd, the last gods alive. Or, perhaps, the first gods of this strange new Midgard, if they choose to be.

"I didn't see this coming," I say to Munin.

Munin chases a moth near the treetops and snatches it out of the air.

The dominoes are spread out before us, not just in lines but in endless convolutions. They fall and rise with no pattern I can discern, as if they have a will of their own. I find them very discourteous. Ragnarok was the long-anticipated end of everything. And now Hermod has given us an unknown tomorrow.

Which means today, anything is possible.

Below, Hermod whistles for his dog, and Winston runs to his side, excitedly whipping his tail. Hermod and Mist gather their few things and set off with Sleipnir, eastward, the rising sun bathing the sky in salmon-colored light to overtake the last of the night-time stars.

ABOUT THE AUTHOR

Greg van Eekhout was born and raised in Los Angeles and lives in San Diego. You can visit his website at www.writingandsnacks.com.